DAUGHTER OF MADNESS

Amanda J. McGee

For the ones who light the fire in me.

PROLOGUE

Drummond had need of a man with no respect for authority. He reminded himself of this when the assassin did not kneel.

The man was tall, thin, but all corded muscle. Drummond could not put a finger on his heritage. He had black hair, which was the most noticeable thing about him. His eyes were an unexceptional brown. His skin was not so dark as some of the desert tribes' but darker than Drummond's own, a darkness easily the result of time in the sun. He studied the room with a lazy indifference that rankled.

This was a man who would kill even a god for the right price.

The Lord Regent was prepared to pay that price to finally rid himself of his niece.

He knew that Liana lived. Sometimes, at night, he dreamed of his niece's golden eyes. They sparked with fire, not the pure light of Herkun's own, but red flame, ruin. Drummond had never before feared a woman. He told himself that he did not fear one now. She was a demon, a witch, who had poisoned her own father. Alexander had been his brother. Drummond was prepared to kill him if need be, of course. It was not for a lack of feeling, though he and his brother had never gotten along well. It was merely purification. Alexander was a monster now.

This man was his own type of monster. Drummond knew such monsters, those who delighted in others' pain. They were best treated as tools, not people. If this one could not be useful, Drummond would dispatch him. No point leaving a knife at his own back.

The Lord Regent leaned back in his chair. He had sent the seer away. She was useless. One vision of the princess, one bright point on the map, and she was suddenly unable to see anything at all. She could not give him details, but he had the masters at the Academy pull all of the maps of the lands to the east. Most of them stopped at Herkun's Spine, the impassible mountain range marking Herkunsland's eastern border. Some maps procured from the desert tribes to the south spoke of a great jungle accessible through the southern passes. The jungle was also impassable, the

1

master who informed him had said, but demons did not operate the way people did. His niece should not have been able to escape the castle. To be so far, in some foreign jungle, should have been enough to remove her stain on this land. But the summer's heat remained unceasing. No rain had fallen with spring. He had nobles and commoners alike banging at the gates, demanding food and water. His own table had even suffered, none of the fruits he enjoyed, the butter and milk reduced, the bread no longer fluffing the way he liked. He had demanded an explanation, and improvements. The kitchen had complied, but the cost they required had made him scowl. It was only a matter of time before he would have to start requisitioning.

No, his niece would have to die for true. If she still lived, so far away, then he would have to make sure to remove her.

"What are you called?"

The man looked at Drummond at the question, ceasing to peruse the tapestries on the walls.

"Gino, Lord Regent," the man said. He had a bitter, cocksure smile. Drummond frowned.

"And you will take the offer?"

"I've never killed a princess before," Gino said. His smile became something more genuine, and more sinister. Drummond tried not to feel unease. "I always like to try new things."

"Then I entrust the task to you," the Lord Regent said, trying to keep the distaste from his voice. "My guards will take care of your payment and the terms."

The man bowed, and the sardonic tilt to his shoulders was nearly enough to make the Lord Regent call back his words. Drummond gestured, and one of his two personal guards escorted the man out of the room.

He thought, then, of his wife, dead so many years. It had been years since he thought of her death with guilt. To feel guilt prickle through him now - well, human hearts were weak.

Drummond himself was not weak.

He would do what must be done.

1 THE KING

He remembered the moment that the curse had claimed him.

The king sat in the garden, and the moon shone down. There was a phantom caress on his skin, an ice cold hand. Darkness bloomed in his blood.

He remembered the moment, over and over. Remembered the darkness rising, rising, swamping him.

There was terror there, but for the king it was an old terror. He had lived with the darkness now for a timeless time, and in the darkness he was sheltered. He remembered nothing. He was nothing. That was good, for the man that had been a king sensed that he had failed, that he had hurt. The world beyond the darkness was made of nothing that he wanted to see again.

But no night could last forever.

The man who had been Alexander came back to himself in blood.

It was not the first time he had awakened, since the darkness bloomed in him, since Herka's curse had wrapped its tendrils around his soul. It was not the first time he had sprung back, scraping blood and offal off of his fingers, to strike himself against his cage and scream. Though this time the scream was shorter. There were only so many times that you could experience the horror of awakening to murder with surprise.

She had been a servant who had spilled wine on her lady's dress. Her name was Bryna, and she had pleaded with him, while he sat there with his ears covered, while the sun still hovered over the horizon. She had told him that she would do anything he had asked.

Alexander had asked her for nothing.

The demon had not asked her for anything either.

Now the sun rose, and Alexander stared at the wall its light painted, and waited until the guards came to collect the corpse he had made. He did not even notice the tears mixing with flaking blood on his cheeks.

The guards collected the body wordlessly. The green ones, the ones who cared whether a serving woman lived or died, had long since been culled from their force.

Someone came not long after to scrub up the blood, as best they could. Alexander sat, and said nothing, and watched the time that he was himself tick away. He wished that he had never woken up. They opened the door of his cage, and left water for him to wash and drink.

He did neither.

The sun moved down the wall, steady. He could not stop it.

The door opened again, and a voice said his name.

He blinked, once, and turned his head.

His brother stood in the doorway.

Drummond had aged. His brother was younger than him by some years, though he had always looked the older of them. Now his hair was more gone than not, and what remained was cropped close like an ascetic's. There were lines under his eyes, a gauntness to him that had not been there before. Alexander had felt the aches in his body, had seen the ragged white in his hair. He knew that he, too, had aged, but he did not know how long. There was no time in the darkness, and there was no time in this cell.

"Get up," Drummond said.

Alexander did not move. He watched his brother, thought about how he owed both cage and curse to his betrayal. He wondered what it would feel like to kill him. That was probably the demon talking.

"What do you want?" he said.

His voice was harsh and twisted from disuse. Drummond narrowed his eyes.

"You will bathe," he said. "And you will eat and drink."

Alexander turned his gaze back to the wall. The square of sun had nearly touched the floor. There was only one window. Once that square vanished, he would have only the color of the sky and the ambient light to tell him when night would come. The days were shorter now. The rapidly approaching night was a blessing. He could not think as a demon.

"Get up," Drummond growled, stepping into the door of the cage. Alexander had to crane his neck to look at him.

"I will just kill again tonight," he said. There should have been more horror in his voice, but it came out like a fact. It was a fact.

He could not feel anything anymore.

"You will not," Drummond told him. His fists had clenched at his sides. "There will be no more victims for you."

Alexander blinked.

His brother had made all of those women come to this place. How had he not realized that before?

"You are a murderer," he said to Drummond. "You have used me to murder."

"You," Drummond said, "are a monster. Now get up, and wash."

Alexander did not answer. Soon Drummond left, and closed the cage door behind him. It locked. Alexander was left alone.

The door did not open again that day.

In the morning, no new blood coated his skin. He did not awake curled around a corpse.

His brother came again not long after dawn. The guards came with him, with a tub and new clothes and food. The pressed his struggling, weak form into the hot water, and scrubbed him until he was red.

"You can eat," Drummond said, "or I will have them force you to eat."

Alexander ate. Little by little, he felt himself return.

He was a man who had been a king. He had a daughter, and a son. He had a kingdom.

At night, he was a demon. Locked in his silver cage, he raged and wailed.

By day, he was Alexander.

And he was very, very angry.

2 THE CAPTAIN

Bertrun, former Captain of the Guard for King Alexander, current fugitive and revolutionary, disliked the tunnels underneath Herkun's City with every fiber of his being. The tunnels were close and tight for his wide-shouldered frame, and though there was no fire above his head as there had been the night he first stumbled into them over a year ago, he always felt as if the phantom smell of smoke hung in his nostrils. These tunnels were where he had said goodbye to his king, where he had fled with four nameless Shadows while wracked with pain and shock. He was reminded of that, every time he entered them.

Yet the tunnels were his freedom, too, and perhaps the freedom of all of Herkun's City.

In the months since he had discovered the entrance within his brother Maldun's wine cellar, Bertrun had, with the help of the Shadows, explored path after path through the maze of these subterranean passages. They had mapped those paths, as best they could. Bertrun was not a cartographer, and neither were the Shadows - their hands were better suited for wielding swords, as his were - but they had developed a system of navigation, identifying paths from one destination to the next. From Maldun and Lisa's house, he had traveled to the safe house he now resided in, a former boardinghouse on the southern side of the city, far from the castle walls. It was a narrow, wooden two-story with four small bedrooms above a dining room and lower bedroom, and with an attached kitchen to the rear of the house built all in stone. Marie, once Maldun's maid, managed the house, taking care of all of the necessary tasks in her retirement, and Bertrun was the only boarder. He spent his days memorizing the maps that the Shadows had made, copying them over and over on a large slate they had procured for his room, and pacing the halls that sheltered him.

Bertrun left that safe house now that dark was safely fallen. Marie, her silver curls piled atop her head, was preparing for the morning's meal before she retired to bed. The kitchen fire kept the room warm, and sweat beaded on the thin wrinkles of her forehead.

"Will you return tonight?" she asked, concern on her face. Bertrun touched her shoulder, reassuring her.

"I always come back, do I not?" he asked. Her smile was thin.

A Shadow waited for him outside the back door, scarred face impassive. They walked together through the darkened alley, dodging refuse left out for the soil collectors. Bertrun was glad for the newly chill air, since it cut down on the smell of the alleyway. They kept their alley clean, but refuse was still refuse.

The entrance to the tunnels was narrow and low to the ground, a crawlspace beneath a bakery. Boxes stacked to conceal the space kept the ground clear of refuse leading to the entrance. Still, Bertrun winced as he clambered down to his hands and knees and crawled forward. He was not as young as he once was, and his scarred hands ached to bear his weight against the cold cobbles of the alley.

Herkun's City had been built on secrets. The crawlspace held an entrance long abandoned, as many of the old buildings in the city did. Though new construction in the city was largely done in wood and brick, the tunnels were made of quarried stone, from what quarry Bertrun knew not. Master historians and the clergy agreed that Herkun's City had stood on this spot since the dawn of the world, though they might disagree on the details, but Bertrun wondered at all that had been lost. How could a whole maze of tunnels exist below the castle and the streets, one that expanded even beyond the old city walls and out into the surrounding growth of impoverished communities that had grown around them?

Exploring the tunnels had, in the end, only given Bertrun more questions without answers.

Pursuing those questions was not his goal tonight. Passing once more into the subterranean maze of the tunnels was something he did now only in order to continue his quest. He would carry out Alexander's last order to him. He worked to make a way for Liana's return. Whenever that return might be.

Passage through the tunnels was uneventful, in the way that any routine discomfort often was. His breath was tight in his throat, his heart pounded in his chest, but nothing of moment occurred. The Shadow's soft steps followed behind him, and the light of his single lamp flickered against the old stone walls.

At last, they came to their destination.

It was an unexceptional entrance, an unused door in the back of a building that seemed to go nowhere. The door led to what might look, from the outside, to be a root cellar, but which was in fact a tunnel entrance. It had been boarded up, and to the Shadows' credit it still appeared to be when Bertrun closed it behind him.

They were in a long hallway, which was stacked with boxes and barrels of goods. Bertrun waited quietly by the door as the Shadow ranged out ahead and vanished around the end of the hall.

As always, he held his breath. This particular hallway, forgotten and relatively unused though it was, was in one of the class buildings of the Academy. One never knew when a restless student would decide to get into mischief and exploration.

When the Shadow emerged once more and beckoned, Bertrun exhaled and followed.

The Academy was a wide complex of multiple buildings. Each held classes for students of various disciplines, most among the lesser nobility and merchant class. King Alexander had mandated programs to teach trades to the public. Working with the various tradesmen in the city, he had created courses which were paid for by the crown. The tradesmen were paid for classes they taught, and the students received room and board, the last a heavy expense. Yet Alexander had felt that it was important to train the public. He was tired of seeing people go hungry.

Bertrun had been in one of the first classes of the Academy dedicated towards the training of civic guards. The previous captain of the guard had been a war veteran of a minor house. Bertrun had been a landless merchant's son who stood to inherit nothing, grandson of immigrants. Was it any surprise, he wondered darkly as he picked his way through the hall, that his men had betrayed him?

Such thoughts would not do him any good here.

The hall bent, ending in a door. Beyond it, he heard voices. The Shadow opened the door, and the captain entered.

Voices stilled as the door swung open. There was palpable relief when he appeared.

"Bertrun," Syria said, smiling. He crossed around the table at which she sat to hug his sister. Maldun was there as well, seated beside her, and hugging that man was a long awaited thing. Maldun had been traveling in the summer months, cultivating contacts in the south. He would leave before Bertrun saw him again, to take one last train of goods before winter struck in earnest.

The rest of those seated at the table were not so dear. Jessa was absent, having made her report to the Shadows themselves. It had become too dangerous for her to leave the castle regularly, and someone must be their eyes inside those walls. It was she who had told them that food was being brought to the high tower where they expected Alexander was kept, and she who would relay news from the seer, whom Drummond kept at his side and called Nicolus. Bertrun remembered meeting her in a different guise, and still shivered sometimes at the memory. No one had seen the seer for weeks, and gossip said she had fallen out of favor. Jessa did not yet seem worried. Drummond was mercurial. Still, it was worrisome that a key agent had been so isolated, for all that Nicola had her secrets.

The remaining two individuals seated at the table were near-strangers, though the Shadows vouched for their loyalty. One was a master, and the reason that they were meeting in a hidey-hole in the back of the Academy in the first place. His name was Wrothfurt, and he had been tutor to the twin princess and prince. The masters as a group had been horrified at the execution of Master Corvin, who had been a loyal servant to two kings and respected peer in his retirement. Most of them had banded with the resistance, if very, very quietly. Wrothfurt was their voice, for now.

The other person seated at the table gave Bertrun more discomfort. It was not because she was a woman - Syria and Marie were both women, and Jessa. No, it was because of her rank. The Baroness Masana, a matronly widow, had the soft folds of a woman who had known little in the way of hardship or hard work. It was easy to dismiss her for that, if you did not meet her eyes. Her gaze, when she met Bertrun's own, was forthright and assessing. It reminded him no little bit of his grandmother's.

"Good evening," he said to both of them, and took his seat. The Shadow was already standing guard at the door.

"Good evening," Wrothfurt said. The baroness merely nodded her greetings. Bertrun could see laugh lines around her mouth, but he'd never seen her smile in their brief acquaintance.

"What news?" he asked.

"There are rumors that the clergy mean to move against the Academy," Wrothfurt said. The table shifted.

"Surely not," Syria said. Her voice was high with shock. "The Academy helps so many of the common folk. They couldn't."

"They will," the baroness said. "And Drummond will say nothing. It is only a matter of time."

Syria sucked in a breath as if to protest. She still volunteered with the temple, still believed in its charity, for all that she knew the corruption at its heart. Bertrun felt his shoulders sag when she held her silence.

"Do we know when?" he asked.

Wrothfurt shook his head.

"It's only whispers as yet," he said, "word from among the staff of the court financiers that the Usurper would begin to cut costs. The harvests have been poor, and even the royal coffers feel the strain." That was troubling. Bertrun knew that food costs were high, but for it to be impacting the Crown so deeply spoke of further instability.

"Will this meeting place still be safe?" Maldun asked.

"It will depend on the nature of the attack," Masana pointed out. "Do we have an alternate meeting location?"

They stared at one another, aware that the answer was no.

"I could -" Bertrun began.

"It's too dangerous," Maldun said.

"But -"

"I will provide a venue," the baroness said, breaking off their incipient argument. "It is too dangerous for you to host us, captain. I personally would rather not know where you are staying at this time." She cast an eye around the table. "There is a good chance the Masters will be purged. I am surprised it has not happened already."

She issued the statement with a matter-of-factness that made Bertrun's blood cold. He stared at Wrothfurt, who shrugged, a surprisingly informal gesture.

"There have been a few relieved of their positions, but none have outright vanished," he said. "It will get worse. We will need to make arrangements to hide those that we can."

Bertrun looked at the Shadow, who nodded.

"Then we will begin preparing," he said.

"Is there any news from the castle?" Maldun demanded.

"Nothing new," Bertrun said shortly. Jessa brought news only of strange rumors regarding Alexander's tower, and of abuse of the servants. Bertrun had not told all to the council where the king was concerned. He could not bring himself to.

"The crops have been poor," Masana said. "My own holdings will barely make their tithe, and I know some who will not. It may be that more lords will come to our cause if this continues."

"The price of bread will rise again," Maldun said.

"They can't keep raising prices," Syria hissed. "People will starve. Are starving."

"Peace." Bertrun ran his hand through his curls. She was not wrong. Yet he could not see a way to help. He could not do more than he was doing through the people at this table. "We will do what we can."

It was all they could do.

The rest of the meeting was uneventful. They each slipped out, one at a time, into the night. Bertrun was one of the first to go, and when he hugged Syria goodbye she clung to him too tightly.

"Are you alright?" he whispered, but she turned her face away with a small shake of her head, and Bertrun would not press her here before the others.

He cast one last glance at her, and at their small council. Then he stepped out into the dark, cluttered corridor, the Shadow at his heels.

It was a long walk back.

3 THE SEER

Once upon a time, she had been able to see dreams.

Nicola stood in her room. She had not left its confines in days. But it was time for the change in the guard, and Matthius came when the guard changed. She waited each morning for that visit, for him to step inside the room in the spare moments before the rest of the castle woke.

She waited now, dressed already in her livery. The air was gaining a chill at last, and the livery was safe. Matthius knew she was a woman, but the rest of the castle did not. The rest of the castle thought her a strange boy, with the bright red hair of a witch, with blindfolded eyes that nonetheless saw everything.

They were only wrong on the first count.

The livery, she saw through her closed eyes, was green, a deep, forest green. Drummond's colors, this forest green, and she knew that he hated that color, which reminded him of Perlen, as much as he loved the gold that embroidered it. He longed for the golden banner of the Sun Throne to be his, and knew that he could never have it in truth. He was not Herkun's own. He was just a man. This, too, he hated.

The Lord Regent was a man of violent passions. That was why she was locked in this room.

There was little other color here - green fabric, golden embroidery, the plain white of the bedclothes. The floor was bare stone, the walls stone as well, large, deep gray blocks of it with ancient, blackened mortar that pebbled under her fingers. The bed itself was a dark wood, polished to a high sheen but otherwise unprepossessing. Only Nicola was color. Ironic, that she knew all of these things even with the golden cloth on her eyelids to hold them shut. Ironic, because Nicola had once been able to know much more.

She fingered the smoothness of the locket at her throat, feeling pain behind her breastbone, swirling in her stomach. The green inside her pulsed as if in comfort. Gratitude mixed with resentment in her heart.

The green, the green god. Her divine lover, who had given her back her eyes. His essence rested in her belly like a lead weight. Like a weight it kept her from the roads of the future and the past.

All she had left, with the green god riding her, was the now. Not for the first time, Nicola wondered if she regretted their pact.

When she thought of him, she thought of smooth skin, apples and smoke. She thought of the fire on her skin when he touched her, how her whole body had arched into him, the rushing force of her pleasure.

She thought, too, of grief. How could she not, when only three months prior he had dissolved in her hands and left her alone? The sand of him she kept still in a box beneath her pillow, but she did not open that box. She could not stand to.

This is what came of loving gods. Gods were cruel. She of all people should have known he would leave her.

And yet, he had not left. He remained lodged in her, and she twisted around him and became something else. Not a seer, not anymore.

This alone would have been terrible and wonderful at once. Nicola's visions had never given her happiness. She would have yielded to the fate, most likely.

But there was Drummond to consider. There was always Drummond to consider. How long since the twins had left, spirited away on the night the castle caught fire? Nicola had never been good with the passage of time. For fifty long years she had lived in the bowels of the castle, where time seemed not to flow at all. Now, above, she knew only that the sun rose, the sun set, and that since Midsummer she could not see her visions at all. It had not taken long for the Lord Regent to become cognizant of this.

How she had pleaded to be allowed back to the well, certain that a touch of that heady, heavy water would open her inner sight as it had always done. But Drummond was crueler even than a god, and he did not let her go. Instead, he had locked her inside her room, a new one. It was small, smaller than the room she had kept when she had held favor, but not so small as the closet he had kept her in when he had first brought her up from the depths, the one on the back of his bedchamber. She was grateful for that, at least.

The sun rose. The sun set.

Yet, today, as she waited for Matthius, Nicola felt the hair on her arms prickle with something like premonition.

There was a knock, quiet as a whisper. The door opened, creaking on its hinges. She could see the wood of it, the fine grains just as clear as if her eyes were open but without the conscious focus of eyes. This new sight gave her details at whim. What she would give to not see them.

Matthius' face appeared in the crack of the door, trouble brewing behind his brow. His light brown hair hung over his eyes.

"The lord requires his breakfast," he said, voice low.

Nicola started, opened her mouth to speak only to be interrupted by the snick of the door closing. Her heart pounded in the silence. Days since she had gone out, weeks or months since she had lost favor with the Lord Regent. Now, the lord required his breakfast. Nicola moved to the door quickly, flung it open and hurried out. She hissed thanks to Matthius as she passed.

The Lord Regent was fond of tests. It was the one thing for which he could be counted on, his lack of reliability. Nicola herself had not eaten for days, had not drank, and needed neither. But a man needed food and water, and he needed to trust the one who brought it to him. Nicola had once saved the lord from poison. Perhaps his pique with her inability to serve him had passed. Perhaps he had found another way to keep her useful.

She hated how much it mattered to her.

She moved quickly down the corridor, her steps unerring despite her blindfold. The stone here was covered in a wide runner of carpet, newly made since the fire. She could smell the dye in the fibers, and the green told her the dye was red and gold. Once, she'd been able to walk these halls without being troubled by so much detail catching at her attention. Nicola felt tears prick her eyes, and did not know what she was mourning.

The kitchens were a bustle that felt overwhelming after her isolation. Pans clacked, fires roared, workers scuttled and hurried. At first, no one noticed her. Then a familiar voice called out to her.

"Nicolus!"

Nicola started at the name, though she shouldn't have. Still, it had been weeks since anyone called her by the name Drummond had chosen for her. Matthius called her Nicola, in the privacy of her room, when he sat with her for moments in the mornings. And the Lord Regent had not wanted to see her.

It was Jessa who had called to her. Nicola had not seen her since the green god had planted his light in her, and now she was struck by the girl's beauty. Long, brown curls were bound in a single braid instead of the elaborate styles the royalty favored, and brown eyes looked at her expectantly. There was worry there, fear even, Nicola could feel that, but it was hidden behind a bright smile.

"I've come for the lord's breakfast," Nicola said, her voice stiff and low as a boy's might be. How much did Jessa know? Matthius had told her the court took bets about what she had done to displease Drummond. Even Matthius wondered, but she had not told him the truth. To admit aloud her inability was more than she could manage. The visions she had gained from the water of the well, the visions that cut through time and distance and made her a power, were gone. Drummond thought her useless. Maybe he was right. Maybe Jessa would think her useless, too.

"Well, it's not done yet," Jessa said, interrupting her thoughts. "You'll have to wait with me awhile." It was teasing. Nicola felt herself redden.

"Unless you'd like to help me," the girl continued, her tone turning sly. "I just finished peeling these potatoes and need to go fetch more. Surely you'd carry them for me?"

Nicola fidgeted. "Surely," she said.

She followed Jessa down a handful of steps into the cool root cellar. The green flared as Jessa turned to her, fire in her eyes. Nicola gasped as she was pinned to the wall. Jessa leaned close. She smelled of horses and some flowery soap - perhaps lavender, though it was faint. The lavender surprised Nicola. It was not the scent she would have thought Jessa to prefer.

"Where have you been?" Jessa demanded, her voice a harsh whisper. Nicola was grateful for the question. She had never been close to a woman besides Jessa, not for fifty long years. She did not know what they felt like to hold, to touch. The green inside her pulsed and spun.

"Locked up," Nicola said, gasping around the power's weight. "He locked me up."

"What for?" Jessa asked. She had a dangerous look on her face, and for the first time Nicola realized that Jessa saw her as a threat. It shouldn't have hurt.

Still, she did not answer.

"Drummond needs his breakfast. If I don't get it to him on time, my head will be the next thing he asks for." She did not mean to sound tired, to sound anguished. She must have done both, for Jessa's fear shifted to concern. She leaned away from Nicola.

"What happened?" she asked again.

What had happened was that she was not what she was. Jessa couldn't know that.

"He hired an assassin," Nicola said, changing the subject. She knew Jessa had taken it as explanation when the other woman swore. Nicola felt relief, guilty and sweet, still the tremors in her hands.

"When," Jessa demanded.

"A few weeks after midsummer, I think."

"Did you tell him where she was?" It was a pointed question. Nicola swallowed.

"I had to," Nicola said. She had told Drummond where to search, tried to buy herself time. She had hoped the distance might discourage him - no one made the passage over the Spine, even she knew that - but it had not. Drummond burned with obsession, with need. "He thinks if he can kill Liana, the weather, the resistance, all of it will go away."

Jessa went still. She made a small sound in her throat. Nicola reached out to her, catching her shoulder.

"They're alive," she told the girl who had once been Liander's lover. "There is no way the assassin will find them, Jessa."

Jessa pushed her into the wall then, voice rough with anger.

"Hope that your visions directed you aright."

There was a shout from above. Jessa jumped back, grabbed the potatoes and dumped them into Nicola's arms.

She didn't wait for Nicola to follow her back up to the

kitchens.

4 THE PRINCESS

There were lights, and sound. Voices hovered above her in the bright redness, echoing across a distance cavernous and vacant. A rusted prism of sound set its hooks into her numb skin and drew her upwards with a rush of crimson. Lights sank between her eyelids, prying them open.

There was a face above her. Blue, familiar eyes. She frowned at them, blinked, turned her head towards the beloved face that held them.

"Liana," the man said. "Liana! Do you know me?" She didn't answer. It seemed as if her voice had left her. She felt tears in the corners of her eyes, cold as they ran down her skin. The room was cool. For some reason that frightened her. She reached for the hand of her twin, feeling the familiar calluses there. The movement left her weak.

"Liana," he said, and she saw tears in his eyes.

"Liander, why are you crying?" she whispered. Her eyes travelled past him. The ceiling was strange. Where was she?

Voices arose outside, somewhere beyond her vision, muffled by distance. Liander's eyes tightened, and he made as if to stand. Instinctively, she held onto him, feeling fear rising in her throat.

"Liander, what is it?" His eyes returned to hers, his expression carefully still. He was waiting, fearfully waiting for something he couldn't change. She couldn't remember him wearing such a face before, but she knew the expression intuitively. She always knew her twin. Strength she didn't know she had flooded her grip. She saw him wince.

"Liana, look at me," he commanded. She fastened her gaze on him desperately. The fear was a rising tide in her, though she could remember no cause for it. Liander was safe. He was her brother. He would take care of her, always, would protect her from whatever it was her mind was shying away from. He wouldn't leave her.

The door opened, and her twin's grip tightened on her hand, as if to keep her by him. Steps came towards them across the floor and suddenly she felt her heart kicking frantically in her chest, flashes of images dancing on the edge of her thoughts. She recognized, in some vaguely animal way, that the sound of these steps was something to fear. Liander held her still like a startled rabbit in the wood, holding her breath, praying she might not be noticed.

"Liana," Jeilalu breathed, and his voice shattered the stillness.

She jerked upwards, her eyes finding him, memories returning in merciless waves of too vibrant color. Their banishment from the kingdom and her subsequent isolation. The evidence of her half-sibling's attraction, the division of her self before his attentions. The rape beneath the moonlight, the world disjointed with magic and pain. The child, lost in the depths of the black water, his cries swallowed forever. Relentless, her life returned to her, and she pressed herself into the wall, ripping her hand from her twin, stopping her ears to block out the sound of his voice, that hated, sultry sound that worked its way beneath her skin mercilessly.

"This isn't real," someone whispered desperately. "Stop it, stop this." The voice was familiar, shuddering, quivering, a weak and useless thing. It was unable to convince her, to drown out the truth of him inside her head. Her hands were unable to drown out the voices which rose up to bind her to the now. She cringed against the wall, tears coursing down her cheeks, hoping that they would release her, spare her. At last, they passed by.

"Liana." She didn't look. The other voice kept whispering, telling her not to look up, to keep her eyes closed and stay safe inside the shelter of darkness. Her hands trembled weakly against her ears like fluttering leaves.

"Liana, please," the voice said again, breaking on the words. Hands found hers, wrapped around them and steadied them, drawing them away from her ears. Familiar, warm hands. She kept her eyes tightly shut. The whispering voice had stopped, and silence fell. Dizziness swamped her, but she kept her back against the wall.

"Please, don't do this again. I can't..." her brother murmured, sounding broken. Her brother. She knew him.

"Damn him," Liander said. "And damn me, for failing you. I should be damned to the deepest, darkest hell."

Liana opened her eyes.

His head was slumped towards their clasped hands, his sandy blond hair hanging down over his eyes. The cold of the room pressed around them, and she shivered once, then leaned awkwardly towards him.

"It's not your fault," Liana whispered, her voice harsh and stiff but hers. An awareness of herself, absent for so long, settled back into her body gently, filling up a void she had forgotten existed. Liander jerked his head upwards, his eyes fastening upon hers, his hands going to her cheeks. She twisted her lips into something like a smile.

"I'm sorry. I left you alone for too long," she said.

Liander embraced his sister, and his sobs shook them both. But her eyes, her face above his shoulder, were as dead as the face of the moon.

The first thing she asked for was warm water. Her body was unclean, her hair matted, and her bones peeking through her skin. Liana did not ask her brother how long it had been. There was no desire in her to know. What was done was done, and she could not go back. At the bottom of the lake, an infant's corpse rested. What was done was done.

She washed herself alone. The small room of the hut was chill with the fall and the water was not much warmer, but she sat in it for some time, watching the water turn gray around her. She submerged her hair in it and scrubbed. Vague stretch marks across her stomach became visible as the grime vanished from her too pale skin. Momentary panic filled her at the sight, and she closed her eyes. The world was spinning.

She pulled herself out of the dirty water with effort. The rugs on the floor absorbed the water from her bare, gaunt feet, from her too-pale skin. She wondered how long it had been since she had seen the sun. That question, like the others that haunted her, she shunted to the back of her mind.

Fresh clothing had been laid out before her. It was white. She ignored it and wrapped herself in a blanket. The cold danced across her unfeeling skin.

Liander entered as she had finished cutting her hair. There had been a knife at his belt, and it had been easy to pawn it with him so addled. That knife had a glinting question to ask her, and Liana had looked into it a long time before she told it no. She saw the fear in her brother's eyes when he saw it in her hands. It snicked once more through a coarse, matted lock. She heaped the remains of her long braids on top of the white cloth.

"I won't wear white," she told her brother. Her short hair left the base of her neck bare. The breeze from his entry tickled her skin. He nodded and picked up the pile, throwing it into the fire pit.

"I'll go get you something else," he said, and picked up the tub of water with effort, carrying it outside the door. She heard him dump it unceremoniously on the ground before bringing it back inside and leaving again.

Liander returned with buckets of lukewarm water, soap, and a set of clothing in pale gray which he placed on the bed. She looked at him questioningly. He shrugged, and she knew it was likely from his own wardrobe. He handed her the soap and dumped the last of the water into the wooden tub.

"I'll be back with more," he said. His gaze said that he was waiting for her to break and vanish beneath her madness again. She smiled bitterly at him.

"I'm not going anywhere, Liander." He nodded, though there was no certainty in his features, and exited again. She watched his back expressionlessly. "Though you may wish I had," she muttered in the empty room. The water steamed, and her hands went subconsciously to her neck.

The pendant was not there.

Suddenly, triumphantly, a fierce joy spread in her. The pendant was gone. It was as if a chain had disappeared from around her. She imagined the shining orbs of the lake goddess blinded and dripping black blood. Liander found her grinning madly. He stopped in the door, horror on his face.

"Don't worry, brother. I am not going to go mad and eat you," she teased, her voice ugly. Her fingers stroked the spot where the pendant would have lain and she sighed outwards, letting the expression slide from her features, though a slight smile remained at the corner of her lips.

"You ripped it off," Liander said, breaking her concentration.

She looked at him, her expression once more stiff and blank.

"I'll need food next," she replied. He turned to walk away once more, but her voice stopped him. "Liander? If you happen to know where it is, I'd like you to burn it. With the things in the pit." He didn't look back at her as he walked out of the hut.

With the bath, and proper clothes, she began to feel better. The men's clothing hung on her wasted frame loosely, swallowing her. Her strength had long since left her, and she remained standing only through extreme force of will. But she did stand. She would have to build up her strength quickly. That creature would come back soon, try to take her. Liana knew this as surely as the stars rose in the east. It was inevitable. He was what he was.

Liander returned then, interrupting her meditation. He brought food. Liana felt her stomach twist in rebellion, felt her legs shake. Her steps were at least even, if not steady, carrying her across the room towards him, to the fire pit in its center.

"Whose home is this?" she asked, calmly, but Liander flinched slightly, as if the question were a blow. Liana regarded his face, scruffy and lined with fatigue. He had aged years while she had been lost in the red sea behind her eyelids. No doubt she had as well. Neither of them would be mistaken for the youths their age suggested. For a moment, she regretted the pain she had cause. But only for a moment.

She knew whose home it was. The voice that had almost driven her back into herself had belonged to a man confident in his ownership, to have entered this place without question. The round room in which she had awoken was the central room of a village house, a small one that an unattached man with no sisters would call his own. For all that it was well-made, not the veritable hut that she and Liander had been given when they first came to this place. No, this was like the house she had built with Akala. The bottom floor was all painted white, though oddly bare of decorations. Liana suspected distantly that the austerity was her doing. She had not been passive in her distress. In her madness.

She did not plan to be passive in her sanity.

"Answer me."

"Liana-" her twin began, twin in only years and parentage now.

"Why?" Her voice was iron.

"I had no choice," Liander told her. "Jeilalu-"

Voices rolled in her head, a wave without ending, drowning her. Liana fought them, fought to rise above them. When the room spun back into view she was gasping for breath, but she had not lost. Her feet remained firmly planted underneath her, anchoring her to the floor. Liander watched her as if she were a stoneware figurine about to shatter, but he had obeyed her out-flung hand and still stood near the door, tray of food held before him like an afterthought. The smell wafted to her again. Liana swallowed convulsively.

"Continue," she said. Liander took a step towards her, then thought better of it.

"He is still the son of their god. They say they saw Her, when-" he broke off. She didn't think her face had changed, but from the way his own face had paled it must have. "I couldn't take care of you without their help."

She saw the grief in his face, the guilt and revulsion. Liana held still in the face of it, studied it with detachment. It was punishment enough, that look of self-loathing. Yes, he had failed her. But he still could have use. A broken tool was a wasted one. That was why she spared him further punishment. It was not because she loved him. Surely she had outgrown things like love.

She took a step forward and forced her shaking, exhausted legs to lower her to the shallow bench beside the central fire pit. Soon. The fire pit before her yawned, begged to be lit, the evidence of her failures piled within erased.

"I will eat now," she said. Liander handed her the tray. She sipped the warm, salty broth, and thought of death. She would have vengeance. It was a promise she made, staring at the evidence of her failure, forcing herself to live. There was a life that had been cut short. A child she should even now have been cradling.

She would have vengeance.

5 THE PRINCE

Liana looked at him. She knew his face.

It had been so long since his sister had fallen into madness, so long since her brain had been burned up with grief and terror that almost Liander had given up hope. He had watched for three months as her flesh had wasted away, as she wept and screamed and stared silently at nothing. Her golden eyes had gone flat, no longer shining with their inborn light. Her long, lovely dark hair had become brittle and gnarled. Nothing Liander had tried would get through to her, and what care he managed was minimal compared to what she no doubt needed. She would let no one else near to help him. He bathed her, when he could stand to or she would let him, and brought her meals she would refuse as often as not. He could do little else. They had not even been able to go back to their own house in the village. She had screamed and screamed when he had tried to carry her across that threshold.

Instead, Jei had mandated that they stay in his house. The man had kept his power with Herka's children, power that had grown in the wake of the moon goddess' appearance only days after they had ripped Liana's child from her arms. Liander remembered the eeriness of that night, how the whole village had been summoned from their beds and moved like sleepwalkers to the side of the lake. The sound of them, of so many moving feet shuffling in the dirt, had woken him. He was sleeping fitfully in his own bed, in the house they had built with Akala and her brothers. Only a handful of days since they had dragged his sister out into the mob as she labored, and the horror still sat in his stomach like a weight. But there was nowhere else for him to go. He could neither leave her unconscious form, nor set her free.

But when he had stood, skin crawling, in the doorway of their home and watched the unseeing villagers pass him by, a strange, disjointed movement had drawn his eye. Liana. It was Liana, staggering as if fighting each step, the talisman around her neck shining like a brand with white light. Her legs were stiff, her eyes rolling in her head, but still she walked towards the lake, while the villagers remained calm, almost as if dreaming. Only Liander had been himself. Even Jei merely stood, expectant, looking out into the water, to the light that grew there. It had curves like a woman.

Liander had raced towards his twin, pushing aside the bodies of the watching villagers, and pulled her back from the water's edge. Her clawed hands had come up, and for a moment he had feared that she would fight him. Then she met his eyes, and a low moan like wind in the trees on a dark night had come from her, like the creaking of a ship about to break beneath the pressure of the currents, and she had grasped the shining light around her neck, her face a rictus of pain, and pulled the chain that bound it to her until it broke. It dropped to the ground. She stamped on it, her bare feet grinding it into the mud of the mount, and screamed to wake the dead.

Since then she had not known him. Her body moved, but her mind had fled. The memory of it made Liander sick, like it was trying to crawl its way up his throat.

Jei had forced them back to his house, where Liana had been kept as the moon swelled and waned, swelled and waned. Four long months had passed, each more hellish than the last. Liander was the only one she would touch, but he was there on sufferance. The villagers knew he would gladly see them dead. His hate shone in his eyes, whether he willed it or no. They feared him, some, and despised him, too. But they feared to defy their god and Jeilalu wanted Liana alive.

Now, he would have his chance for vengeance. Now, after months, Liana had returned to him. She looked at him and knew him, and her eyes flickered with fire. He should have been overjoyed. He had been, at first. Until he had begun to understand just how much Liana's madness had changed her, Liander had been almost ecstatic in his relief. But he began to see that nothing would return the Liana he had known, his twin, his other half. Her eyes saw only fire and steel.

He had not said no to the task she had set him.

Liander touched the hunting knife that hung at his belt. His sword hung across his back, where it was less likely to catch on a tree or bush. The weapons were not so well-balanced or useful in the underbrush he passed through as his daggers might have been, but those Perlenian weapons had not escaped the castle. No doubt his traitorous uncle Drummond had them locked away somewhere or melted down. He'd always maintained that the Perlenian weapons were beneath a prince of Herkunsland, no matter that Liander was half-Perlenian himself. It was a shame, because while Liander was capable with a sword he had always been better with his daggers. The symmetry moved him.

His opponents would outnumber him tonight, daggers or no. If he was forced to fight, he would lose. No weapon would be enough to win him home. It still didn't make him long for his daggers any less.

He had crept out of the village at dusk, when the dying light might hide his comings and goings, and now, hours away by foot, he crept through blackness beneath the heavy leaves of the trees. The forest he walked through was green still, though some of the few deciduous trees had begun to change. Though he could recognize many of varieties of tree and plant by daylight, and name them in the villagers' tongue, they had been totally unfamiliar when he and Liana had first arrived, victims of his uncle's coup d'etat. The foliage was thick and unrecognizable in the darkness, obscuring his surroundings.

Liander wasn't sure how far he would need to go to reach his destination. He'd brought only a small bit of jerky and water with him. Liana had told him to walk south, and pointed out the stars which would show him where south was if he became lost in the trees. There were clearings, occasionally, though there had not been one for a while, places where large trees had fallen and destroyed their smaller neighbors. When he'd last checked his bearings, he had still been headed more or less in the right direction. This was easily the furthest south from the village that he had ever been, but he would have to turn back soon or risk discovery of his absence. Jei always came in the mornings to see his sister, no matter that he wasn't welcome.

The forest went quiet. Liander straightened. He heard a rustling to his left, and then to his right — intentional noises, distractions. He released his dagger, and held his hands over his head.

"I mean no harm," he said in the language of the villagers, the ones who called themselves Ma'alu's children, children of the moon, Ma-peli'a. It was close enough to the language of the Quet'le-Ma that he would be understood. He felt the hard line of a sword press his neck, heard the strike and hiss of a spark becoming flame. Light bloomed amidst the shadows of the trees. The prince was ringed with warriors, their faces made fierce in the flickering light. Dark cloth wrapped their braids, no doubt strung with bells. Liander would have heard their approach, without that cloth.

"What do you here, stranger?" The one who asked the question was somewhere behind him. Liander could not turn his head, so he addressed his answer to those he could see.

"I've come with a message from my sister."

There was silence. No doubt the men were taking in his golden hair and figuring out exactly who his sister was.

"What does Fa'elu-peli want with us?" said a man in front of him. Liander met his eyes.

"We have a common enemy. She would have your help destroying them."

"She saved them before," one of the men scoffed, his accent making the words almost unintelligible. Liander grimaced.

"They repaid kindness with treachery," he said. The sword was still at his throat, but they were talking, thinking over his words. Liander didn't relax — that would have been foolish — but the conversation did give him hope.

"We will have her words, have her here," the original speaker said at last.

"I am her words in this matter," Liander said. The sword at his throat bit into skin, and he flinched in reaction, a bare shivering of muscles.

"She will come, or there is no bargain," the Quet'le-Ma told him. The sword vanished, leaving a line of warm wet at his throat that a breeze rendered chill. "In three days, at moonrise, you will return here." Liander heard a sword slid into scabbard, heard the rustling of the woods behind him. One by one the Quet'le-Ma vanished into the darkness between the trees, leaving Liander alone, or as alone as he was likely to remain while still in their territory. He drew his dagger and scored a jagged mark in the nearest tree, invisible against the shadowed bark.

"Three days," he said, his voice swallowed in the leaves. There would be no returning to the village afterwards, not without the Quet'le-Ma. Liander shoved his dagger into its sheath and started back the way he had come.

It was long past time for leaving.

6 THE CAPTAIN

The coins sat on the table between them, glittering as only metal could. Bertrun eyed them, heart heavy. He misliked taking his siblings' charity, but necessity was necessity. Marie spared him from staring further by gathering them up and disappearing with them into the kitchen.

Bertrun leaned back into the chair, then, and looked at his sister.

Syria was not usually the one to bring him his monthly funds. Usually, the Shadows ferried them back and forth, trading on their knowledge of the passageways below-ground and their tendency to slip from the eye and mind of passersby when they wished to. For all that the pile of coins had looked large, what had been contained therein had not been much. It was only copper and some few silver moons. Spending anything larger would raise questions, and questions were not what Bertrun needed, hiding here. Then again, visits from his sister were not a thing he needed either, no matter how welcome they were. It was too dangerous. He could not guess what she had been thinking.

Still, he forbore to ask. Let Syria tell him in her own time.

"Would you like a tisane?" he offered instead. Syria nodded, and Bertrun got up to get mugs and the kettle. In the kitchen, Marie counted coins into piles on the counter, following some alchemy he did not know. Bertrun left her to it.

Pouring the tisane took a moment. Syria stared at the steaming, falling liquid, eyes dark. When he handed her mug to her, leaves swirling and browning the water already, she cradled it close. For warmth, he thought at first - the vast dining room was cold, the fire banked in the grate despite the damp chill of fall. But her face remained grim, and Bertrun soon realized that his sister needed the comfort, too.

"How is Rufus?" he asked at last. Syria started, as if she had been lost in thought. Her gaze focused on him.

"Rufus is fine," she said, gesturing the question away. Her husband had bought into their cause with strict conditions - Syria was supposed to be mostly kept out of it, excepting funds. But his profession as a merchant took him away on trips to Perlen often, and Syria had never been one to be kept in a box. She remained active with the temple, volunteering among Herkun's priests. The intelligence she brought the Shadows was only the kind that let Bertrun see the lay of the political landscape, as the priesthood kept out of the Lord Regent's management of the city for the most part. They were interested in their tithes and little else, as least for now, though he knew Wrothfurt feared future action against the Academy.

"Then why risk this trip, Syria?" Bertrun said, his impatience at last getting the better of him. "You know it's not safe to come here, not for you."

Syria gripped her mug more tightly, looked away. Then she sighed deeply, and looked him in the eye.

"The priests are planning a large event, some days from now. They're rounding up all of the volunteers, and all of the regular parishioners. The temple is to be opened to the city entire."

Bertrun sat back, blinking. An event at the temple was rare, no matter the time. The throne had kept its own counsel as long as he had been alive, with the temple being opened only for major events at high holidays, for weddings, and for -

"Is the king dead?" he demanded, his throat nearly closing around the words. Syria looked at him in surprise.

"Would the Shadows not have told you?" she asked. Worry clouded her face, drawing lines there that he would not have seen even a year ago. Then she shook her head. "I don't know. Whatever it is, they haven't told me yet. Only asked for my help in passing out bread."

"They'll feed whoever comes then?" Bertrun asked.

"They always do." Syria's voice was bitter. "Everyone who makes it to the midday service is fed. Why do you think so many people go? They have to close the gates on more people each week."

She put the mug down then, wrapped her arms tight around herself. "Every week I see starving children, Bertrun. They come halfway across the city for their loaf of bread. Every week they are thinner. Yet the priests stay fat. I stay fat, and well fed."

"Syria," Bertrun began. He reached out towards his sister,

though the table lay between them. She did not take his hand.

"I'm pregnant, Bertrun."

Bertrun was grinning even before he fully understood Syria's words. Pregnant, with a niece or nephew that he could hold, one day, when all of this was over. He felt his heart swell with the joy of it, imagining those small hands.

But Syria was not smiling.

"What's wrong?" he asked. She shook her head, took a deep breath.

"I can't help you if I'm pregnant, Bertrun. The priests would never hear of it. And I-" Her voice died in her throat.

"Syria," Bertrun said, standing. If she wouldn't take his hand he would go to her. He walked around the table between them. She leaned into his chest, and he felt her shudder.

"What will happen to this child? How can I bring a child into this?" Her voice twisted at the last. Bertrun tightened his arms around her shoulders, letting her cry.

"I won't let anything happen to you," Bertrun said, but he knew the promise was false. He could not stop everything. He could not protect everyone. Someone would die before this was all over, people had died already, and he was just one man.

But she was his sister. He would do what he could, whatever he could.

"Have you told Maldun?" he asked, when Syria was breathing again. She leaned away from him, and he let her have her space. His shirt was wet, and it clung to him coldly, so he crossed to the fire and built it up. They could both use a little comfort.

"I haven't." Syria's voice was hoarse. He saw little bruises on her eyelids when he turned, and wondered that he had not seen them before. "Nor Rufus. I have a few months yet, before it will be obvious. Then they will insist I go into confinement, as if I might break just from bending over."

"I'd ask you to stop going to the temple now-" Bertrun began.

"And I'd tell you no." Syria shook her head again, looking wry. "I'll help as long as I may. Lisa could help, once I'm confined."

"Lisa is still frail."

"She's stronger than you think."

"Maldun will never -"

"Do you want your queen or don't you," Syria interrupted, eyes burning. "Liana will be your queen, and underestimating her got us into this mess. Don't underestimate me, or Lisa."

"Liana is god-touched," he began.

"The Queen is a woman first, and god-touched second. The Lord Regent has made that clear." Syria sighed, a deep breath out. "You need whatever help you can get. Don't discount us, Bertrun."

Bertrun nodded his head, accepting the point. It chaffed, to let his sister and his sister-in-law risk themselves. Lisa had already paid a hefty price for her spying, with her illness. But if this was to be a country of women and men, who was he to tell them no.

After Syria left, he sat and thought about starving children, and her worries. The memory of the coins she had brought him was cold and heavy in his thoughts. The merchants in the city supported unseating Drummond, though their support was quiet. It was not, likely, because all of them cared for starving children, like Syria did. It was because each tariff and tax imposed by Drummond to feed the groaning tables of the castle and the temple, each piece of aid not given when drought or flood ravaged the countryside, cut into their profits and their livelihood. Bertrun knew this, but he had never thought on the fate of those he could not see. He had never thought about parents who were too poor to feed their own babes. Had such been the case when Alexander ruled? He did not know.

Would Liana do better? He did not know that either.

All he could do was hope.

7 THE PRINCESS

The night was dark, and chill. The cold moved through her too-thin body like a knife, despite her warm layers. Liana did not shiver. It would be seen as weakness and she was done cowering from anything.

Liander had awoken her from a restless slumber some hours ago, just after darkness had settled in around the village, driving most of its inhabitants indoors. With her gray clothes and hacked off hair, Liana didn't look much like herself, and Liander said the villagers had taken to ignoring him. He was not their friend, and they knew it. It dimmed the resentment she held towards him. That ill feeling was still there, and she'd have to deal with it if she planned on getting them both back to Herkunsland alive. It would be a long journey, not the sorcery they had experienced before. Liana's hand spasmed towards the place the talisman had hung before she could stop it. She forced herself to exhale slowly but her nails still scratched idly at the dip in her collarbone.

"It's gone," she whispered to herself.

"What did you say?" Liander said, his voice low.

"I wondered when they would come," the princess said, dropping her hand. She couldn't see her twin's face. Was she imagining the skepticism, the worry? It didn't matter.

"They'll be here," he said at last, his voice containing only a hint of worry. She believed him. They would come if for no other reason than to kill the trespassers on their lands.

As if summoned by her thought, a figure melted out of the shadows of the trees. He let them adjust to his presence before others stepped out, surrounding them. Liana smiled grimly, glad the blackness hid her expression. If they let themselves be seen, they were less likely to kill her out of hand.

"Fa'elu-peli," their spokesman said, and Liana started. She had thought the figure before her a man. The shadow of the profile was tall and wide-shouldered, but the voice was high and unmistakably feminine. She felt Liander tense beside her as well. Her twin was also unfamiliar with the speaker, it seemed.

"You may call me that, if you wish," Liana said, in the tongue of the villagers who had subjugated her. The words were flat and dead in her mouth.

"It is what you are," the figure said, "though your fire burns low."

Liana bared her teeth, feeling rage smolder in her. "I am still capable of burning."

The figure barked a laugh. "With enough tinder, any spark can burn." As if to emphasize the words, a spark appeared between them, and a flame. Liana felt her eyes dilate with the light, and looked into the speaker's face.

The shoulders, as the shadow had suggested, were corded with muscle and wide-set, the skin the golden color she had seen on the other Quet'le-Ma whom she had encountered. But the fine features of that face were feminine, the hands long-fingered and small, the wrists tapered despite their muscle. They were, possibly, a woman, though their hair was wrapped in the same black cloth the warriors around them used and their hips were narrower than Liana's own. There was something undeniably masculine in the set of those hips, in the posture of their body. Even their breasts were nonexistent, barely pressing against their leather vest - hard leather, and formed with raised designs that caught the light and cast strange shadows. It was leather for warring in.

"Who are you?" Liana demanded. The woman who was not a woman smiled.

"I am a...priest, of a kind. You may call me Ma'tela." Liana nodded in acknowledgement, and only then noticed the contraption perching in the priest's palm. It was a bowl of flame.

The bowl was copper, she thought. It had that bright color, not quite dull as bronze. Bowl was, she realized on further inspection, a misnomer. It was a small vase, top mostly covered, the hole in the top filled with what appeared to be a cork of some kind. She could not tell what the substance was in the dark, but from that cork sprouted a wick, which held the bright, clear flame that lit the priest's face. As it had since she had awoken, the fire felt distant from her, but Liana remembered its closeness. She remembered how it had filled her with warmth and life when her son had shared her body.

No more. He was gone.

"I would kill the villagers. I would end Ma'alu's children" she said. It was a raw pronouncement. The priest's lips twitched. Liana didn't know if that abortive movement would have been smile or frown. She didn't care. The time for dancing around these things was past. She was tired of politics.

"You have been treated poorly," the priest said, and the echo of Akala's words so long ago made Liana tense. "In our village you would have been kept safe, revered for your knowledge. Fire's knowledge cuts when handled unwisely." A shrug rippled muscles, shadows flowing in the light of the flame held between them. "But it is only a boon for us. The goddess is also remorseless. She has told us that if we retake the mount, we will be Her children again. Our cousins will pass into history. The question remains if your fire is bright enough to do the deed."

Liana smiled bitterly. Jei had taken both her sword and Liander's, but Liander had known where they were. He had stolen them away during the day, when the villagers were out in the fields harvesting. It was that time. Every hand was needed. There had been no one to see when he reclaimed what was theirs. They had left before the weapons could be missed. Her rapier hung across her back instead of in its customary perch at her hip, the better to shield it from the grabbing arms of the brush. Its presence kept her spine straight even as fatigue settled into her bones.

"Vengeance is a heady enough elixir to feed an exhausted soul," she rasped.

The priest's eyes flickered, again unreadable. "As you say." Was the tone of that pronouncement more reserved? Liana hoped so.

It would be a hard enough task to kill her current enemies. She had no desire to make more. But they would all meet the same fate, should they cast themselves against her. She would burn them, or burn herself to ash.

There was no longer any room in her for compromise. It had not served her.

They left with little fanfare, heading back the way they had come. Liander made her eat something first. His face was stone-like, his eyes distant. Even now he did not quite believe in the justice she would mete out. But he followed her as they spilled through the woods, the warriors around her silent, her own feet crunching leaves and loam with a gentle crackle.

At last, at last they would burn. A trembling exhilaration filled her - not quite joy. She didn't know what it was named, but it rose up in her, twisting her lips, baring her teeth to the night. She heard her breath rasp in the night air, felt her muscles burn in agony with the effort of her steps. So weak still, her body was so weak. They had taken her youth, her vitality, her innocence. They had taken her son.

Now they would have back one thing she had taken from them. They would have fire. That was the great weapon of the Quet'le-Ma, the thing they feared.

They should have feared her more readily.

Her heart picked up in her throat as they neared the village's edge. The Quet'le-Ma, hair bound to hide the clinking of bells, flowed ahead of her silently. There weren't many of them. If someone found them, sounded the alarm - but the villagers slept, exhausted from their labors bringing in the harvest. Liana thought of the old woman who had taught her to weave, of the children she had once watched at play. She thought of Akala. A moment's regret washed through her, sudden as a spring storm. The princess clenched her fists. It would pass.

They came to the edge of the village. The houses hung in the darkness, smoke from cooking fires painted the air. There was no returning. The priest of the Quet'le-Ma appeared beside her, androgynous face unreadable in the shadows. The contraption of flame was pressed into her palm, and something else. A clay pot, its top filled with fine rushes, not the slower burning woven wick. Liana stared at it for a moment, feeling the fire closer than it had been since she had put the pieces of herself back together.

"Liana," her brother said, "we don't have to do this." She started, looked back at him. It surprised her to see the look of anguish on his face. Her own lips were twisted up at the ends, smiling with sudden euphoria. This, at least, the song of the fire, this she could have back if only the children of Herka would die.

She turned, and lit the little clay pot. It flared in her palm. Her arm pulled back, and she threw.

8 THE PRINCE

He watched the object sail, trailing flame. Watched it shatter.

The fire blossomed immediately, roaring as it consumed the air. Someone let out an eerie, high cry and suddenly fire was everywhere. The night lit up, bright as day. In the light, he saw Liana draw her sword.

The flames flared brighter as she tipped back her head and laughed. Liander gaped at her. Chills crawled across his skin. The moment prolonged itself as his heart throbbed in his ears, as the first of the screams began. His feet had turned to lead, his hands were numb and still she laughed.

The first of the village warriors reached her, face obscured in the poor light. Liander saw the sword come up in the man's hand before he realized what was happening. He gathered breath in his stiff lungs to shout a warning.

Liana sobered, and stabbed the man through the throat.

It had happened so quickly. The warning died on his lips. The village man - no doubt someone Liander had known, someone he had hunted with once - went down, his blood black in the firelight. Liander felt his stomach twist, and reminded himself that the same man had helped sacrifice an innocent child. It didn't matter how unnatural that child may have been. His sister had deserved a choice.

He drew his own sword, and followed Liana forward into chaos.

The flames burned unnaturally hot, searing his skin. He could not see a house that wasn't in flame now. People ran screaming. The Quet'le-Ma cut them down, all but the children. He heard a toddler sobbing near him, heard a person pleading for mercy in a voice that suddenly ended. The fire roared. Ahead, he glimpsed Liana.

Her gray clothing looked sooty in places, singed in others. Her brown hair flew about her head wildly in the wind from the fire's heat. In front of her stood Jeilalu.

The man wore white, as he always did. His chest was bare, glistening with the sweat the inferno had called up, his long hair unbound. His white pants shone in the reflected light of the flames. One might have thought he was the hero of this story - and perhaps, Liander thought bitterly, he was. His sister had destroyed a people for her vengeance. What more would she take?

But this man had made choices just as horrible, and the hatred that Liander had felt upon looking at his face drove any qualms he still harbored down deep. There was no time for that now. He saw how Liana trembled, her gaunt form losing the strength it had been able to muster for this fight. He could not lose her to this man a third time. Liander lunged forward - and came face to face with Akala.

There were burns on her face, her shoulder. Liander had time to notice that before she swiped at him with her knife, its gleam hard to track in the changeable light. Her dark eyes were hooded in shadow, her mouth snarling. Liander moved to the side, feeling the knife bite at his arm through the cloth of his shirt.

"Traitor! Murderer!"

The allegation brought an answering snarl to his own lips. "To me? You say that to me?" The anger in his voice surprised him. She came for him again and he moved, quickly this time, no longer held back by surprise or sentiment. And when she drew back, he struck forward. She moved past his blade bonelessly. Her cry of rage tore through the night.

She didn't see his other blade.

It sank up beneath her ribcage. Liander heard the gasping, wet suck of her breath, felt the knife in her hand tumble against his side and to the ground. This close, he could see her eyes. They were full of tears, reddened with smoke and wild with terror. She was as beautiful as she had ever been.

"Akala," he said. He didn't know why he said it, what he planned to say. There was no apologizing. She sneered at him with bloody teeth.

"I knew," she said, "that you would kill me for it."

He lowered her to the ground gently. She breathed her last.

Later, he would feel this. Now, the prince stepped around the corpse of a woman who had once been a lover, who had once been a friend. He did not think of the grief that had moved her to attack him. He did not think at all. His feet moved, and his hands tightened on the bloody hilt of his knife, the larger grip of his sword. Liana was in front of him.

She was surrounded by flame. Inside that ring was Jei.

They fought - or she fought. Jei seemed only intent on avoiding her blows, turning the stabs of her sword's point. There was blood on his face, along his forearm. He had not always been quick enough, and no wonder. Liana moved with focused efficiency, with precision that gutted her usual grace and made mockery of it. No move was wasted. Nothing was elegant, only clean and brutal and cutting.

A village man threw himself in front of Liander, eyes wild. The prince cut him down. He did not even stop to see who he was, to see if he had known him.

Liana cut and stabbed and pressed Jei into the ring of flames. Liander saw the ends of the man's hair dancing upward with the heat, saw the moment that he knew that he could no longer act only on the defensive. He struck out with his sword. Liana was forced to block, forced to back up a precious half step. Then he pressed her back another. His reach was longer, his weapon heavy. Liana's light rapier could barely turn it safely. The focus on her face did not change, though. There was no fear there.

Liander ran. The form of the priest arose before him, catching the downward stroke of his sword with ease.

In the light of the flames, the in-betweenness of the priest's face was even more pronounced. It stopped Liander, caused hesitation long enough for the priest's words to reach him.

"Will you take her vengeance from her?"

Liander swallowed at the question. The person before him was considered holy, he had seen that quickly, a font of wisdom to the Quet'le-Ma. Reason told him that they needed the priest's support. They needed, when this battle was over, to petition for the food and supplies they would require to cross the mountains.

But Jei was close to cornering Liana now. His sister was weak from her madness and grief, weak from the harm the man had already done her. He could not leave her alone. He pressed his opponent's blade aside, pushing past - and barely dodged the strike that followed. He spun towards the priest, startled.

"You will listen to me," Ma'tela said. "If she does not kill him herself, she will not heal. The fear of him, the knowledge of him, will fester like a canker. You will let her kill him, or let her die. This is her crucible to pass through, not yours."

Liander gritted his teeth, nostrils flaring. Those words could be true. He turned to look at Liana again.

As he watched, she slipped past Jei's guard and skewered the meat of his bicep. The sword went clear through, but she didn't pull it out. She swung up, tearing the muscle with fiendish effort. Liander saw Jei stagger. His back was to a roaring block of fire, once a house. Jei's sword at last dropped from his hand. Liander saw his mouth moving, pleading.

Liana brought her sword forward again. The point rested above Jei's heart. She backed him towards that inferno, towards the all consuming fire. And then she kicked him, hard, in the stomach. He was a big man, and she thin and haggard with her illness, but he staggered backwards. Perhaps he had not expected it. It didn't matter.

Liana gestured. The fire roared, and the building framing it collapsed on Jeilalu, burying him.

When she sagged, Liander lurched forward, and Ma'tela did not stop him. He sheathed his sword and dagger so that he could gather her in his arms. She didn't fight him. There was a cold look on her face as she stared at the fire that had consumed Jeilalu, murderer of her child, rapist, and son of a god. What strength had kept her fighting Liander did not know, but her eyes were clear despite the exhaustion of her flesh. They sparked gold as they looked into his own.

"This is only the beginning," she told him. He picked her up, and carried her out of the remains of the village for the last time.

9 THE KING

He awoke in his cage. That was the way of it. Every morning, just as the sun crested the horizon, Alexander, deposed king, madman, became once more himself. The darkness that had housed itself in him receded and his body was once more his. How he longed for it to be otherwise.

He wanted the curse out of him.

He felt its film as he lay, curled in his cage, the silver bars beneath him cutting into his side. It was greasy, like rancid fat, and left a taste on his tongue like old blood. That blood was not his own. It was the blood of all the women he had killed in his madness, all of the women the darkness had torn apart with his hands. Their deaths blurred together. He could not even remember how many there had been. No matter how much he was bathed and dressed, no matter how he was fed and watered, he could not get rid of the memory of waking up drenched in their blood.

For weeks they had brought no new offerings, and for weeks Alexander had rebuilt himself. It had taken time to remember what it was to be human and to be king. It would take more time still. Alexander had nothing at all to do but try.

Once he awoke, there was some time to wait before a guard would come, and more time if it were overcast. They liked to be sure that he really was himself before they stepped into the room to open the locks that held him bound securely. It made his days even shorter, and he no longer thought the night an ease. This dawn seemed bright, so his guards would be along soon. He pulled his aching body upright, felt the dry rasp of his throat and the dull ache of his bladder competing with the discomfort of lying on cold bars and stone. His head pounded. Vaguely, he thought that he must have spent some time banging it against the bars. A probing hand came away maroon with half-dried blood. Alexander hissed despite himself and crawled to the back of the cage, propping his back against the bars to wait.

The door opened. A soldier entered.

He did not meet Alexander's eyes. Once, the king would have

known all of the soldiers in the castle, at least by sight. He did not recognize the man today, did not recognize any of the guards who cycled through as his jailers. In a way, it was a comfort. But it left him wondering how many of the royalty must have supported his traitorous brother, for his resources to be so many.

The soldier cleaned what there was to clean in the room, checking it for unsightly presents the demon might have left. The cage kept Alexander's body confined during its possession but did not keep the demon from throwing what it could get its hands on, if the mood struck it. Alexander had often wondered how the malevolence inside him could have a mood, but mood there was, derived perhaps from a careful calculation of what would cause its observers the most distress. Quiet days were necessary for instilling fear. The guard proved this - he was by turns guilty and apprehensive, his shoulders hunched, his gestures sharp with tension. Alexander wondered what the demon had whispered to the man in the night.

But that way lay madness.

Eventually, when he was done with his chores, the guard came to stand in front of the cage. With hands that trembled, he lifted a set of keys that rattled and clinked with the motion. There was no way for them to tell for sure that he was once more Alexander, no matter that he had been waking up himself for what must have been months, if the chill air and the shortened days were any indication. The king knew the guards dreaded this duty. After all, it made no sense to them how he had returned to himself. It made no sense to Alexander either.

The lock clicked open. The man jerked back in reaction, his hand on his sword.

Alexander watched this, too.

After a time, the man backed out of the room. Alexander stood, feeling the ache of old bones too long misused, and staggered through the door of the cage. There were new clothes laid out on his bed, and on the bedside table rested some bread and cheese, and a flagon of watered wine. All of it was good quality, but not fine. There was no point in wasting fineries on such as him. Alexander ate, drank, changed. He felt exhaustion drag at his eyelids and spilled himself across the musty mattress of the bed. The sleep was dark and troubled and endless.

He awoke when the door to his cell swung inward.

The footsteps had nearly reached him by the time he pried open his eyes. The groggy, ill taste of sleep lingered in his mouth and head. He could not force himself up before his brother loomed over him. Drummond, betrayer, would-be kinslayer, stared at him with a faint frown, a bemused expression which Alexander's exhausted mind could not interpret. Forcing himself to inhale deeply, Alexander pushed himself into a sitting position with shaking arms. The room reeled and then settled.

Alexander had always been of a more spindly build than his brother, though adulthood and a crown had lent him a regal air in his prime. His unkempt hair, once long, brown, and wavy with health, was brittle, streaks of coarse gray running through it, and tangled. Even his face was narrower and longer than Drummond's, though they shared the nose. Drummond had the look of their father. That bitter old man was likely turning in his grave at the audacity of his younger son, no matter that he had often wished Drummond his firstborn and heir. Alexander could almost hear it, those words from his father's throat.

His eyes had closed, he realized. Alexander pried them open.

"Are you done napping?" Drummond demanded. Alexander felt his eyes try to roll back in his head. His exhausted body did not want to give up on sleep, and a meal of bread and cheese would not be enough to give it the energy it needed. He hadn't slept for days, and it was not like the demon did anything so serene as nap. Memories welled up when he closed his eyes, memories of things his hands had done, and kept Alexander from true rest until exhaustion had rendered rest inevitable. He took another deep breath, forcing it into his chest with effort, and sat up straighter.

"Brother," he said. Drummond grimaced at the word.

"When was the last time you slept?" Drummond demanded. Alexander shifted where he was propped against the headboard, chipped and battered thing that it was.

"You care." It was half a question.

Drummond shrugged. "You are needed." He watched Alexander silently. The once-king felt himself come awake under that regard, shaking off the sleep if not the crisp, too-bright film of exhaustion. His brother had something he wanted. Alexander had hoped his new state was merely a kindness. He should have known better.

"I would have you crown me king," Drummond said.

Alexander laughed.

It was a wheezing thing. Drummond waited stonily until he was finished.

"This is no laughing matter, brother," Drummond said, grinding out the last word. "The fall is come but the crops have died in the fields. The land is still under its curse. The people need leadership."

Alexander felt his lip curl. "If this land is cursed, it's your doing," he said. He didn't believe that. Not really. The land had been cursed long before that, and for no reason he knew. Otherwise why would Herka have included him in her machinations so easily?

"Don't patronize me!" Drummond roared. A fleck of spit struck Alexander's face. He wiped at it reflexively, finding himself unimpressed with what his brother's anger might mean for him.

After all, he could do no worse than he had done already.

"Why should I?" Alexander said.

"I had thought you would be more grateful," Drummond said. "I can always put you back to trying to make heirs."

Alexander paled.

"Liana lives," he said. "And I cannot -"

"Liana will be dead soon enough," Drummond said. "I will see to that. You will crown me regent, or you will regret it."

Alexander stared at his brother.

"At least I have a demon inside me," he told his brother. "What is your excuse?"

Drummond did not answer. He left, and locked Alexander away once more.

10 The Seer

She had been fetching the Lord Regent's breakfast for three weeks before he finally revealed the cost of his regained favor.

Nicola moved down the corridor, the heavy weight of the breakfast tray in her hands. Matthius had managed to sneak inside this morning. Normally, they spoke of his son, and his wife. Matthius believed himself loyal to Drummond, but he was kind, and Nicola reminded him of his sister, who had died when he was young. She, too, had been blind.

Nicola had never told Matthius that the green god had given her back her eyes. It was better that way. Nor had she ever tried to bring him into the rebellion that she knew depended, to some extent, on her. For months, no one from Bertrun's network had spoken to her. It was no wonder that Jessa had been so angry when she saw her at last.

It was selfishness that had kept her from asking Matthius for his help, selfishness and fear. She did not want to lose this small bit of comfort. She did not want Matthius to be killed on her part. More, she did not want to risk Jessa. The girl was loyal, and she yet had a part to play. Without her visions, Nicola could not tell what the outcome of introducing the two might be.

Still, sometimes Matthius gave her news that was useful. It had nearly stopped her heart when he said that there were rumors Alexander had regained his mind - at least in the day. Nicola well remembered the power of the curse that had wrapped itself up in him, set upon him by Herka herself, and she thought it was surely a trick of the demon he had become. But day after day passed and Alexander continued to awake. The demon claimed him still at night, Matthius told her. As long as no one entered the tower room by darkness, they were safe.

That was news that she wished she could pass on to Jessa, and from her to Bertrun, though it might be news better unshared. Nicola could not shake the feeling that this was but a fleeting reprieve, leading to some new horror. She remembered too well the fetid odor in the tower where he was kept, the way that blood had soaked into her clothes.

No, perhaps it was better that she not pass on such a hope.

Today, when Matthius ducked in to speak to her in the brief moments before she went to the kitchens, Nicola sensed that he would not speak of the happy comforts of home. He smelled of sweat and he moved quickly, like a man excited or afraid.

"There's rumor," he said, sitting on her bed, "that the Lord Regent is planning an event at the temple."

Nicola did not have to ask which temple he spoke of. There was only one temple of note in Herkun's City, though there were small shrines to other gods, she knew. Her own parents had kept a small shrine as well.

No other temples, though, no other place that was believed to hold Sermund's bones.

They were wrong, of course. Sermund's bones were not in the soaring building that grew from the other, small hill in Herkun's City. The temple was a beautiful building, as beautiful as the castle had been before fire wracked it. Unlike the castle, it was not built for defense. Its towers sprung up like trees, straight instead of sprawling, reaching for the sky. Nicola had seen it in her dreams, though rarely.

What could Drummond want with an event at the temple?

Not for the first time, she reached for her vision. It felt as if someone grabbed her hand and pulled her up short. No matter how she tried, she could not break free of that grip.

She thought on Matthius' news all the long way to the kitchens. Jessa was not there, and Nicola did not dare ask after her for fear that she be seen taking too much interest in the girl. The fat cook that Jessa got along with so well laughed at her searching expression.

"You're like a dog sniffing for a scent," he said. "The girl's off to the stables for a stint. Seems one of the fool grooms got his hand chopped off for disappointing a lordling."

Nicola bowed her head, duly chastened. Lord Drummond's breakfast was heavy in her hands as she fled the cook's gaze.

She entered the Lord Regent's rooms just as he settled down to the table. It was fortuitous timing - she was not always so lucky. Nicola busied herself with placing the tray on the table, then setting out the dishes as she knew he liked. Forks to one side, spoon and knife to the other, glasses just so. Today's breakfast was a soft-boiled egg, a rasher of bacon, herbed butter and bread. Nicola felt her stomach turn at the smoked bacon smell as it mixed with Drummond's forest scent.

"Sit with me, Nicolus."

Nicola froze at the command, then forced herself to move again. She hoped he hadn't noticed, but Drummond enjoyed fear. No doubt he would be aware of her own.

"My lord," Nicola said, and sat.

It was easier to tolerate silence in the confines of her room. Here, with Drummond before her, her mind kept darting, looking for reasons, fleeing memories. With his scent in her nose, it was hard not to remember the pressure of his hands on her wrists, the weight of him. The green god had been there to protect her then, whether she knew it or not. Now?

Now she was at the Lord Regent's mercy. It made her skin crawl.

Drummond ate, for a time, without a word to her. He was a wide-shouldered man, Drummond, though not so tall as his brother had been. He kept his hair cropped short to his head, and wore few adornments. A circlet, golden buttons - not much to indicate his position besides the fineness of the cloth. His eyes were sunken, the skin tight to his head despite his size. He looked like a man burned up from the inside, and Nicola knew that he was just that. She had preferred it when she did not know these things. She wanted to reach up and rub at her blindfolded eyes until she could wipe the sight of him away. Wipe the texture of his thoughts from her skin.

"In seven days time, Nicolus, I will require your attendance at an event," Drummond said. "It is very important to me that this event go smoothly. Do you understand?"

"Yes, my lord," Nicola said. She opened her mouth, then closed it again quickly, biting off the question that had been rising in her throat. Drummond saw it, of course. She could sense his amusement, cruel and sharp.

"You have questions, Nicolus?"

"My lord," Nicola said, then swallowed. "It is only that I wonder what kind of event I will be attending."

"Why Nicolus, can your sight not tell you such a thing?"

Nicola swallowed again. He knew it could not. There was nothing to say, so she said nothing. It was safer, with this man, to say nothing.

"In seven days, my brother will crown me King, Nicolus." He paused. Nicola felt her heart flutter at his proclamation. Drummond could not be king while Alexander lived. He did not have the mark of Herkun to ensure his divinity. Nor did he wish to marry and make an heir. What he spoke of was blasphemy.

And yet, there had been unrest while she was locked away. A few small riots at market, but there were rumors of greater strife. She had heard nobles speak of it in the halls, when they thought there was no one to hear. Servants didn't count, of course, and she seemed a servant until they saw the blindfold. Her ears were better than most.

What would Drummond not do, to keep his seat? Righteous men were often the most corruptible.

"Your brother, my lord?" Nicola asked then, registering the other half of his statement. "My Lord Regent, Alexander is dangerous. He is-"

"None of your concern," Drummond said. His voice was hard. "Alexander is well enough to pass his crown. You will attend. Perhaps your quivering magic will find itself emboldened enough to tell me why Alexander is once more himself."

"Yes, my lord," Nicola said, her voice faint. She remembered, once more, the darkness of Alexander's tower. The screams of the guards.

"Remember whom you should fear, Nicolus," Drummond said to her. His voice was storm clouds and iron.

"Yes, my lord," Nicola said. There was nothing else to say.

11 THE PRINCE

Liander watched his sister in the light of the fire. She was sitting too close to it, but he did not pull her back. The fire didn't seem to cause her feet any discomfort, not matter that her toes were almost in the embers. The pregnancy, ill-fated thing, had changed his sister. If he had had any doubt of it, it had been erased the night before. Those changes were permanent.

They were camped outside of the remainder of the village. The smell of old burning hung in the cool evening air. The Quet'le-Ma were combing through the wreckage that was not still smoldering, looking for things of value that may have survived the night before. Those objects might replace their stores, help to provide for the extra mouths they would be taking in. The children that had not succumbed to the chaos of the fires had been spared. Their weeping hung in the air, grating at Liander's nerves. Not as much crying as there had been in the night, but it still shattered the quiet. A guard stood over them, not far from where Liana contemplated the campfire. He was a nominal presence. The children of the village had nowhere to go now. Thankfully, Liana had not said a word about the Quet'le-Ma keeping those children alive.

In truth, Liana had barely spoken at all since the night before. She responded to direct questions, but otherwise stared into the flames, her expression mercurial. One moment, her face would be filled with a sort of quixotic glee, a grin that reminded him, chillingly, of the expression she had often worn in her madness. Then, rage would suffuse her, hard and impassive, and the fire would flare. Sometimes she would reach her hand towards that fire, a look of longing on her face. Then the hand drew back. Her expression shuttered, and she receded. It was hard for her twin, once so close to her, to understand what she pondered.

Liander, for his part, had taken a turn clearing the village of the dead. The unburned bodies were scattered primarily in paths between houses. Gashes scored their flesh, blood dried across skin turned blue-gray in death. Liander had helped pick them up, their cold flesh clammy against his palms, and place them one by one on a stretcher made of scavenged blankets and branches. They pulled the bodies to the lake, depositing them on the mount. The priest spoke over them, long hands fluttering in benediction. Then the corpses were tossed ungracefully into the lake by two of the warriors. Liana had left the fire for that, stepping lightly through the woods in her half-burned shoes, to watch the bodies of those she had helped kill consigned to the waters.

They should have floated. Liander had been unsettled when they sank instead, pulled into the liquid blackness of the lake. Jei's body was not among them.

He could not say why it bothered him that their twisted half-brother had not been consigned to the lake, but it did. Liander had seen the fire consume Jeilalu. The building that had fallen on him still smoldered. Liana herself seemed stoic, and Liander could not bring himself to ask his twin about the man. Still, it would have done him good to see the body. To see Jei slide into the water as Akala had done. He thought that sight would be with him until he died.

The prince brushed away the thoughts of a woman who had been a one-time lover and a friend, brushed away thoughts of his blade sinking into her flesh, though they clung like cobwebs, and stood. Liana's eyes flicked to him, and then back to the fire. He waited to see if she would break her silence. When she didn't, he went to look for Ma'tela.

He found the priest standing in what had been the central square of the village. Once, Jei and Liana had danced here, Liana all unsuspecting of his intentions. The memory crawled through Liander, twisting his stomach. It made the wreckage around him easier to bear, remembering what this village had conspired to do.

"You need something," the priest said, calling him back from his thoughts. Liander shifted.

"My sister and I need provisions," he said at last. "We have a long road before us."

The priest was silent for a moment, face pensive. "You will return to the home of the sun then. It will indeed be a long road. The mountains between this village and your home are a monolith. You cannot go due west. You must pass south, far to the south, before you seek a crossing. And the passage to the south leads to deserts. If you have dipped down too far, the deep deserts will suck the water from you and leave you dead. Cross too far north and you will not find the pass. You will wander the mountains forever.

"The jungles to the south contain tribes that war fiercely and take no prisoners. The trees are as tall as mountains. Every day it rains. The tribes there will kill you and use your entrails for their auguries. The land will suck at your shoes and set your feet to rotting. You must pass through all of this to reach your home, and your sister is not well."

Liander cast a glance towards Liana reflexively. She was invisible behind the burned out husks of buildings. "She aided you well enough last night," he said.

"Ah, this is true. But a long journey takes much from the body, and from the soul. She has nothing to give."

"She would take months to regain what she has lost." Liander left unspoken the bitter thought that followed. Some of it would be lost forever.

"Yes," Ma'tela said, face serene.

"She will not take months." It was a truth that sat in him like a stone. The need that burned in his sister was all-consuming. That same need had driven her to torch this village, to set all its inhabitants to the sword. She had asked him to return with her, but he did not doubt that she would go on her own. If they had overstayed their time in this place, done irrevocable harm to her - well, that was his fault. He had doubted. He had not listened.

This carnage was the result.

"No," the priest said, looking at the prince's face, "I suppose she will not. I will send runners to provision you from our tribe's stores. Pass quickly through the jungle, stick to the mountain ranges, and you may survive. Your god, after all, is ascendant."

Ma'tela stepped away, shouting for one of the men. Liander stared after the priest for a moment, pondering those last words.

Pondering, against his will, his sister's fire.

12 THE KING

The crowd was eerily quiet.

That was what struck Alexander as he walked across the balcony high above them. The temple courtyard he had looked down on for his own coronation was packed, and silent. His steps, muffled by carpets, were still audible to his ears, despite the press of people that filled the square. The walls of the temple spread to either side of him, white stone that glimmered softly even on this overcast morning in late fall. The building itself was forbidding enough, but walls emerged from its sides and wrapped the crowd. There were large gates in those walls. If things went poorly, those gates would close, and trap people within. They would not withstand an army, but a mob would not faze them.

Those walls had always bothered Alexander as king. They bothered him now. It seemed strange, to wall in a place of worship. Yet even from this height he could sense the tension in the air, tight as the manacles that bound his feet.

His brother Drummond did not trust him to behave.

There were guards on the balcony, just out of sight of those below, and there were guards along the walls as well, their livery gleaming gold and white, more of them than Drummond would have bothered with if he expected this to be peaceful.

Then again, Alexander expected his brother needed the reminder of authority far more than he ever had. Many of the faces that stared up at him from below were gaunt with hunger. They watched him cross the stage, watched him between the hulking shoulders of his own guards, and their faces were unreadable. They were ghosts in their own flesh.

Drummond was behind him, somewhere. He had seen his brother briefly as the bindings on his hands - gold, because he was a king, but manacles with hard iron at their core - were unlocked and he was led onto the platform. A waifish figure had stood next to him, green livery a bright spot amidst the golds and blacks that surrounded Drummond. The gold and black were the colors of the Shadows, which these men were not, and that burned at Alexander unexpectedly, made him grit his teeth so tightly they ached. It distracted him from the pale form in green, and his jailor had swept him past quickly. Alexander suspected the chains had only been taken off his wrists because of public perception. His brother did not trust him to keep the monster inside in check, but Drummond could not take the chance that seeing their king chained would incite the people to riot. A king in Herkunsland was the avatar of their god. One did not chain divinity lightly.

Alexander did not blame his brother entirely. The demon was a wild, unpredictable thing, and though the sunlight had kept it at bay, he now knew, since the summer solstice, it still held Alexander's nights. He had seen what it could do.

He turned to face his subjects, standing tall on the wooden platform that had been provided. A page appeared next to him, carrying a red velvet pillow on which sat his crown. Alexander stared at it, at the golden rays which speared upwards, the diamonds inlaid in its surface. He had not worn this crown every day. It was ceremonial. Only the sun-crowned could wear it.

Drummond meant to be crowned with the king's own crown.

He would have laughed at the audacity, but there were too many people watching and their wellness was hostage to his own good behavior. Regents had been crowned before. Drummond should have had a circlet made, something commensurate with the position he could legally assume. Alexander would not be the only one to think so, no matter who had once supported his brother.

Still, some rats would cling to the ship until it sank.

There was a blast of trumpets - a second blast, his had come first when he mounted the platform - and Alexander watched his brother approach. The Lord Regent's expression was suitably grave, but his brown eyes sparked with triumph. He had worked so long for this moment, had upended a nation. Today Alexander would at last give him what he had killed so many for.

A moment of worry for his daughter sparked in him, and Alexander forced himself to breathe evenly. Liander was with her. She wasn't alone. His children would fight their way back to him, surely, if he could hold on. If he could keep a place for them.

His actions today would undermine that place. He grit his

teeth. Drummond stopped before him, eyes wary. Some of Alexander's anger must have shown on his face, giving his brother pause, and with good reason. The demon was fearsome, but the sun was high. Its darkness was quiescent. The king met his brother's eyes, smoothing his expression. He would do this thing. For the people in the courtyard below, if no one else. A crown was merely a crown.

A flash of green caught his eye. Alexander turned his head to look. That same small figure stood behind Drummond, a wisp of a person. No doubt she was meant to be disguised as a boy, but Alexander knew the form well.

The demon knew it, too.

Drummond had turned his back to Alexander to address the crowd. He did not see the change.

The demon came howling from the depths of him. He saw Nicola turn, saw her mouth open to shout a warning. Saw the warning die in her throat.

It was day. It was day, but his muscles did not belong to him. He could watch, but he could do nothing.

"You," the demon said, its voice high and wavering. Alexander fought to clench his teeth, to restrain it. Nicola took another step back. Drummond began to turn.

"You shine," the demon said, and Alexander's mouth warped into a grin.

The guards weren't fast enough to stop him. But then, he didn't leap for Drummond. He leapt for Nicola.

The demon moved with speed that cracked old joints and ripped muscles. Alexander felt the pain of it distantly. Drummond was shouting, his words slow as honey. One step, two, thudded through Alexander. He hit Nicola so hard he heard her teeth clack in his ear. His clawed hands scraped at the cloth that covered her, gouging. His mouth gaped, jaws popping as they spread wide.

A green light welled out of her and hit him like a hammer.

The demon receded sharply. Alexander felt as if the ground had risen up inside him, giving him purchase. He bucked the demon off like an unwanted rider, reached into his limbs, forced his muscles to an instant stillness. Nicola was panting, her breaths on his face, her warm skin merely inches from his mouth. He felt his control begin to crumble.

Her guard, unseen before, slammed into him. Alexander tumbled. As the soldier hit him again, the only thing the king could feel was relief.

He had not killed her. She did not deserve that from him, after all he and his had done to her.

The demon flared, pulling him upright. It had recovered, and it slavered after Nicola again, moving with his body, his legs. Someone tackled him. Alexander felt his sensations again receding, felt his body becoming even more tightly possessed by the darkness within. His arms were wrenched back. Drummond was still shouting. There were shouts from the square, too, he thought, echoing in his ears like the crying of birds. The body that was not his strained. It screeched and cackled with his throat.

The light would make it whole. The light would feed its hunger. That bright, green light.

Alexander, too, had light. A spark that was his. He could feel it inside him, and he hid it from the demon thing lest it realize. Lest it come and eat this last bit of him that remained. He had been hiding, it seemed, forever.

In the quiet corner of his mind that he still held, the king made a vow. He would not let it rule him. Now that he knew it could be defeated, could be knocked back, he would find a way. The fragments of him that remained in the face of the ravenous void of the demon tightened and solidified. It would not rule him. He would find a way to overcome this curse, or die trying.

13 THE CAPTAIN

There was chaos in the streets. Bertrun pushed through the press of people surging towards the temple gates, keeping his head low. There were guards, but not enough of them, and he was heading away from the unrest. He didn't think they would pay much attention to him. He kept his hood up regardless. It would not do to be caught now.

The house he shared with Marie was blocks away yet, but he could see the crowds thinning out not far ahead. A pickpocket darted into the jostling crowd, taking advantage of a protester's distraction. Once, a lifetime ago, Bertrun would have been a guard on the street, would have been honor bound to detain such a child. Now, he was not that man. He watched the thin form, the quick fingers, and let the child be. There was nothing he could do without drawing attention to himself, and he was drawing enough attention heading against the surge of the public, though he wasn't alone. A handful of others close enough to the back of the courtyard had managed to push through the crowd to escape what was rapidly becoming a riot. Those who hadn't fled would be locked in, and no doubt arrested. Many of them would be released, Bertrun hoped. Many of them had done nothing wrong but not move fast enough to escape, trapped by the angry mob behind them. The priests and the guards would likely spare those who had not rushed the doors of the temple itself. Drummond and his retinue had fled safely in the chaos. They had escaped.

They had taken Alexander with them.

Bertrun thought on the king who had trusted him, and his heart twisted. The man had been willowy but strong, wise and fair, with strong features and dark hair and eyes that burned a warm gold. That was the king he remembered. But on the balcony above he had seen a gaunt thing, hair streaked with white. Those sunken eyes had lost their spark. Even from across the packed courtyard the captain had known his king a man changed. His stiff steps showed that the year had aged him. Bertrun had thought, at first, that that deterioration had been due to captivity. He had hated Drummond with a fire then, a burning in his chest and gut that made his throat convulse. The man had done this thing to his own brother. He had held him captive like an animal, waiting for age and stress to do what he could not be bothered to do himself, and now paraded the captive king in front of a crowd for his own ends. Bertrun had longed for a weapon then, a crossbow, perhaps, something that could reach the distance. Drummond could die, and Alexander be freed.

The Lord Regent had marched onto the stage, his stocky form unmistakable in its rich furs and brocades. Behind him trailed Nicola, her red hair stark beneath her green cap. Bertrun had watched them, feeling that struggling rage twist in his chest, and gritted his teeth. He had reminded himself that Nicola had saved Drummond, once. Bertrun reminded himself that she was loyal. Her loyalty was not to Alexander. It was to Liana, and Liana could not come to power without her father's death.

It was an unworthy thought. It did not make it any less true.

Drummond, traitor that he was, had stood in front of Alexander and professed some pretty sentiment to the king of Herkunsland, mostly inaudible despite the acoustics of the courtyard. A crier from a high wall behind Bertrun repeated his words, no doubt from a script. At a pause in those words, the lord had turned to kneel. In that moment, the king had leapt - and struck Nicola's thin form with force. His high, mad voice echoed in the stunned silence of the square. A guard had moved before anyone else, knocking the king off of the seer. Someone had screamed.

The crowd erupted. Bertrun could still feel the wildness of the moment. People all around him, encompassing him, shouting maledictions and obscenities, screaming and crying, their voices a roar. They thrummed through him. Waving fists obscured the balcony, but he saw Alexander thrashing against his bonds. He had not been loved when he was king in truth, but he had not been hated either. Drummond was hated. These people saw only a man who had been fair to them brought low by one who had ruined them.

Bertrun saw a man that he had loved. One who was riddled with a curse that had transformed him. It was worse than if he had died.

Drummond's party descended from the balcony, vanishing from view. Guards took their place, training their crossbows at the crowd. More guards were arriving at the courtyard, beginning to push into the crowd even as the doors behind him creaked with motion. Bertrun had seen it all through blurry eyes. He wanted to move forward with the crowd, to face death. To find his king.

Instead, he had moved leaden feet to escape the trap curling around the crowd, pressed his numb body against the tide of bodies. He had not believed, before that moment, the rumors. The things people had said of his king.

He believed now.

The crowds thinned out, finally, into the normal, muted traffic of this new city. It was not the same place the captain had grown up in and patrolled. That place had been lively, full of chatter and gossip and the smells of cooking food. This place was dull and silent. There were shapes huddled in the alleys, eyes glinting out at him beneath tattered blankets. The shutters were all closed, even on a warm, unseasonable day like this. Through the haze of his grief and dismay, Bertrun registered the fearful expressions. No one was afraid of him, though. The thought came that if he had still been one of those guards in uniform, that would not be the case. What must it be like, to be feared so instantly by those you were supposed to protect? Some of those guards had been good men, once. He had recognized one or two of them, and steered well clear. There was no telling if they were good men still.

A shape came up beside him, matching strides, and Bertrun looked up to see the Shadow that he thought of as the leader. They walked in silence for a time. Then Bertrun raised his head.

"Did you know?" the captain asked. The Shadow looked at him sidelong, his face grave in its usual, stoic way. The scar beneath his eye flashed white.

"We knew," he said. "It was the price." Bertrun thought back to that night, the last night he had seen his king. It seemed ages ago, now, but he remembered. The king had said that he would not be fit to rule. He had known.

"The price?" Bertrun asked, almost unwilling.

"For the life of the prince," the Shadow said. "It was necessary. The goddess wishes for the prince's death. Her curse was to insure that."

Bertrun felt his stomach grow cold with dread. What could anyone do in the face of a goddess' intent? Yet his king had withstood it, in his fashion.

When they were sure that no one was following them, they turned back to the house where Bertrun was staying. With the focus on the square, no one would be watching the streets they walked now, and Bertrun walked more easily. They came to the house, and Bertrun stopped at the door.

"I will return," the Shadow said, "with news."

He left. Bertrun stepped inside.

He spent the afternoon sitting at the table with Marie, listening to the sounds from the city. The riots had spread, like a fire. It was tinder he himself had set, but Bertrun could not help but cringe from every distant shout. People were dying.

He had not been made to be a revolutionary. He was a civil guard, he was supposed to keep the peace. How had they come to this?

Marie reached across the table, took his hand. He gazed on her lined face in the flickering light.

"It will be alright," she said. "Or rather, it won't be. But we do what we must."

It was all the comfort she could give.

14 THE PRINCE

They had been traveling for days. Liander watched Liana closely for signs of fatigue, but could see none. She rode her hardy Quet'le-Ma pony, its nose pointing unerringly south. She must have felt pain - even he was saddlesore, between a year without practice and the padded blankets they had been given for saddles - but she said nothing. If her movements were stiff at night, well, his were, too. There was nothing to comment on.

There were stirrups sewn into the blankets, and rope bridles, but no bit. The ponies responded to pressure from his knees and the reins laid over their necks. He had ridden both of them when Ma'tela brought them to him, and given the calmer one to Liana, an older mare with white socks to her ankles and a sandy coat. His own mare was young and spirited. She was a beautiful bay, not a spot of white on the reddish brown coat, and if she had been taller he would have had no complaints. When he sat her without stirrups, he felt as if his feet would brush the ground at any moment.

Still, they were both solid mounts. The diminutive things climbed the deer trails of the rolling hills they encountered as they moved south without any trouble. Ma'tela had said the hills were the foothills of the Spine, or what Liander guessed was the Spine. They would know they had reached the jungles when they found themselves at a cliff. Liander had pressed the priest for more exacting directions, only to be met with laughter.

"You will find it," Ma'tela had told him. Liander was beginning to wonder. They had as much in the way of provisions as they could carry between them, and the ponies made good time. But they had traveled days. What if they had veered off course? He told himself there was nothing to worry over. Liana certainly didn't seem worried.

He cast a look back at his sister. She had her head cocked, a furrow between her dark eyebrows. When she met his eyes, he almost jerked. It troubled him to meet her gaze anymore.

"Do you hear that?" she asked, her voice gravelly from disuse. They had hardly spoken since leaving the village. He had to clear his own throat before he could answer her.

"Hear what?" he asked, straining to listen. All Liander could hear was the wind in the trees. Except - he looked up. The tops of the trees around him, some kind he did not recognize, were still.

"The roaring," Liana confirmed. He found himself frowning, his expression mirroring hers.

"Perhaps there's a river," he said.

There was more than a river.

It took them all that day and half of the next to reach the source of the sound. The land had leveled as if they had reached a plateau or ridge, but the dense green leaves surrounding them gave little indication of what might be beyond. Around midday, Liander began to see blue sky between the trees to the south where they were headed. The roaring was so loud it made his teeth ache, and so he was distracted when Liana kicked her pony into a canter and swept past him.

"Wait," he shouted inanely. His own mare tossed her head and broke into a bone-jittering trot. He wasted a few moments reminding her he was there. When he looked up, Liana had vanished between the trees. He growled and forced the bay after his twin.

Liana appeared from the undergrowth suddenly, and he drew back hard on the reins, forcing the bay to a halt. His sister was looking down at something, her pony prancing and rolling her eyes. Liander looked beyond them and felt his stomach drop.

There was only air.

"This must be the cliff," he said, because he needed to say something. His voice was almost swallowed in the roaring. Vertigo spun behind his eyes, and he slid off the now nervous bay, tying her reins to a low-hanging branch. He went to grab Liana's reins, to pull her back from the edge. She cut him a glance so sharp that he jerked his hand back. Fear and guilt and revulsion were not brotherly emotions. He swallowed them down. Akala's dead eyes flashed in his vision.

"More than a cliff," Liana said. Her mare had stilled at last, though her sandy flanks heaved. The pony leaned her long neck against Liander's hand, her ears flicking. Liana slid from her back, and her twin exhaled a breath he hadn't known he was holding.

"Look," Liana said, pointing west. Liander looked.

He felt vertigo strike again, and leaned his weight against the pony, gasping.

The vision that greeted them was surreal in its magnitude. Mountains rose to the height of the sky, ice blurring their peaks against the pale blue of the horizon. They were the mountains he and Liana had been traveling parallel to, the Herkun's Spine, grown large with proximity. They were underscored by the cliff's edge, curling away to the west and south. That cliff was intersected by a river. It was not just any river. It was, Liander thought, the greatest body of water he had ever seen, barring the ocean. It hurtled from the heights and cast itself into a froth of cloud, vanishing from sight. The roaring of that impact throbbed in his ears.

Beyond the mist, a lake as clear and blue as any sapphire sparkled beneath the sun. That celestial sphere's heat and brightness belied what would have been, should have been, a coming winter. Its searing light reflected harshly enough to cause Liander to shade his eyes. Beyond the lake, Liander could see a vastness of emerald green, bisected by a single, shimmering swath of water. The river cut south and west, following the arm of the cliff and extending beyond until the mountains marched down to meet it. He could not see what happened to it after that, but a dip in the peaks likely marked the only safe passage through the Spine. Between that hoped-for passage and their current vantage spread a dense, green swathe of distance that might take them more than a month to traverse. Liander felt his heart quail.

If Liana was daunted, she gave no sign.

"Look for a path down," she said. Liander nodded, eyes still fixed on the vista beyond.

It took them hours to find a trail that descended into the mists below. It was tentatively wide enough for the ponies, but only if their riders led them. Liander contemplated it, feeling his gut twist. There was no way to tell if it narrowed or worsened before reaching the jungle below, and it was a long way down.

"We'll make camp tonight," Liana said, looking to where the sun had dipped towards the sharp points of the mountains. "We can try the trail in the morning." Her expression was hard to read.

He looked for signs of fear, but couldn't say if he found them.

"Alright," he said, aware that the silence had stretched too long.

They retreated into the trees and went through the habitual motions of readying themselves for nightfall. Liander wiped down his bay with a brush, cleaning her fur of sweat and grime that might make sores if left to accumulate. The familiar odor of horse was a comfort, no matter that the mare was small and flighty. He wondered if she would make it through the next day. The worry chased itself around his head like a snake biting its own tail. The bay nibbled at his hair as he checked her dainty hooves.

When he carried his saddlebags and blanket to the fire Liana had made, he found his sister staring contemplatively. The fires at night seemed to sooth her. The prince tried not to find that disturbing and failed. He had seen her run her hands through the flames and come away unburned.

She turned away from the fire tonight, though, and lay down amidst her blankets.

"You need to eat something," he told her, putting steel in his voice though talking to her held its own kind of vertigo, its own sense that he might fall from a cliff.

"Ah," she said. "Yes." She sat back up, took the jerky and hard bread he handed her with a murmur of thanks. Almost, she was his sister. It was a strange sensation.

"Get some sleep," she told him when they were done with their small repast. He blinked and acquiesced, lying down to stare at the shifting branches above. Exhaustion could not quite shepherd him to the lands of dream. He lay there, silent, listening to the roar of the waterfall. Wishing that he could hear her breathing, the only proof that his sister had not vanished.

15 THE SEER

"You have ruined me!" Drummond's voice echoed in her small chamber. Nicola crouched before him, her cheek still stinging where he had struck her.

When he buried his hand in her hair, she was not even surprised.

"What did you do to antagonize him, witch?" Drummond shook her, and she let him. She had known from the moment that Alexander wrapped his hands around her neck that she was undone. Even without her sight, she knew Drummond well enough to know. Who else knew him better? Waiting for hours for him, she had used up all of her terror. She could not feel fear of him now, though pain ripped through her scalp, though she cried out.

Far more terrifying was Alexander, with the darkness in him, smiling at her.

"You are mine!" Drummond shouted, as if he could see her thoughts. "Your powers belong to me! You should fear me."

He threw her onto the bed then. The world spun with the force of it. She slid into the wall head first, and put her hands to the pain despite herself. That cursed vision, the green god's vision of the here and now, showed her the blood on her hands from where her scalp had torn, showed her the texture of the stone, showed her the lord, panting, anger and fear and avarice warring in him as he reached for his belt.

The green inside her, near forgotten, lurched.

She did not know if she did it. She did not know if she reached into it herself, pulled the power herself, or if the green pressed its power into her. She found her hands planted on the stone of the wall. She found the world behind her eyes going to grass and nothing.

Below her, the earth began to shake.

She thought it was Drummond, at first. He was on the bed, she could feel his weight as the mattress sank. Her heart was pounding up into her throat, pressing its way out of her mouth. She screamed, or started to, and he pressed a hand over her face.

She tasted ashes, and the salt of his skin.

Then the bed beneath them bucked.

Drummond cursed. His hand disappeared from her mouth, his warmth from over her. He was shouting. The door opened - she heard its creaking, and the clatter of men in armor.

"My lord, it is the earth!" someone cried. Drummond staggered out of the room as the walls around her groaned, the bed beneath her swaying as if on a restless sea.

She lost track of things, then. Fell, somewhere deep and distant.

Darkness was all around her, scentless, soundless. She could not feel the bed beneath her back. Even the throbbing of her cheek and scalp had gone.

Then, a light.

She looked down, and then farther down still.

At the heart of the world burned a fire.

The fire looked back at her.

Nicola awoke with a gasp, drenched in sweat. The green god's sight was slow to come back to her, and her own was as dead as it had been since midsummer. But she knew that someone was in the room with her before she had drawn a second breath.

When those inner eyes opened, she realized that it was Matthius.

"This is familiar," she croaked. Her mouth was dry, and that frightened her. She was glad not to be alone.

"Nicola," Matthius said. She heard him shift towards her, saw the concern in his expression. "Are you alright?"

If she reached behind his eyes, she could almost make out the fear there. It was like a shadow on the room.

"What happened?" she asked.

"The Lord Regent thinks," Matthius paused, his voice strained. "He thinks that you caused the shake. The shaking of the earth. Nicola, it damaged the temple."

She absorbed this in silence. Matthius was scared for her. What would Drummond do to her? Execution? Or something worse?

"Nicola," Matthius said. "Did you?"

"I don't know."

Her admission was quiet in the room.

"I need to get back -" he began.

"Matthius."

"I asked Russel not to say anything but someone will notice I'm not with him soon -"

"Matthius!" The sharpness of her voice surprised her. She had never raised her voice to anyone before. She swallowed. "I need your help."

"Nicola," he began. Then he stopped. She felt the conflict within him as if it were in her own chest. He wanted to help her.

But he did not want the consequences. And there would be consequences.

"All I ask," she said, "is that you bring me the water. The Lord Regent has denied it to me, since I displeased him, but if only I had it, I might help him. I might prove my usefulness."

He said nothing for a long moment.

"Nicola, it will prove nothing to him," he said. Then he walked out the door, leaving her.

She sat, alone, for a long while, and thought.

Her body was sore, and her mouth dry as bone. Her pale skin was sticky with sweat, her throat prickled with pain. She was small, and alone, and she did not want to die. Neither did the green inside her.

Yet she knew that when Matthius had denied her, she had run out of options. Whatever Drummond had decided for her, whatever death, it would find her.

So it was a surprise when the door opened and it was not the Lord Regent come to pass judgment.

"Nicola." Matthius' whispered summons drew her from the bed. She could smell the fear on him, sour in his sweat.

"You have an hour, two at most," he told her as she slid through the door. She realized that it was night, and that Matthius was alone. Neither should have been true. He had just been guarding her that day. Had he even gone home? Was her situation so dire as that?

There was no time to think on it.

"Matthius," she said, pressing her locket into his hand. It held the only thing that she had of her parents. She would never leave

66

it. Matthius must have sensed its importance, for her took it readily, his grip tight. "Keep this for me. A promise I'll return."

Then Nicola was gone, running on silent feet down the corridor.

The darkness of night meant nothing to her. She wore a blindfold after all. It was always dark. Yet she could see every detail of these corridors with what was left of her sight, could sense everything around her. She moved quickly, and her heart did not pound in her chest despite the unaccustomed activity.

It felt, at least, as if the lodestone at her center were cut loose. As if she were, finally, doing what she was made to do.

There was a wall before her. Her fingers dug into a niche of it, and a door sprang open that had not been there before. There was no one to see her step down into the tunnels. No one to see her vanish. Not that she would have known even if they had been next to her.

The depths were calling her, and she answered.

Nicola spiraled down, down into the tunnels hidden beneath the castle. She knew, from when her vision had been her own, that these tunnels stretched below the entire breadth of the city, everywhere inside the outer walls that had been constructed in Sermund's own time. Though the poorest of the city's inhabitants had spread out, beyond those walls, only the space within them was truly called Herkun's City, and everywhere that was Herkun's City was connected by a subterranean spiderweb, a network that had been built to house two things: the well that called to Nicola even now, and the sarcophagus that was truly Sermund's tomb.

It was the well that she searched for.

Yet as she passed through the corridors they twisted beneath her feet. She felt certain that she was moving towards the well, so certain. But soon she felt the heat of fire on her face. The fire at the center of the earth, twin heart to the chamber that had held her.

Nicola shuddered, stopped. Every inch of her rebelled at walking towards the flame. The green inside her had gone small and quiet, and ahead she heard a crackling.

Then steps, soft in the corridor behind her, made her turn.

It was Jessa.

Astonishment was not a new feeling for Nicola. Her visions had never been perfect, even before they had been lost to her. Yet she could only remember such a sheer disbelief filling her heart on a handful of occasions before this. To be astonished, for Nicola, was to be surprised at how the pieces fit together. Not to feel the floor drop out beneath her.

"Nicola," Jessa said. She sounded resigned. "Of course you would be here."

"Jessa," Nicola said faintly. The fire's calling made a terrible sense, now. Jessa was being called to the fire.

There were seven Shadows that stood by the king at all times. Seven, and yet three had died to protect Alexander. They had fallen almost without a fight, as if their deaths were simply accepted. At the time, she had not questioned it. No, Nicola had not been good at asking questions, with the visions to distract her and the rapidness of the changes around her pulling her attention.

Now, she at last wondered why the Shadows had allowed themselves to be so depleted. One did not simply get tapped on the shoulder and join. In her time below the castle, she had witnessed only three inductions. The Shadows were as much Herkun's own as the King, two parts of the same power, for every light made shadows. They lived unnaturally long lives in service, and those who undertook the ritual gave themselves completely. They did not always survive. Even Nicola did not know why some burned in more than spirit.

"You will go to Liana?" Nicola asked, throat still pricked with that awful dryness. "To protect her?"

Jessa nodded. "I thought you would have known."

"I should have," Nicola said, half to herself. This was her fault. She had told Drummond where to send his assassins, and she had told Jessa of the threat. "You will be a Shadow? Are you sure?"

The dim light of the tunnels did not shield Jessa's expression from Nicola's bound eyes. Her face had twisted.

"I have watched Drummond kill my friends," she said, and if her voice was level Nicola knew the deceptiveness of that. "He tried to murder Liander. I have no future in this country, now - King Alexander would have let me inherit as stable master, eventually, or Liana would have. Drummond wants every woman in the castle playing scullery maid in the kitchens. He kidnaps girls like me and no one knows what he does with them."

Nicola felt chilled at that. She knew what had happened to the girls the Lord Regent took. But she said nothing as Jessa continued.

"I tire of doing nothing, Nicola. When Liana comes, I will help her with everything I have."

The seer bowed her head. With the green near-silent inside her she could almost look out, could almost see the light of the princess. Almost, but not quite.

She longed to see it again, longed for the hope of it.

"Let me walk with you," she said. Jessa took her proffered hand, grip dry and firm.

Together, they walked towards the restless fire.

16 THE KING

His tower shook, once, like a dog settling its fur. He heard one of his guards shout, then silence.

Alexander waited, curious, to see what would happen next.

For a while, nothing did. It was late, the light gone, and normally the demon would have gripped him. That particular darkness had not bloomed yet and he did not know why. No one had come to lock him in his cage despite his outburst in the temple, which worried him because he preferred to have an extra barrier between him and anyone who might come inside this isolated tower room.

He had failed to crown his brother. Drummond could make good on his threat.

But when the door opened, it was not his brother. Nor was it some new sacrifice to be slaughtered at his hands.

It was his own Shadow.

Alexander stared from where he sat inside his cage, his brain refusing to comprehend. Then, because he believed in the Shadow, the Voice of his Shadows, their leader, more than he believed in anything else, he stood.

The Voice bowed. The scar near his eye crinkled with the ghost of a smile.

"My king," he said.

"How?" began Alexander, and then, "Why?"

"You are needed."

Alexander found he could feel the fire.

It came on him suddenly, like someone had been distantly calling his name for days and he had only just turned to look. Below him was an light at the heart of the castle, one that always burned, forever. But Alexander had only felt it a handful of times before. Once, when he had become king, and been inducted into its mysteries.

And again when he had brought this man to its embrace.

He realized that the room was nearly black, that the night had almost fallen. The demon in his veins remained quiescent, even so. The fire thrummed in him instead.

"Come," the Shadow said.

Alexander went.

They made their way quickly down into the dark, silent passages beneath the castle. Alexander saw people in the corridors, but their eyes slid off of him as he passed in the Shadow's wake. A hidden door took them from these populated places into the secret spaces that only the king and his Shadows traversed.

There were many secrets below the sprawling halls of the castle, as many below as there were above. Alexander was sure he did not know all of them. The seer had been one, placed in the labyrinth of passages by his father to look into worlds separated by distance and by time, to channel, sometimes, the words of the gods. He thought of Nicola, as always, with a pang of shame. There had always been a keeper of the water. She was, however, the first to have been found so young. He had often thought it a cruelty that his father had brought her at all.

The passages that led into the city were another secret that he doubted many amongst the residents of the castle were aware of. Certainly there was no one in the city who knew how quickly the nobility and their guards could be among them. While Herkunsland itself had only rarely experienced unrest, Alexander knew that it was only a matter of time before his brother led the country to civil war. He was not sun-crowned. And the gods walked this world as they had not done in an age.

But then, the gods had never truly left. If the well was Herka's hand upon the world, then the bones of Sermund were certainly Herkun's.

The priests, in their soaring, gold-flashed temple, maintained that Sermund was interred within their altar. The temple, despite its beauty, had been built after Sermund's death. The bones in the altar, if there were any, may have belonged to his firstborn son, the first truly mortal of the sun-crowned kings. But they were not Sermund's. No mortal stone could keep the body of Sermund at rest, because he had not been truly mortal. No womb had born him. And because he had never been born, he could not truly die.

The Shadow's steps were silent before him, but Alexander's own footsteps sounded on the stone, echoing back dully. The hall here was narrow. Always before he had brought a torch, some light to beat back the darkness. Never had he approached Sermund's resting place without it. So the king was surprised when he realized that he could see the blacker outline of the Shadow before him. He could not say when he had begun to see it, but it soon became undeniable. There was a light, up ahead. Moments later, he realized how warm the air had become. The damp air was now dry. There was a breeze pulling towards their destination. Alexander felt goosebumps on his skin.

They came to a room that was roaring light.

This was not the light of the sun, but the light of fire, the sun's hand on earth. It consumed desperately, growling with need. Yet it also sustained. Alexander could feel the heat of it pass through him, and for the first time in over a year felt himself. The curse was curled up inside him, yes, but it was as if he had never walked into the courtyard, had never let it blossom like some poisonous nocturnal flower. He gasped in relief, and pressed a hand to his chest.

The Shadow looked at him, his eyes knowing. Then he stepped into the room, and Alexander followed.

There was an inferno in this room, one that dwarfed the sight. Stone set at the heart of it, a blankness in the flames. He could see the shape of his ancestor's face, the proud brow and strong nose resting in eternal slumber. That face was the center of a maelstrom. The heat rendered sweat from his skin, but he felt no pain. A warm hand cupped him close in the flames. Alexander blinked and the feeling was gone, but the desire to advance into the heart of the fire remained.

There was a dish between the hands of the stone effigy, and Alexander knew that was from where this fire issued. That dish had held a small, ever-burning flame in the times that he had visited the tomb before. Alexander remembered the fire in its home upon the sarcophagus, the torches in the hands of his Shadows, the way the flames licked upwards almost unnaturally in the still air. Stories abounded about Sermund, the first of the sun-crowned, but the kings and their Shadows were the only ones who knew his secrets. Sermund had not simply been arisen from Herkun, he had been the god, a fragment of divinity given form.

Even in death, his bones remained focuses of that power.

Now, they burned unceasingly. Alexander felt his heart catch in his chest.

"This is the cause of the weather," he said. The fire caused a wind that almost drowned his voice, but still the Shadow heard him.

"Not the cause," the Voice said, "but a symptom. The same as your own awakening."

Alexander felt a chill that had nothing to do with the air. This flame was mirrored, in some small part, by his spark, by the blood of Sermund that flowed in his veins. He wondered if his father's bones also smoldered somewhere down in the catacombs below Herkun's temple. He wondered about his daughter, and flinched from the wondering.

His feet had paused upon entering the chamber, transfixed as he was by the impossible, unburning fire. Now the king looked about, noticing the silhouettes waiting, patiently, for him to join them. The Voice had already taken his customary place, facing out while the others faced inward, four lonely Shadows where there should have been seven. There were circles in the stone for each of those seven to stand in, with paths leading back to the tomb - and to Alexander's own space, now in the heart of the flames. He swallowed the dry air. The Voice nodded to him, face black against the backdrop of light. Firming his shoulders, Alexander stepped between his Shadows and began to walk towards the flame. The Voice did not turn to watch him. It was just as well. Three other sets of eyes recorded his progress, and it was slow. His heart thudded with terror.

Alexander stepped towards the fire. Sweat started on his brow. He felt the heat like a weight, an anticipation of pain, but somehow it never became unbearable. The flames leaped and jittered, licking closer to him with each hesitant step. He inhaled, exhaled. They seemed to grow to fill his sight, impossibly bright. Before he had realized it, he was among them.

He felt no pain. The fire rasped his skin but did not burn, flames licking like the tongues of great cats. They recognized their own.

Alexander came to a stop before the tomb of his forebear,

looking at his hands in wonder. The tight skin along his knuckles, over tendons and flesh, was a rosy gold in the light of the flames, not crackled and charred. He raised his gaze to the heart of the fire. Sermund's bier burned as white as the sun. He had to look away.

"The time is come," the Voice said. Alexander started, turned around. The three Shadows watched him, faces rendered harsh and orange with firelight. The Voice still had his back to the king, as was proper, but he spoke ritual words to a form outside of the fragmented half circle of Shadows. Two figures stood in the entrance, a small, distant outline. For a moment, Alexander was confused, but the figures stepped into the room, and their faces became known to him.

One was Nicola, her eyes bound in golden cloth, her livery green, her red hair nearly a flame itself. She watched him unerringly despite her blindness, the effect as disquieting as it had always been. He was able to look at her, without the demon's clammer now. There were bruises on her wrists and cheek, bruises he had left, but guilt had no place in the heart of the flame. With the exception of the bruises she was as she had always been.

Her companion was not.

She stepped into the room, wearing breeches and a tunic as Nicola did, so that at first Alexander's eyes deceived him into thinking she was a man. But her hips were unmistakably rounded and her chest as well, even in the moving light of Sermund's fire.

"The flames rise," the Voice said, "will you stand in their way?"

The woman stopped, at last close enough that Alexander could see her face. It was Jessa, the head groomsman's daughter. Almost, he opened his mouth and called out, but silence held his tongue. Her eyes met his for a moment, and there was only determination there.

That gaze reminded him of Liana.

The vision of his daughter, here in the arms of this pyre, was a knife to his heart. He felt the flames around him shift unquietly, as if catching his pain.

"I will stand, as the god of fire and light has bidden," Jessa said. Alexander dragged his focus back to the moment.

"Then come, and join us in our circle," the Voice said. "The price is steep to cross the threshold."

"I will pay the price the fire asks," Jessa said, her high voice firm and unyielding. The Voice stepped aside, as if opening a door. Jessa walked through the place where he had been. The Voice returned to his station, turned now to watch her. He did not look outward for this. In this moment, there was too much at stake.

Jessa stopped a handful of paces from the flames. Her head was raised defiantly despite the apparent fragility of her features. Alexander had always though her an impish child, though she had blossomed into the short, dainty body with curves that made her beautiful in the eyes of men. His Liana had been lanky and strong, coltish enough that he had sometimes thought she should have been the groomsman's daughter, and Jessa the princess. She would have been happier that way. But it had not been the wish of Herkun, to place the fire of the sun in a form so easy for his people to love. He wondered, watching Jessa, if she came to this circle for the sake of the gods, or for his daughter.

Either way, it did not matter. The strength of her conviction would carry her, or not. She had said the words. Alexander reached out his hand.

Fire leapt from him.

This was a fire not like others. It had a need to burn other things besides flesh. As the flames reached her, Jessa's eyes widened. Her back arched, and they burrowed into her, slid beneath her skin not into flesh and bone, but into soul.

For a moment, she hung suspended, surrounded by gold. The king felt his heart twist, watching her. Watching the agony that could not touch him transform her into something not quite mortal. Many did not survive this part of the ritual. The history of the Shadows was littered with the names of men who had burned entire, their bodies pillars of ash. The Voice, their leader, remembered them all, Shadows and the lost, without regard for one over the other. They had all given their lives in the end. One did not retire from being a Shadow.

Jessa hit her knees, curls swinging forward to hide her face. The flame rushed out of her then and passed by Alexander, its color the bright heart of the inferno. It nestled in the brazier behind him, returning to its source. The flames around him died back slightly, a barely visible contraction, springing away from the newest Shadow.

Jessa, when she looked up, met his golden eyes with her brown ones. Her face was distant, expressionless.

"Do you regret it?" he asked, though it was not something he had asked before. Did the words come because he had known her, or because of her sex? He stepped forward, out of the flames, as she stood.

"No," Jessa said. Her voice, though, was hollow. "I am more than I was. I remember too much."

"I am told that is the way of it," the king told her. "It will take you some time to work your way back to yourself."

Jessa looked at him as if from a great distance. "I will come back?" she asked. Her voice was so soft he almost could not hear it over the roar of the fire. The Shadows behind her stirred like trees in a wind.

"You are still Jessa," the king said. "The Voice and the other Shadows do not use their names. It is uncomfortable for them. I know them all, though." He smiled. "You know them now, too, no doubt."

Jessa nodded. Her eyes were still unfocused.

"The other Shadows trained long to be what they are. You are something new. What you will become is anyone's guess." To be honest, Alexander wasn't sure why she had been commended to the fire. She was barely more than a girl, and known for mischief and frivolity despite her wit. While the shadows could be personable - he had used them as spies before - they were by nature taciturn, watchful and violent. Jessa had been none of those things.

"Little you know, king," she said, as if answering his thoughts. Her eyes had sharpened for a moment, but then she drifted away again, lost. Her body turned of its own accord, and she took her place in the circle.

It was one more link in the chain that protected the world. Two Shadows still remained to be found, but at least they were one step closer to that.

He turned to Nicola.

"You must take a bone," she said.

Her voice carried over the sound of the flames.

"Is that why you've come?" he asked. She turned away from him then.

"I think so." She was standing with her head tilted, as if listening hard for something on the edge of hearing. "It's hard to see anymore."

"The green light I saw," Alexander said. "It's blinded you?"

Nicola went very still.

"I do not understand what I saw, before," he said, the memory of the abortive coronation making him wince. "I felt it reach into me, I think. That green light."

"It's not for you, Alexander," Nicola said. Her voice was hard, but not cruel. Afraid, he thought, and fighting that fear. It was noble of her, to try.

He was, in the end, fearsome.

"Thank you," he said.

He returned to the stone tomb of his forebear. The sleeping face carved in the stone seemed almost familiar. Alexander stroked its brow.

"Forgive me," he said.

Then he leaned forward, and pushed the stone until it slid.

It did not take as much effort as it should have. The fire moved his hands, and the tomb slid open, just a crack. A golden glow emanated from within, and Alexander reached down.

For the first time, he felt pain. The gold within burned.

He choked off the cry as it fought to escape him. The fire grew fitful around him. His questing fingers brushed a thing that scalded, something small and round. He grasped it and pulled it free.

It was a knucklebone.

"What now?" he turned to ask Nicola, but she was already gone.

17 THE CAPTAIN

The riots ended when the shaking struck.

Bertrun had laid down to sleep, but sleep did not come. Every spare sound had woken him, left him certain that at last the guards had found them, certain that the riots had come to their door. He knew, from the reports of the Shadows over the afternoon, from the distant sounds the wind brought, that the area around the temple continued to experience unrest. Every time he closed his eyes, he saw Alexander lunge with gnashing teeth. But dark fell early, and so Bertrun struggled gamely to sleep, knowing that a summons might come any time in the night. He would want to be rested.

He had just begun to doze when the shaking struck.

At first, it seemed as if someone had grabbed his shoulder and shook it gently. His eyes opened, bleary gaze falling on the ceiling. He saw nothing in the room with him, and the room itself seemed to be swaying.

Below, Marie screamed.

Bertrun shot out of bed. The coals in his fireplace were scattering across the floor, and he kicked them back away from the wood with stockinged feet. The building around him swayed as he pulled on his boots and grabbed the basin of water he kept for washing his face in the mornings, splashing it on the embers. Steam rose, but the heat died. Bertrun was glad his paranoia meant he slept clothed. He grabbed his jacket from its hook on the wall, pulling it around his shoulders, and stumbled and slid into the hall and down the stairs.

"Put out the fires!" he shouted to Marie. He couldn't see her but there was smoke coming from the kitchen. Their small cistern was there as well, so he ran in that direction, snatching a bucket from by the stove and moving to fill it. Marie was there already, throwing sand in the stove, swamping the fire. He left her to it, running back to the dining room's fireplace and dumping water on the coals. The world was still shaking, and he almost fell into the fire.

"Is that everything?" she called, emerging, her hands braced on the doorframe.

"Your bedroom?" he asked.

"I put it out first." There was a burned spot on her arm, he saw, a raw wound.

The shaking stilled, all of the sudden.

They stared at one another in the silence, listening to the sound of their breath rushing in and out of their throats. The house creaked and settled around them.

Bertrun heard the clanging of the fire alarm out in the street.

"Go," Marie told him. "I'll stay and watch the house."

He took his bucket and went.

The street in front of his house was dark and rimed with frost, the streetlights only spottily lit. Bertrun heard a woman wailing, saw a man stagger through white with dust in the dim light. The house across the street had caved in on itself. Bertrun crossed to it, shouting into the pile of boards and beams, listening for a response. There was nothing.

He followed the sound of the wailing to a woman a few houses down, also partially collapsed. She didn't seem to feel it when he put his hand on her shoulder. In her hands, she clutched a doll. It was dark with something. He realized with horror that it was blood. Bertrun felt his stomach clench, and moved on.

The smoke smell was growing stronger, the fire bells louder. Bertrun found himself running. His scarred hands ached. He clenched them into fists. He took a corner so fast his feet skidded on the cobblestones, and came face-to-face with an inferno.

It froze him. He almost tripped, brought himself to a stumbling halt. The fire roared. It had taken three buildings, old wooden things, in the time between the start of the quake and his arrival. Another was beginning to smolder, though it was farther away from its lost neighbor. He felt his mouth go dry, felt his body tremble, and only then truly understood the depth of his fear.

The fire in the castle had marked him in more ways than one. His travel through it likely should have killed him. His instincts sensed this. The smell of smoke incited panic, an animal thing in his belly, even as logic told him he must move. If the fires in the city could not be quelled soon, they would take over, burning everything in their wake. Unlike the expanse of the castle, the houses in these neighborhoods were mostly made of wood.

A woman jostled him as she ran by, shaking him from his stasis. A chain of men and women had assembled, and buckets had been brought forth from the surrounding houses. It was a long way to the nearest cistern. They would need all of the assistance they could manage. No city guards had come. These people were all residents of this neighborhood, his neighbors, the people he had served as captain and hoped to serve as rebel. Bertrun fell in line, and began passing buckets.

It took little time for his arms to ache. Smoke stung his eyes, made him cough. It affected the others around him little better. Time and again, Bertrun grabbed a full bucket from the woman on his left, passing it to the youth on his right. Time and again, an empty bucket came back to him on his right and moved to his left. There were nigh twenty buckets being passed up and down the line. Occasionally he would end up with both at once, and force his tired arms to juggle the heavy water pail.

At last, the fire was contained. A shout went up down the line. Bertrun put his hands on his knees, feeling the breath pant in and out of him. Around him others did the same, soot-covered and exhausted. Bertrun gazed at them, and they gazed back, men and women and adolescents, grief and weariness on their faces.

A hand fell heavily on his shoulder.

"Sir, you'll need to come with me." It was a voice of authority. A guard stood there, in the uniform Bertrun himself had once worn. Beneath the helm was a face dimly familiar. This man had served under him.

His uniform was clean, unmarred by wet and dirt.

The crowd began to mutter, the people nearest Bertrun straightening.

"What're you detaining this man for, then?" someone demanded.

The guard looked up, surprised, as if only just then seeing the crowd that was growing around him.

"That's none of your concern," he said, grip tightening on Bertrun's arm.

"He helped us put out the fire," a woman cried. "Why are you

AMANDA J. MCGEE

bothering him instead of saving people!"

Someone threw their pail at the man. It clanged against the metal bits of his armor, and the guard staggered, losing his grip on Bertrun.

The man who had once been captain did not think. He ran.

The crowd let him pass, closing up behind him, leaving the guard shouting invectives.

It took him hours to find his way back to his house, but he did. The city had already dealt with enough unrest, and any riots that may have been rekindled by his altercation with the guard had died back quickly. The calm that settled over the streets was a bitter, ashy thing.

It only hid the fire beneath, Bertrun knew.

He made it to his home, and vanished inside.

18 The Prince

The descent to the bottom of the cliff took two days. They were nerve-wracking, endless days that left Liander clenching his jaw until it ached, certain that each step would be his last. The ponies took it no better. Their home was relatively flat, dense woods. Even though their unshod hooves and stocky builds made them well-suited to the steep, narrow path, the precariousness of the footing and the open view of the jungle beneath them was foreign and unwelcome. Liander, walking between his bay mare's bulk and the jagged wall, was in agreement. It didn't make it any less terrifying when one or the other of the ponies balked, snorting and pawing at the thin ledge that kept them from air.

The path widened from time to time in switchback turns. They camped in one of these when darkness made it too dangerous to continue forward. All that first night, Liander expected to roll off the edge into blackness. His mind painted pictures of his body shattering on the trees below. When dawn came, he had barely slept at all, and the heaviness of a second restless night dragged on his limbs, an iron weight. That second day, he was almost too tired to be terrified. It should have been a blessing, but instead the exhaustion and anxiety combined to make him nauseous and clumsy. Several times he slipped, stopped from sliding under his mare's hooves only by luck.

When he and Liana at last reached the bottom, it was nearly dark. The trees towered over them, impossibly tall, as they had for half the day. Thick green growth clung to the spaces between their trunks. In the twilight, shadows gathered under every strange leaf. The clamor of insects, birds, and other exotic creatures nearly deafened Liander, mixing with the distant roar of the waterfall to become cacophony.

They made camp in a small clearing by the vastness of the lake, too tired to set watch, but they kept a fire burning and the horses close. Between the roaring of the waterfall and the wailing of the jungle, Liander thought he would be unable to succumb to his exhaustion. Mosquitoes whined in his ears, and the horses snorted and stamped, but at some point in the darkness he slept.

The morning dawned with a heavy rain that woke both of the twins and set them on wet ponies without breakfast. The rain stopped as suddenly as it had come, leaving them breathing air so warm and humid it was like soup. The sun was swamped by the treetops, leaving the green depths of the jungle swathed in permanent half-light. The rain returned suddenly in the afternoon, a deluge as if an enormous bucket had been overturned on their heads. Only their cloaks were water-proof, made of the oily, long hair of the Ma-peli'a cattle, washed only enough to make it soft for weaving. They were half-cloaks only, nothing like they would have had in Herkunsland. The parts of their bodies which remained uncovered were soaked through instantly. The parts beneath the cloaks became hot and wet regardless. Soon Liander gave up on being dry at all. Even when the rain relented, the air was too saturated for anything wet to dry.

He began, that first day, to realize just how improbable it was that they would survive this journey. Liander stared into the fire that night and contemplated the enormity of their task, of the world they still had to traverse. Liana had started the fire. Liander could not get the wood to light, could not even find wood dry enough to think of burning, but his sister laid a spark to the damp tinder and it flared with a crackling roar. It was the first time he had considered her new strangeness a blessing. The thought sat uncomfortably in him that they might not survive without these new powers.

His sister had changed with the child in her womb. Liander remembered her crooning to it, feeling no chill despite the winter, her flesh always warm to the touch even on the coldest day. At the time, he had felt only his fear of the changes in her, gnawing at the lining of his belly, twisting in his throat. Now, he thought on how happy she had been. How, despite the trauma she had undergone at the hands of someone she trusted, despite her isolation in the village, she had found comfort not from him, but from the vestigial life inside her. How even now the remnants of her motherhood continued to comfort her and provide succor.

Perhaps he had been wrong to fear. Perhaps if the villagers had not done what they had - but done was done. He remembered how Akala had thrown herself at him, the sick feeling of his blade sinking into her body.

Done was done, and dead was dead.

They pressed deeper into the jungle. The ponies sank into the mud of the footpath and hung their heads dejectedly, but went where they were bid. Liander rubbed his bay down meticulously each night, knowing the toll the heat and the mud were taking on the poor beasts. Each day his eyes were dazzled by green and shadow, and at dusk his ears were battered by foreign cries that disturbed his sleep.

The sun rose late and set early, down amongst the mountainous trees, and tiny bright birds in scarlet and sapphire flitted about their heads as they traveled. Mosquitoes and biting flies struck any exposed skin. Brilliant, jewel-like snakes and frogs hung from the leaves around their heads.

Food was questionable, despite the verdant greenery, and Liander began to wonder if the ponies would starve to death. He caught fish in the streams when he could, and one night Liana cut off the head of a snake that reared up to strike her mare. She skewered it for the fire with no squeamishness, and if the meat was odd tasting, it was still filling to his empty belly. But the ponies had only the grain, mostly dry in its packs, and neither Liana nor Liander knew what else in this strange landscape might be safe for them. Even the prince grew gaunt on a diet of only meat, but Liander knew well that they couldn't dare the occasional fruits they did find. There was no telling if they were poisonous. Princess and prince subsisted on dried fruit and were careful to boil their water. When the dried fruit dwindled and disappeared, they subsisted on meat alone. Liander felt his belly snarl at him from sun up to sunset.

Despite the path they followed, they saw no one. Liander knew someone could be only a handful of paces away and lost in the greenery, but he had thought the natives might at least warn them away. The forest, though, remained inscrutable. Its shadows and foliage told them nothing. After a time, Liander was not even sure which direction he traveled in. When he pressed Liana on that subject, she simply cast her eyes to some portion of the occluded sky and said, "There's the sun." He inferred from her auguries that they were still headed south, and tried not to hope for a sign that they were not lost besides his sister's word.

Hoped for or not, he got his sign eventually.

In all the endless green, speckled as it might be with other bright flashes of color, Liander had lost track of the days quickly. He rose in the morning to rain, or mist so heavy it was almost rain, darkening everything to twilight, and rarely saw a beam of sunlight. This morning was no exception. Liana saddled their ponies, which looked gaunt and bedraggled in the wet. Liander packed their meager belongings, dwindling quickly now that they could not trust the foraging, and tried not to think about how he hungered for something sweet. Honey or fruit, or grain cakes, it didn't matter. His tongue watered, and his stomach cramped.

They mounted up and continued down the winding path through the undergrowth. They had been traveling barely more than an hour when the attack came.

Forms melted into existence against the foliage. Liander had time to see that the people were small, brown, with black thatches of hair. They seemed to appear from nothing. He heard a sound, a sharp burst of air. Liana's mare reared, screaming, its hooves sending mud flying. His own bay startled. He pulled on the reigns, feeling his teeth jar as it kicked out its hooves. The jungle folk were giving high, singing cries. He heard Liana shout, and turned to look for her desperately. He could not see her. The bay heaved underneath him. He pulled the reins sharply, trying to keep her from bolting. There, Liana stood, sword out, the metal flashing in the gloom. Small figures slipped out of the way of her strikes like ghosts. He saw the golden mare dead next to her, its body rigid and unmarked. His hand reached towards his sword.

He didn't even get the blade pulled free before she died.

19 THE SEER

Nicola raced through the depths below the castle.

How long had Jessa's induction taken? How long had Alexander searched? Why had she not left? Above Matthius would be waiting, and she could not even reach through, could not see. Was he safe? Had they discovered her absence?

Her feet were sore from the running, her lungs straining at last. The power that moved her could only take her so far, no matter how immortal she seemed. Nicola was tired, and desperate to find the water she had come here for.

The mazed labyrinth of tunnels under the castle was as navigable as it had been before. This time it was the well that drew her like the tip of a compass needle, and she followed it through the subterranean passages unerringly.

The damp air touched her bare cheeks, moved through her hair. She was close.

Nicola stepped into the round cylinder of the well chamber. The air, the echoes, enclosed her, easing a tightness in her chest that she hadn't known existed. The well was often murmuring, the subtle slosh of water against stone. It murmured now, the sound a rising susurration. She paced towards it as if it were the only thing in the world.

That was why she didn't sense the guard in the opposite passage. He didn't notice her, either, not until she had lowered her hands into the well and drawn the water up into them, drawn it up as if it were a muscle she could flex, an extension of herself. It settled into her palms and she tilted her head back. Liquid flowed down her throat, thick and viscous. She did not question its aliveness in her hands, in her mouth. She drank.

The guard shouted. She didn't have time to consider running, and the water coursing through her delayed her fear. He had made it across to grab her arm almost before she processed his voice.

"What do you think you're doing?" he demanded. His voice said that he was barely into manhood, but he must be loyal, to be down here. He must know who she was.

Nicola should have felt terror, or at least some kind of anxiety for what was to come. She felt nothing. The water was alive, and it filled her now with life that buzzed and rocked in her veins. Like with the fire, she could hardly feel the presence of the green god in the face of it. Unlike with the fire, it did not feel foreign. It felt like a missing piece of herself had come home.

The guard's fingers dug into her arms as he drug her up the stairs. They were the same stairs that Alexander had come down so many times, to bring her food and ask her counsel, curving along the wall of the chamber. Her head swam with the motion of climbing, with the throbbing of her heart. Almost, the seer could hear Alexander's footsteps descending past her. She thought, if she could see with her human eyes, that she might look down at the well and see her own self there, dressed in a thin shift, blind eyes open and staring at nothing.

She was aware of it when they moved through Alexander's burned out chambers, still haunted with the ghosts of flames no matter that she felt new rugs beneath her feet. Those flames crackled in her ears, and shouts and footsteps rumbled distantly like thunder. It was as if all the past were happening at once, and maybe the future, too. Nicola could not separate it from the moments that stretched as the guard drew her forward, and forward, and forward, unending.

Until, at last, it ended, and she was before a familiar door.

It was the shock that brought her out of her haze, the shock and fear she felt from Matthius. She knew the taste of him on her mind after all these long months, and she turned towards him, remorse rising in her at the cost that even now began taking shape in her mind. The young guard pulled her back, his grip biting into her arm. His knuckles rapped at the door.

Nicola realized, then, what was coming. She went still as the door opened, as murmured words were exchanged, as Drummond, once sleeping, awoke.

She was shoved unceremoniously through the door. It closed behind her.

There was a lamp burning somewhere to her left. Its wick hissed in the silence. She could not see it, as she had seen when the earth was all the power she had. Blindness was not something that she had forgotten, but it was unsettling to have neither the power of her visions nor the power of the earth god's senses to guide her. The sound of the wick, the press of stone and rugs beneath her feet, the sound of her own breathing, each of these sensations were given to her, and then broken, interrupted, by the presence before her.

Drummond's scent of forest pines, his cold, banked rage, his violence - she could taste it on the air.

The silence stretched between them. Nicola knew it was meant to intimidate, so she stood quietly and did not let her breath rush in her chest or her hands shake. If it took more effort to stop the latter than it should have, well, that was the nature of sharing a room with the Lord Regent. She remembered when he had thrown her to her bed, the breadth of his shoulders, the overwhelming scent of him in her nostrils. The shudder that fought to ripple through her was almost too strong to suppress.

"I would hear your explanation," he said at last. His voice was conversational. The seer swallowed.

"I have none," she said.

He shifted, as if her admission surprised him.

"What exactly did you do, in the well?" he asked after a moment. His voice was still deceptively calm.

"I drank the water," Nicola said. The thick, living water that now moved in her like some strange appendage, clenching and unclenching as her hands would not.

He stood, chair sliding across the rug. She had not realized he was seated, and she felt her skin tighten at the thought of him on his feet.

"You were not to leave your room," he said. She felt the heat from his skin, opened her mouth to offer some explanation, some excuse.

He hit her.

It was not a casual blow. It was not the same as when he had shaken her, or when he had thrown her, not meant purely to intimidate. This blow was made for damage. One second she was standing, and the next she was on the floor, her face pain only, more pain than she had felt in a long time.

But even as she thought this, the water flared. The pain dissolved.

It was hard to tell if Drummond noticed. He was already lifting her up by the hair, her cap lost somewhere in the scuffle. Her scalp screamed as he hauled her upright, but that pain, too, was temporary.

"You are no longer of any use to me," Drummond said. He opened the door, and shoved her out into the hall.

"Detain her guards," he said, and one of the men who stood to either side of his door stepped away. The young man who had brought her caught her in a hard grip again. "Return her to her room, and lock her in. I will deal with her on the morrow."

Drummond slammed his door shut. Down the hall, Nicola heard Matthius arguing, heard him being dragged away from her even as she was returned to the door he had been tasked with guarding. It opened. The man shoved her inside.

The door closed before she could reach it, and locked tight.

20 THE PRINCESS

There was mud everywhere. Mud coated her doeskin pants, her boots, squelched between her toes. She'd streaked it across her face and over the narrow silver streak that had started in her dark brown hair. The cold wet of it helped cool the fire in her skin.

Her head ached, not the pounding of impact but of fever and blood loss. It was a persistent, hazy pain, one that coated the too-green world in fog. The air was oppressively hot, the dampness doing nothing to assuage the dry, dead taste in her mouth. She wanted water, clean water, and rest. She would get neither. Her water-skin was gone. The only things left in the clearing with her had been the gleaming metal of her blade, holding onto its shine despite mud and the humid climate, and the broken husk of her pack, slashed to tatters. Liander, and everything he had been carrying, was gone.

The misery of her body, the wavering of her vision, kept Liana from focusing on the absence of her brother. If she thought on it too long, the darkness of loss might cover her up and drown her as quickly as the bogs sometimes nestled amongst the roots of these great, impossibly tall trees. She put one foot in front of the other, grasping at the hole in her side. Another scar, if she lived, one to add to all of the others she was accruing. She smiled grimly. The pampered body of a princess was long behind her. She didn't want it back.

But she would get back that which belonged to her. Liander was waiting. She could sense him before her, or, perhaps more accurately, sense the fire of those who had taken him. It was a long way away, but she would make it there eventually.

It began to rain.

It was the heavy, drumming rain so characteristic of these jungles. The vegetation around her shifted and jittered with motion, blurring before her eyes. She allowed herself to kneel in a rapidly swelling puddle, to set her sword across her knees and reach towards a wide, flat leaf filling up even now with water. Water pounded the leaves above her head, fell in rivulets from the trees. She set her mouth to the edge of that leaf with the eagerness of a child. Water flooded her throat, and she swallowed, gulped. Her side ached with the motion. She let the leaf refill, then poured water into the wound, trying to clear out the black, bloody mud which filled it. It was agonizing. She had known worse agonies. But she was tired, and the world swam with it. Her vision blackened. Only the wet kept her upright. She felt her hands bury themselves in the mud, barely catching her weight.

Well, so much for that. The wound would stay dirty. If she lived through the next few hours, then perhaps she would fight off the inevitable fevers that even now began to grip her and manage to cross to the deserts. Perhaps not. The gods, after all, were cruel.

She stood, with effort that made black spots dance in her eyes. She walked.

It was a familiar situation, shambling through the wilds with some violence done to her, looking for her twin, who had escaped, she hoped, unscathed. Liana wanted to laugh. How many times had she, injured and in pain, looked for succor from him, looked to find safety with him. Before, she had thought it was her weakness, but no. Each time she survived. No matter what wounds she accrued, what harm was given, she survived, and became more aware. The fault lay in those who did harm to her and hers. They deserved to burn. The fire inside her had told her how easily the world would burn. Sometimes that gave her pause. But each time she thought to try living again, living without fire for blood and sinew and self, some new harm came. She needed the anger.

Her feet tangled in a vine. Liana staggered. This footpath was clear enough, for a jungle. It was traveled often, the path they had been following. Perhaps that should have been a warning, but it was one unheeded. She had thought that they could pass unmolested. Her mistake.

They would pass once she was done. The fires were closer now. She could feel them speaking to the flames inside her heart. Perhaps the feverishness was what let her sense them so clearly. Her head lolled. She righted herself. How far, how much distance left? The heat came off of her in waves, radiated from her and left her cold.

She would have the fire. She would reach it. She would lie in it and let it tickle her whole body as it had tickled her toes that morning after she had slaughtered the villagers.

Liana shook her head, feeling her consciousness waver. The fire would help, yes, but not that way. Fire was for burning.

These people would burn just like everyone else. She had promised. She had promised vengeance to her son, and now she promised it to herself.

She was delirious.

The fire was close.

Liana had the sense to pause, swaying. Her shoulder was wedged against a tree trunk, her body wrapped in the leaves of some verdurous growth. The world spun, and then slowed. There was the path. Beyond, what appeared to be a wall of green. But her senses told her that there were people on the other side. There was the fire, of course. But the jungle was quiet here, and in that quiet she caught fragments of sound. The small cries of children, a murmur of conversation, a footfall. And there, the nicker of a horse. She had arrived.

She had made it here. Now, to recover her twin.

Her sword was heavy in her hands as she pulled it into guard position. Liana pushed her leaden feet into motion, quickening her pace. The jog jounced her wound, and she let out a coughing battle cry, pushing through the pain. The greenery spat her out. There before her were the flames of a campfire. Liana reached for them, drew with the lodestone of heat inside herself. They came, swirling around her head like a crown.

"Now," she panted, raising her sword, "burn."

"Liana, wait!" The sound of her brother's voice halted her momentum. The flames were a haze, and her fever made them blur. He was running towards her, arms outstretched. These fires would kill him.

Liana let them go, and staggered as the power left her. The flames settled about her like a blanket, and vanished. The energy had kept her upright. She could feel herself guttering with them.

"You would spare them?" she ground out. The tip of her sword was on the ground. She wasn't sure how it had gotten there. At the edge of her vision, she could see shapes, rounded brown faces, a reddish brown like clay in a fresh-turned field. Their black eyes watched her. But it was Liander she forced her gaze to, Liander who stood before her, so near, but did not touch her.

"I can't watch another village burn, Liana." His blue eyes were hard, desperately determined. She felt the urge to laugh. Now, at last, after all these weeks, he looked at her. It did not matter that she had won them both free of the prison the villagers had made of their lives, that she was taking both of them home. Her brother's heart was not made for vengeance. He hated her for what she had done.

She had promised.

But the fire had gone out, and her legs trembled. She bared her teeth at him, feeling the inevitability of her body's betrayal.

"It's on your head, then," she rasped. Then her legs folded, and the ground rose up to meet her.

21 THE CAPTAIN

Bertrun was sleeping deeply, his hair and skin still smelling of smoke, when the knock came on the front door. It was not a hard knock, not a threatening one, but with the memory of his near miss the day before fresh in him, he awoke all at once and made his way down the stairs before he had fully realized where he was.

He undid the latch and cracked the door open cautiously to see a small figure on the other side.

It was, he realized as the person turned, Jessa.

The groomsman's daughter turned cook's assistant turned spy was not dressed as a woman. He could see this even in the dim light of the street lanterns. Her hair was tucked away, the front chopped short so that it hung in her eyes as a boy's might. She wore pants, and had used some trick to obscure her breasts beneath her jacket and cloak. But Bertrun knew her face, shadowed and obscured though it was. He recognized her, for all that the face wore an expression that he had never seen.

Bertrun swallowed. "What-?"

"Inside," the scarred Shadow said, emerging from the wall next to him. Bertrun had not even seen him there. He stepped back, letting them inside.

"Why are you here? What has happened?" he demanded, groggy still.

The door had barely closed. He heard the door open to Marie's room, saw her white hair at the corner of his eye. He rubbed his palm across his face, feeling awareness come back. It was dark, still, and he turned to the fire, crossing before Marie to do so, and put a few logs on it. The heat and light would help to wake him.

"There is news. We have been with the king."

"King Alexander?" Bertrun demanded. His voice shook. "He is mad. I saw it."

"He is well enough to be counted on, now," the Shadow said.

Beside him, Jessa stood unmoving, impassive. He had never seen her so. He looked from the Shadow to her, and back, the similarity striking him. Her eyes were flat, her expression still. And as he looked at her, he found his own eyes wanting to slide away.

"Jessa," he said, then. Unable to grapple with the sight, he rubbed at his eyes. "Why are you here?"

It was the Shadow who answered.

"Jessa has been called to the fire," he said. His voice was soft, Bertrun thought, and then wondered if he had imagined it. Marie made a choked noise to his right. The captain licked his lips.

"Women are not called to the fire," he said. Women did not become Shadows.

The two Shadows met his statement without comment. It was patently untrue.

Bertrun let out a sound, half shout, half snarl. He turned away from Jessa's blank face.

"You knew you were going," Marie said, her voice shaking. "You didn't come say goodbye."

Bertrun looked at her. There were tears on her cheeks, and she was staring at Jessa. They had been friends, of a sort, as much as circumstance would allow. He crossed to Marie, and put his arm around her. She sagged into him, looking every inch her age in the dim light.

"Why come now?" he asked the Shadows. Did he imagine the flicker of grief on Jessa's face?

"Jessa will go south," the Shadow said. "Liana is coming, even now. She will prepare a way for her."

"If Alexander is well -" he began.

"The wellness is temporary," the Shadow told him. Bertrun shook his head, rubbed his face again. The scruff of his beard pulled at old scars. "He will succumb to the darkness. That is the cost. But the fire can make him useful again, for a time.

"Useful," Bertrun said, choking on the word. "For what?"

"The Lord Regent confides in him."

Bertrun shook his head. "That's what Nicola's for, she's the spy," he said. "You can't -"

He stopped, took a breath as his mind caught up with him.

"Where is Nicola then?"

The Shadows said nothing. Bertrun thought of how Alexander had leapt at her.

"Has she betrayed us?" he demanded.

"No," the Shadow said.

"Then she's not safe." He released Marie, paced to stand in front of the scarred Shadow, and Jessa. "You must get her out."

The Shadow nodded acceptance. He, too, knew the usefulness Nicola could have, and what she had sacrificed. Bertrun realized that he only had Alexander's orders to motivate him, but the Shadow had a broader vision, knowledge he no doubt kept from Bertrun even now.

Could he trust the Shadows? He wanted to. And in the end, he supposed it did not matter. If he could not trust them, then he was dead in the water. They knew too much.

"I want to see Alexander," he said.

It was not a demand he had planned to make, but when it left his mouth he knew the truth of it. He wanted to see his king, the man he had pledged his life to all those years ago. They were not so many years - Bertrun was still not an old man - but they settled on him now like a weight. Was he doing the right thing? Had he done well? He felt certain that if he saw Alexander's face again, he would know.

The Shadow nodded, once. Bertrun could not tell if it was a nod of acknowledgement or acquiescence.

"Jessa will stay here tonight," he said. Then he turned and left the way he had come.

Marie fetched a candle and took Jessa upstairs, her voice quiet and hesitant. The girl did not speak, and Marie did not ask questions. She closed the door behind Jessa, then turned to Bertrun where he stood in the dark hallway. Her expression was one of grief.

She pushed past him without a word, and he let her go, stepping into his own bedroom door and closing out the cold night.

22 THE PRINCESS

She awoke beneath an unfamiliar roof, and for a moment she was back in the village. Panic filled her, and she jerked in her bed - only to have the panic subsumed by the pain in her side and the fire in her flesh. The world spun and rocked. Liana leaned to the side and vomited. There was nothing much in her stomach to vomit up. Her wound pulled with every heave. She spat bile and thin, yellow liquid on the hard-packed earth below her.

Exhausted, Liana collapsed back, staring at the ceiling again. The world slowed its rocking as she gazed upward. This roof was nothing like Jei's ceiling. Her bleary eyes registered sheaves of impossibly large leaves hung on thin poles, not thatch from the rice fields over thick beams. There was a finely woven net hanging under the roof, filled with odds and ends. Storage of some type, obviously, and her bed was not a bed at all, but something more like a sling. Suspended from the ceiling, it rocked when she moved, adding to the dizziness in her head. She was lucky she had not dumped herself out of it.

She was lucky she was alive at all.

Her mouth tasted horrible, but she was too tired to do anything about it. With effort, she turned her head, looking about the small, one-room shelter. There were no tables, no chairs. The walls were made of more of the giant leaves, with the thin poles that looked up close like reeds to hold them up. She felt as if it would all come down around her head with a strong breeze.

The door was a small, curtained aperture. She couldn't tell at this distance what the curtain was made out of. Some kind of plant fiber again, or at least she thought so. It was too far, and despite the ambient light filtering into the hut, it was dim inside. She laid her head down again. Her eyes closed.

For a time, Liana drifted in a quiet, dreamless darkness.

A rustling woke her. She opened bleary eyes, stared in the dim, directionless light. There was an old woman in the hut with her. Her hair was white and straight, cut to frame her face and otherwise as short as Liander kept his. Her old breasts were brown and held tight by a band of blue cloth across her chest, and her loincloth was covered in knot of many colors, forming intricate patterns. She carried a water-skin and a wooden bowl. Her face was remarkably smooth, but wrinkles hung in the crease of her mouth, rippled the black lines of ink that rendered her face like a mask. Liana stared at her, certain that she was an illusion. But the old woman walked to her bedside and pressed the bowl to her lips. A warm, salty-bitter liquid flooded Liana's mouth. She swallowed it because it tasted better than her mouth had before, and because she sensed that it would do her good. Tiny old women rarely poisoned the wounded in their beds.

Perhaps that ascribed too much logic to the feeling in her chest. Perhaps she just wanted to be cared for, to be touched by a person who did not mean her harm. The princess knew in her gut that this woman would not harm her. If her brain threw up reasons for it, they were no substitute for that instinct of safety, not when she was so tired.

She slept.

When Liana woke again it was dark. The woman was holding a small lamp, little more than a twisted wick floating in a bowl of oil. She opened her mouth and spoke.

"You are awake," she said. "Good."

Liana blinked into the light, into the lines on the old woman's face. She heard the words, but their meaning did not come through her ears. It settled in her mind, a familiar sensation. It was how she had first communicated with the villagers. It was a gift of Herka. The princess tensed, heart pounding. Any ease was forgotten as she grasped frantically at where the pendant had hung with weak hands.

"Shh," the old woman said. "I know what you fear. Your brother has told me much. We are no more the moon's people than any other's. Peace, sun-child." The mention of Liander and the bitter welling of feeling his name brought almost distracted Liana enough to miss it when the old woman held the little lamp out to her. The light, though, was strong in the dark, and the flame called to her insides. The princess took it with trembling fingers. Only her earlier certainty, her unreasoning trust, kept her still, though this woman had just handed her a weapon that begged to be wielded.

"There. A little bit of fire to help you heal," the old woman said. She reached down, and Liana realized distantly that the elaborately beaded loincloth was in fact an apron. Its patterns concealed pockets, and when the old woman withdrew her hand there was a powder in it.

"And a little bit of earth," the old woman said. She pinched a few granules of the stuff, sprinkled it on the flame. It flared, and Liana jerked her hand to the side instinctively. It was hard to remember that flames could no longer burn her after a lifetime being sure of the opposite. So focused was she on the spitting, crackling fire of the makeshift lamp, the sloshing flammable oil, that she was not watching the old woman.

That old woman held her palm flat and blew dusty powder into Liana's nose and mouth.

"There now," she murmured as Liana coughed and spat. She had taken the little lamp back into her wizened, brown hands. Liana stared into its impossible brightness. "Follow the flame."

Liana did.

It was a long way down, but familiar. She traversed the staircase into the depths with weightless feet. Some part of her rebelled against the journey, knowing that there was no longer anything in the deeps waiting for her. But she could not deny the hope. It pulled her like a fish on a line. The pain of it drove her onward.

The descent was timeless, its cessation abrupt. The room she found herself in had neither water nor light. The shock of that absence made her want to weep, but her tears would not fall. Her body knelt without her, folding on itself. Her hands buried themselves in the soil.

When had it become soil? The once-stone floor was crumbling beneath her hands. A glow began to rise - from her skin, from beneath the dirt she scooped away, shining more and more brightly. Her hands broke through. The floor fell away.

She floated down into the light. A voice came to her, wrapped about her.

You have suffered much to bear me, it said, in the clear, light tenor of a boy. Her heart leapt in her chest at the sound. *You will suffer more*. She could not see his face. She wanted so badly to see his face. The light was all around her and she reached for it with her muddy hands, grasping at nothing.

Mother, I will be waiting.

The hut was dark. There were tears on her cheeks.

Liana sat up. The old woman was crouched in the corner with her lamp, grinding away at something. She looked up when Liana moved. Her eyes were dark, unreadable in the shadows.

"You have found what you were looking for," the old woman said. "Was it what you expected?"

Liana shook her head. Had she expected it? No. She had seen him die. Even now her mind shied away from that image, the sucking pull of the depths she had followed the body of her son into, to be with him if only in her mind. She could not remember what had been at the bottom of that place she had gone to following the ritual death of her child. Now, she began to have an inkling. It had been the vacuum he had left behind, the dark shadow at her center. A wall she had built between a godling child and herself, out of grief, and fear. Fear that he was too much his father's son. Fear that he would betray, as did the fractious moon.

Perhaps he was more god than child, but he lived. Her son, her firstborn, her light. He lived.

23 THE PRINCE

Liander watched his sister, and wondered at the fact that she had once more transformed in ways beyond his ken.

She sat quietly enough. That lack of conversation had not changed. They had not spoken about how he had stopped her, about how she could have killed him but hadn't. Liander had seen her make the decision, had seen the instant when his life was granted to him. He hadn't realized that danger from his sister was even a possibility, despite everything. He could not, quite, reconcile it in his head. They were twins. They had always looked out for one another.

But in the end, he thought, she was much better at protecting him than he was at protecting her. He had only failed her, since they had left Herkunsland.

There was guilt there. He could feel it roiling in with the anger, with the fear. He could feel his fear of her like an animal inside him.

The old woman could see it, too.

They were forced to stay with the jungle people for several days. Liana was gripped with a fever, an infection in her side that the old woman treated. She was something like a medic, and something like a priest, and something like a grandmother. She channeled the forces of the gods as if breathing. Her dark eyes stared at him, rheumy with age but still piercing between the black lines of her tattoos. Liander did not have the courage to stare back.

None of the other jungle people could speak any language that Liander knew. Liander got the impression that they were semi-nomadic and insular. The huts they lived in were watertight and as comfortable as anything could be in the persistent heat, but not designed to withstand long-term use. He suspected they could be picked up and moved almost on a whim. The long poles they used as the frame were a rib of tall, woody grass that they cut to length and dried. It was almost impossible to damage afterwards, and lightweight. But the leaves grew abundantly, and were flimsy enough that Liander thought they must be replaced often. They made mats out of fibers from the inner bark of trees and used them for seating and for something like doors for their huts. They ate meat rarely, but did eat it. They hunted with poison. It was why the golden pony had died so quickly. His own pony now benefitted from the extra feed the golden one would not be eating. The village children were fascinated by its docility.

None of that helped him to understand why they had done what they had done. Why they had saved Liana, after Liander had thought her dead at their hands. Why they had kept him alive. There was no one to ask.

He learned rudimentary words from the children, who swarmed around him with curiosity, and from a couple of the womenfolk. The men left each morning to go foraging. They brought back strange assortments of plants and fruits that Liander tried to memorize. The women prepared those thing which needed to be prepared, cracking open what Liander could only assume were giant nuts to get at the sweet, white flesh inside, breaking open long, woody pods to spill strange seeds into their large stone mortars for grinding. They practiced almost no food preservation, except to grind those nuts and make a kind of fermented seed cake out of them. They certainly did not need his help doing it.

Days stretched on, and Liander had nothing to do. He watched his sister, and she looked inward, when he saw her at all. Mostly, she stayed in her hut and slept.

The quality of that inward gaze was different, though. It was still focused, still hard-edged and purposeful. But some of the anger, the hatred, had been diffused. Something else took its place. It was an emotion he could not name.

The old woman's name, or title, was Rabati. When he went to her at last, desperate for some kind of human conversation, desperate to understand the sister he had only had one word answers from since she had awoken, Rabati smiled, and beckoned him away from the central clearing of the village, into the jungle that surrounded it.

When she cast the spell that let her speak to him, inhaling one of her strange powders, it was marked by a gust of wind.

"What would you ask me earth-child?" Rabati said, turning to him. Liander swallowed, feeling her power prickle on his skin.

"How do you do that?" he said. She smiled, revealing surprisingly white teeth beneath her black-lined lips.

"The powers that move through the world follow rules. It takes many years of study to learn them." She sucked her teeth and smiled wider. "Men aren't any good at it, boy. Too distractible." The smile vanished as quickly as it had come. The old woman looked at him with that same gaze that had made him look away so many times before.

"Ask the real questions, now," she said.

Liander swallowed, and turned his back to her. The jungle was greener than anywhere he had ever been before. The birds called back and forth over his head. There was always noise here, riotous amounts of it. It had kept him awake at first, but now it helped him sleep. Perhaps that was an example of his adaptability. Why, then, could he not accept who Liana was now?

"How did you forgive her?" he asked at last. "For threatening you?"

The old woman made a thoughtful sound. When he turned to look at her again, she was looking at him with an unreadable expression.

"Would you forgive a snake?" she asked. The question startled him, in part because of his reaction. He felt defensive. His sister was not a snake. The old woman barked a laugh, as if she could read his mind.

"Boy, a snake bites because of what it is. It is in its nature. You startle it, be careless, and it will kill you." She cocked her head. "You sister is fire-touched. The anger will always run hot in her. If you poke a snake, it strikes. You poke a fire, it burns."

Liander swallowed again, his throat suddenly tight. "I am her brother. Her twin."

"You are," Rabati said, looking her age suddenly. "And yet, you are not one thing. You cannot be what she is."

Liander opened his mouth, and closed it again. He had been so angry at her for so long. But who was he angry at? He had been the one who had failed. He had been the one who had not helped her find another way. He could not control Liana. He could only control himself.

"Earth children do not take change well. And you are an earth child, princeling." The old woman stepped away from him. "The fire in Liana would have destroyed my entire clan in order to take revenge for you. She loves you as she can. Repair yourselves, and leave us in peace."

Liander nodded. His chest was in turmoil, his head pounding with the need to think. But the path before him, at least, was clear, even if his heart might need more time. No matter how mercurial his sister, how foreign, he must be her bedrock. He must hold her together.

"What did you tell her?" he asked. "To make her so hopeful?"

"I told her nothing," the Rabati said.

He wanted to protest that, too, but she didn't owe him his twin's secrets.

Liander wandered back to the village without the elder. Liana was sitting in the center of the cluster of leaf huts, staring into the ashes of the fire pit. They only lit it when they needed to cook something, which was rare enough. He wondered if she missed the flames.

Sitting down beside her took effort, but not as much effort as the words that came out of him.

"I'm sorry," he told his twin.

She didn't answer for a moment. Then she looked at him, her golden eyes burning. The fire, the light of the sun that had grown in her, shone out of those eyes. For the first time, Liander understood that it might be hard to keep that fire in.

"I am not who I was," she said. "I can't go back to being the person you want me to be."

"I know," he told her. He did. "But I am not like you, either, Liana."

She nodded.

"We will both have to keep that in mind," his sister said. "I will not ask of you things that are impossible for you. But Liander, I won't change my course either. Not even for you."

It was a warning. Liander swallowed, and raised his chin.

"I won't let you forget that," he said.

She smiled. It was the first smile he had seen on her face since they had entered the jungle, the first honest smile he could remember since her son - his nephew, he acknowledged for the first time - had been killed. The reminder of that event, of his powerlessness, made him clench his fists. Liana looked at him, her smile fading.

"You know our uncle is only the beginning," she said. Liander frowned, glancing at her sharply. "I will kill him, and save our father if he is alive to be saved. But Liander, our uncle is not the one who did all of this, not alone. Drummond is not why we are here."

Liander felt his heart go cold with fear.

"You can't take on a god, Liana," he said, his voice hushed. It seemed that the forest went quiet as well at his words. A chill marched down his spine.

"Do you think not?" Liana asked idly. Her hand trailed through the ashes, and she lifted her blackened fingers, rubbing them together. The odor of old burning came to him.

"Even gods can die," his sister said.

24 THE SEER

Nicola had been confined to her room once more, and the worst of it was that she did not know if Matthius lived or died.

The water had not done what she hoped, not yet, and the green was quiescent enough that she could not sense her surroundings. She had resorted to pacing to measure the room's edges, pacing to disrupt the blackness behind her eyes. She could take eleven steps from one side of the room to the other, but only eight from front to back. She took those steps again, and again, and again.

What would they do to her? What would they do to Matthius?

Inside her, the water bucked and roiled.

Even when it rested she felt it coiled like a living thing. She was heavy and gravid between that new, fractious presence and the equally heavy vastness of the green god's essence. They were twin forces entwined, but one was part of her. One was foreign. She had become used to the green god's light inside her, become used enough to it that she had channeled it to save herself, once, and so though it was not of her, it was the easier of the two to bear. It was the water, this piece of herself, that she hated.

What had she done?

The water sloshed and slipped inside her. Even the smallest of her thoughts left her reeling as it surged, shoving presentiments and visions at her, fragmented and strange. She focused, therefore, on her feet. Walked back and forth until she felt her calves ache and her body tire. Then she lay down on the bed, because no one had come, nothing had changed, and she could no longer stand the counting.

Being still seemed to help. The blue of the water settled as she breathed, letting her mind go blank. Nicola had felt terror before, felt worry, been locked in places she could not escape awaiting unknowable fates, been powerless. She allowed herself to recognize that she was not, in fact, powerless now. Not entirely.

There were two powers pressed up in her chest, bound to her flesh as surely as her breath. There were people counting on her.

Nicola let her mind settle and reached for her visions. Let

thoughts pile together like coins.

Bright coins, they shone of copper. Copper like the rays of the sun.

The field rose up around her, and she tumbled into it.

It was a familiar space. She had been here once before, before she had carried her god-lover inside her. An endless field of tall, trailing grass, wheat perhaps. She had never seen a field like it before or since, but she saw it again now, the alien, endless flat landscape rolling about her in all directions. The question of eyes, of blindness, did not enter into the equation. It rarely did, in her visions.

There was a figure crossing the expanse towards her. She felt his warmth radiating outward, fighting to burn her. It failed. She could not be burned.

"You can hear me now," he said. He was tall, broad-shouldered, far from the boy she remembered. His face was not far from Alexander's in features, and that was how she knew him.

"Sermund," she said.

"For now." He crossed the last of the distance towards her. His hair was golden, a brighter color than the tall grass. It moved as if in a wind she could not feel. The sky was so pale it was almost white with heat. Even his eyes were golden. She felt that she could drown in those eyes.

A spike of pain came from inside her. Nicola put her hands over her stomach. The green energy was sparkling and crackling in her, sending little needles to poke and prod her. She hissed.

"My son is jealous," Sermund said. "My son to be. My son that was." His large, warm hand touched her belly. She looked at him in confusion.

"He is Herkun's son." The correction seemed important, somehow. The hand withdrew.

"I was Herkun, once," he said. His golden eyes met hers. She held on to herself this time, held on against the tide of heat that washed over her, shunted it down and away. He nodded in approval. "You will do well."

"Why did you call me here?" she demanded. A breeze blew up around them. Sermund, once a god, looked out over the endless field.

"I am still a god," he said. "I will become more than that, soon, as will my bride. You understand what we could do to the world, in flesh?"

"I understand what She has already done." It was true. Herka had started this. Herka had begotten war and pain and death, whether that was her intention or no.

"We never do anything without intent." Sermund sighed, and the wind gusted harder around her, pulling at her hair, at the deep, vibrant redness of it, the only color in this landscape of gold. "My mother is looking for me. Will you bring her?"

Nicola awoke panting.

The back of her throat was dry. She swallowed in the darkness, hesitant to look out with her sight. Hesitant to feel the pain of burning. But when she at last stretched out her senses, there was no pain. The green inside her was safe, and the water was quiet, but there was no pain.

"His mother," Nicola said to herself. He had seemed so adamant. Talking to the god - or whatever he existed as, now - was like talking to flames. That crackling was not meant for mortal speech.

She sat up. Her head spun. It was hot in her room.

The earth began to tremble.

This was the god's will, not the green but the gold. She knew this with the clarity of the water. Nicola pulled that power tight into herself, pulled it up behind her eyes so that she could see, pulled it down into her feet so that she could walk. The stone rolled and bucked. She reached beneath the bed, pulled the box of the god's ashes from its hiding place. Stepped towards the door.

There was shouting outside, and a crack from somewhere deep in the castle. Someone screamed. She put her hand on the knob of her door, felt the lock that held it closed. Felt the earth within her pulse as the lock snicked free.

Nicola opened the door to her chamber, and slipped into the chaos outside.

No one was aware of her. They were busy with the shaking ground and the smoke filling the corridor. Someone had knocked over a lantern, or perhaps a candle - the smoke was not heavy enough to be a true fire yet but it was enough to panic a castle that had not yet forgotten how bad fire could be. Nicola found the door to the tunnels quickly, pressed her fingers into the niche that served to open it.

The seer slipped down into the trembling earth.

25 THE KING

The knucklebone had settled to a steady heat, like a mug of hot cider on a cold night. Alexander rolled it between his fingers, sitting in his cage. The demon had not touched him since he had grasped it. Though night had come, the demon had not taken him.

He could feel it, a seething darkness welling in his blood but left, in the end, impotent. The brightness of this sun was too strong. And he could feel the sun, now.

It was rising.

The first crack of dawn was like a shot of warm liquor, lighting him up from the inside. He gasped and gave a shout of laughter. He felt, in that moment, as alive as he had felt at Sermund's tomb, as if all of the sins he had committed had been burned away.

But there was still blood in the grout beneath his feet. When the sunrise passed, Alexander sobered quickly.

When the guard came in, he was waiting for him, the knucklebone hidden in his jacket pocket. They'd let him keep the nice jacket they had given him for the coronation. It was a garment fit for a king, all red fabric and gold brocade, though it was stale and used now. He worried, for a moment, that his brother would come to take it back, and the knucklebone with it.

He could not let Drummond find the key to his sanity. But it might help him, if his brother believed him well.

He sat upright in his cell as the man entered, waited calmly for him to place his tray on the bedside table. For the first time in days, Alexander felt his stomach rumble at the thought of food. The guard took his time with it, obviously unwilling to unlock the door to Alexander's cage. He waited for the man to step back, expression wary as it always was. Then he spoke.

"I would like to speak to my brother," he said.

The man blanched at Alexander's voice, but otherwise did not respond. Alexander knew he had been absent from his post last night, though he did not know how the Shadow had ensured such a thing. He wondered if it was guilt or fear that made the guard pale. Likely both. To be safe, Alexander waited until the guard had left before he made any move to emerge from his cage.

His ability to sleep had not improved, and even with the fire of the sun burning in him Alexander found exhaustion dragging at his eyes. The food was bread and cheese and watered wine, the same light fare. It felt good to eat, good to taste the food without despair numbing his tongue. He sat on the bed, cleaned linens crinkling under him, and waited.

It was mid afternoon before his brother joined him.

"What do you want?" Drummond demanded. He looked haggard, as if he had not slept either. No doubt he was still dealing with the aftereffects of whatever disruption Alexander's outburst had caused. Briefly, the king wondered what had happened in the temple courtyard. It had been set to be a slaughter.

He hoped his brother had shown restraint. He knew in his gut that such had not been the case. Drummond would run his kingdom into the ground, and for the first time in a long time Alexander had the energy to feel fear at the thought.

Alexander brushed at his face, feeling the wrinkles cut into his skin by age and hardship. His brother had never been one for small talk, and he was unlikely to start now. The king considered his options.

"I wanted to apologize, for yesterday. I do not think it will happen again."

Drummond barked a laugh.

"Do not think?" His hands clenched spasmodically. "You have kept your head during the day for months now, and yesterday was the day you failed. The one day when it would cause the most ruin. There were riots through the night, because of you. I wasted good men squelching them."

Alexander sneered.

"That is my fault?" He was surprised at the anger, though he shouldn't have been. It came on him in waves, since he had awoken, and with the fire in his breastbone it came now like a benediction. "You are the one who has led us here, with your actions. You are the one who forced the curse on me!"

Drummond stepped back as Alexander stood, but he rallied

quickly.

"What curse is that, brother?" he growled. "Whose curse? Not mine. Your own actions brought you here. None of this is my doing!" His gesture encompassed the tower, and the cage. Alexander wanted to punch him.

He exhaled sharply instead, fighting the urge to do harm.

"Do you know how this thing came to live inside me?" he said, in the silence between them. "I took this curse to save my son. From you."

He met Drummond's eyes squarely. His brother's gaze was skeptical, angry, afraid. He was a man on the brink of losing, and he knew it. He would not have tried for the coronation if his power had remained stable in the long months that Alexander had been lost to madness.

"We have done horrible things, one to the other. I do not forgive you your greed, Drummond. But I would keep my people safe. A civil war will benefit no one. Let me help you in that, at least."

"You were meant to help me yesterday," Drummond said bitterly.

"You underestimated the avarice of the demon," Alexander said. "It is attracted to things of power."

He hoped that his brother would infer his own value, but Drummond's face twisted with rue. "I see. That will not be a problem in the future."

Alexander wondered what would happen to Nicola then, or if she had used her freedom last night in the tunnels to escape. He did not wish her any further harm, not because of him.

But in the end, he was a king, not just a man.

"Good," he said. Then, "Let me help you, brother. I will support you."

"So that you can win back the throne for your spawn?" Drummond said. His voice was heavy with anger.

"So that I can keep my kingdom whole," Alexander said, "regardless of who rules it."

Drummond sneered. "At least you are honest, Alex."

His brother left then, without a goodbye. Alexander could not say that his voice had reached him. Still, there would be time yet.

He could make his case again. Something would happen that would force Drummond into an even deeper corner, would cause his desperation to peak, even if it were only the slow passage of time.

Alexander sat on the bed, and watched the light outside his window, the sky a pale blue specked with only the barest tracery of clouds. He felt the sun pass its zenith and sink towards the horizon. It felt as if he stood on an endless field, his face turned up to the heavens, his eyes closed and the red behind them full and rich with life. It was a wondrous feeling, and he clutched the knucklebone in his fist fiercely, kept safely within his jacket pocket.

The swaying of the tower, when it came, seemed like a dream at first.

Alexander had been on boats before, though Herkunsland was not known for its boats or ships. Not enough forest, not enough tall trees to shape into mast and keel. Herkunsland's trees were cultivated for their fruits, its orchards wide and varied. Perlen was the place for ship's wood. Still, Herkunsland had its fishing communities along the coast, and Alexander had visited as a young man, that he could know his country better. He had gone out on the calm sea in a small sailing vessel, been tossed about like a cork. That was what it felt like, when the tower around him began to move, like a long, rolling wave had picked him up and settled him back down, and then was followed by another, and another. This was not the quick shake of the day before. Fear rose up in the back of his throat, and he heard distant screams, smelled smoke.

It was like the night of the fire. Alexander, too, had memories of that night, of the fear. He thought of his children, and of the seer, and Bertrun out there somewhere in the city, if he still lived. If any of them still lived. He did not want to die, not anymore.

But he would not be afraid of it.

The shaking passed, after an interminable time, and Alexander sat, silent, in his tower. He waited for his guard to check on him, and then when that was not done waited for his evening meal. He was hungry. They'd fed him next to nothing, and he was not the monster he had been, to live off of terror alone.

When the door opened at last, the guard entered with a tray stacked with food the likes of which Alexander had not seen for some time. Pastries, meats and cheeses, fresh fruit - it was nothing like what he had been fed before. The sun was still an hour above the horizon, but every inch of the guard's body spoke of panic as he placed the tray on a table dragged over beside the cage. Alexander had gone inside immediately when the door opened, ready to be locked in, and he waited patiently while the guard did so with fumbling fingers. The sun was nearly set. His fear was natural. When the guard stood back at last it took him three tries to swallow past that fear and speak.

"The Lord Regent will send for you tomorrow," the man said. He backed out of the room, the door locking quickly behind him.

Alexander was careful not to smile until he left.

It was a grin that was all teeth.

26 THE PRINCESS

Liana straightened, dropping the bay mare's hoof. The pony whickered softly as she moved to the next leg, shifting its weight. She put her shoulder to the furry flesh, forcing the animal to shift again so that she could check another hoof. It was habitual now, though in the beginning the exertion of riding and caring for a pony had made her whole body ache. Now, almost a month from Rabati's clan-lands, her strength had returned. The high air of the Spine passed cleanly through her chest. She stared at the pony's foot pad, checking that it was clean and whole despite the rocky mountain passage, then dropped it.

At her back, she felt the warmth of the small fire she had built like a living thing. In the thick trees surrounding them, Liander's boots made light disturbances in the brush to track him by in the dying light. She could hear each whispering step as she turned to her blankets, spreading them out in preparation for the night. He was much happier in the mountains than he had been in the jungle, and some of the plants here were familiar. Though the final weeks of their trek through that verdurous place had been made much easier by the help Rabati and her people had given them, it was still full of unforeseen dangers. Venomous snakes, poisonous creatures, and parasites were no longer an everyday occurrence. Liana was glad that her days no longer ended in pulling leeches off of her skin.

Each day was strenuous in these mountains, with the thin air and the steep slopes. Snow coated the rocks and trees every morning and melted away by afternoon, though the jagged peaks hanging above them were white still. Liana was able to walk all day now, so they made better time than they had in the beginning of their trek. They and the bay mare moved deeper into the range with little more than directions plotted from the stars as their guide. They had a little feed for the bay, still, supplemented now by its ability to forage on the sparse grasses growing between the rocks. Rabati had given them dried meat, nut-cakes, and some kind of large, round, white-fleshed nuts. Those were all long eaten. If not for Liander's hunting skills, they would have starved to death. Now Liana sometimes took her turn with the short bow, and her arms no longer shook when she drew it. She was able to be proud of her strength.

Would that strength be enough?

Liander's steps warned her that he was at last approaching and she stood. He was carrying a gutted, skinned rabbit, sparse enough fare, but it would do. Liana tried not to think of how the mountain pass was high, of how winter would settle in deeper the higher they climbed. Already the cold of the night near froze her brother, though she found that she was less susceptible to it. Another gift from her son, she thought, and smiled.

Liander saw the smile. He smiled back, thinking that it was for him, and settled down next to the fire.

"We'll eat tonight, at least," he said cheerily. It was a false cheer. They both knew that they were going to be lucky to make it through the mountains. Liana settled beside him as he spit the rabbit on a long stick and held it out over the fire.

"How old do you suppose we are, Liander?" she asked him suddenly, the question grating out of her dry throat. Her brother looked up in surprise, but then seemed to seriously consider his answer. His gaze went to the stars above their heads, so different from the ones back home, though they both agreed that some of the constellations furthest northwest might be somewhat familiar. Looking back down, he frowned in her direction.

"I think our birthday has passed," he mused, taking another bite of jerky. "Should we celebrate?" he joked.

Liana snorted. "Nothing to celebrate with. Maybe when we get back to civilization." She had officially gained her majority whenever their birthday had occurred. At eighteen she was now, if her father was among the living, the Crown Princess and Heir Apparent. If her father was dead? Then she was Queen.

The rabbit came off the fire, and they settled into eating. The sparse trees and thick brush that seemed pervasive at this altitude swayed in the breeze. Liana was sucking the marrow from the small bones when she heard the jingle of western tack.

At first her mind couldn't put the sound into context. Then her body stiffened, and Liana touched her twin's shoulder with her still-greasy fingers, cocking her head to listen.

The jingle came again. Liander stood, dropping his bones in the dirt and reaching for his bow, still strapped to his back. He strung it quickly, eyes scanning the dimness, and knocked an arrow as he raised it to his shoulder. The clomp of hooves carried through the near-dark, and then a voice followed.

"Hello the fire!" It was a man's voice, speaking in their own native tongue. The twins glanced at one another. Liander lowered the bow slightly, but did not unstring it or put away the arrow. Liana nodded in approval.

"Come into the light," she demanded. She heard the creak of tack, strangely loud in the mountain air. A man appeared at the edge of the firelight, his hands held before him. A shadow behind him was likely his horse, but Liana could not see clearly.

"I mean no harm," he said. "Just a trader traveling the mountains."

Liana's hand went to her sword, but she had taken it off and laid it across her bedroll only moments before so that she could sit to eat. He spoke in the language of Herkunsland, and she was sure they were in the Spine. No one crossed the Spine from her home country, and they were south of Herkunsland if the stars were any indication, meaning this man was coming from the deserts. Yet he had hailed them in their own tongue, not the trading tongue of the desert clans. Her skin prickled and her shoulders tensed.

Liander, not sensing what she did, lowered his bow further. Liana had to fight not to hiss at him. She gripped her knife instead, small though it was, where it hung at her waist. The knife had been a gift from the Quet'le-Ma, when they had left the village, what seemed a century ago. It was short, and meant for cutting through meat and little else. Still, Liana thought she could kill a man with it, with luck.

"My name is Gino," the man said. "May I share your fire?"

"We'd rather you went on," Liana said, drowning out Liander's voiced affirmation.

"Oh, now, don't be so unwelcoming, girl," Gino said, and Liana felt rage, never far, rise to swamp her unease. "I told you I mean no harm."

Liana's hand tightened on her knife. She tensed to rise to her feet. Liander opened his mouth to say something, beginning to tighten his hold on the bow.

When Gino moved it was almost too fast for her to see. In an instant, he had crossed the space between them. His knife struck, slicing through Liander's bowstring and towards her brother's chest. Liana screamed. The fire flared behind her as her rage and fear overwhelmed her. She pulled it back before she could burn both Liander and the man called Gino to ash, even as her brother threw himself to the side. Gino had flinched from the surging flames, and that moment of distraction had given Liander a chance to pull away before the wicked, curved knife could complete its journey to his heart.

Liana kicked out with her foot, catching Gino in the side of the knee before he had a chance to go after her brother. Gino's leg buckled, but he turned it into a roll, coming up in front of her. The knife came for her throat. She swayed backwards, caught his wrist. He twisted out of her grip like a fish. The recognition that she was outmatched came a split second before Liander slammed into the man. Liana tightened her grip on her knife. When Gino came up on top of her brother, she kicked him in the ribs. The man rolled away, and came to his feet, grinning. If his side hurt him he gave no sign.

"You are much more interesting than I supposed you would be, princess," Gino said. She heard Liander groan as he pulled himself to his feet behind her. Liana put the relief she felt out of her mind as quickly as she could. She could afford no distractions.

"Who are you?" she said.

"A friend of your uncle's," Gino told her, smiling. She saw his hand move, and dove to the side. A throwing knife flew through the space where she had been.

An assassin, then, and a good one. Liana called on the fire. It was her only advantage here. But Gino had already closed the space between himself and Liander. Her brother threw up his forearm as the knife came at him. The blade opened a deep gash. Blood gushed instantly. Liana felt her stomach drop, felt the world tilt. She pulled on the fire, pulled until the flame went out, pulled the rage inside her. The darkness was near-absolute, as if she had sucked the light out of everything. She heard Liander drop to the ground.

The flames roiled out of her, and found the man called Gino eagerly, like hunting dogs given a scent.

In the light that flared she saw her brother rolling away, covering his face. The muscles in her eyes tightened against the brightness. Gino screamed. There was a wild grin on her face, a familiar sneer of rage and joy. She kicked through the flames that encircled him. They guttered as he dropped to his knees, and she put her small knife at his throat.

"Now, what was that about my uncle?" she asked. Her voice was calm but her blood hummed. The man's coarse, charred hair was wrapped in her grip, his pulse throbbed beneath the backs of her fingers. "Is he expecting me then?"

Gino snarled and made a motion. Liana let the knife pierce his skin, let his blood taste the air. He froze again.

"Liana," her twin said.

"Would you leave him to kill us in our sleep?" she asked him, knowing what her stalwart hearted twin was protesting. She drew the knife across Gino's throat, dragging deep through muscle and veins. The man's body bucked, a guttural, drowning cry escaping him. Liana stepped away.

"You are a good person, Liander, but you are soft in this," she said as the assassin bled out between them. "He chose this path. I merely brought him to his destination."

She knelt and wiped her blade in the dirt, then stood. "Let me see your arm."

Her twin stood on shaky legs. The arm was still bleeding. The cut had been deep.

She sat him next to the remains of the fire and started it with a touch. Some water from their water-skins washed his wound more or less clean, and some powder from Rabati, left over from her own wound, would keep it clear of infection she hoped. She wrapped it tightly to staunch the bleeding once she had treated it.

"You're better with animals than I am," she said. "Will you go find the horse? I doubt it's gone far." Liander, shaky and grey, staggered into the darkness. She watched him go, then turned to the task left to her.

Their own bay pony was tied to a tree, and had pulled at her reins but otherwise not made any fuss, despite the blood. Liana patted her neck and pulled some rope from the saddlebags propped beside her. She tied a simple noose knot in the rope, and looped it around Gino's ankles. She needed the extra leverage to drag him away from their campsite, his body sliding heavily behind her, catching on roots and rocks.

There was a cliff not far. Nothing was level in these mountains for long. Liana stopped on its edge, and searched the man's pockets. He had little of interest. The tinderbox she didn't need herself, but Liander might use it. More knives were hidden all over his person, and his coat, though covered with blood, was heavier than anything that they had. It would keep Liander warm. She stopped, though, at the letter. It was too dark to read it, but she thought it was probably the contract on her life. Liana smiled, and slipped it into the band that held her breasts.

Then she rolled Gino off the cliff.

When she returned to the fire, Liander had the horse tied next to the bay pony. It was a black gelding, and dwarfed the pony by several hands. They made a comical pair. Liander was going through the saddlebags. She could see the hollows under his eyes, made deeper in the firelight.

"Here," she said. "A gift from our uncle." She tossed him the coat. The knives she stowed in her own pack. She couldn't use them, having never trained in throwing knives, but they might be useful for something later.

Liander snorted tiredly. "It's quite a gift. We might make it through the mountains with all of this."

He was holding up well. Liana felt love for him bloom as he staggered under the weight of the coat.

"Get yourself to bed," Liana told her brother, smiling.

There was a long way to go before she could thank her uncle properly.

27 The Prince

They had been moving for what seemed like an eternity.

Liander shook the snow off of his boots, and pressed his heels into the horse's side, urging the gelding forward. Liana walked in front of him, breaking through the crust of ice to keep it from slicing into the horse's legs. The snow steamed off of her. It was a useful side effect of her power, the way that the flakes evaporated before settling on her clothing. She could keep it up for a long time, and call a fire out of the wettest wood. Without that, he did not think that they would have survived this long. The snow at these heights was up to her hips, and never seemed to truly stop falling.

Liander, for his part, was frozen. The only warmth was from his contact with the horse - the insides of his thighs, his buttocks against the leather saddle, these remained a fair temperature. The rest of him was as cold as he had ever been. At night, when they camped, he could never get all the way warm. The thick-coated mare the Quet'le-Ma had given them was handling the weather of this high mountain pass the best, and even she was miserable. She trudged along behind them, her face white with falling snow.

They had a map, scavenged from the horse's packs. It showed the mountain pass they traveled through, and with it they had been able to avoid false valleys and forks. They had climbed and climbed, and been glad of the gear that the assassin had procured to make the climb before them. Thick bedrolls, a tent, gloves - all of these were impossibly valuable. They had made what they could in terms of clothes, once they had realized what they were climbing into. Liana sported a rabbit fur hood that would likely disintegrate in any kind of warm weather. Happily in the cold they could not smell it. Muffs of fur wrapped her legs as well, and his, keeping snow out of their boots and adding extra insulation. It wasn't enough.

The cold had climbed into him and set up a home. Liander could feel it, and knew that he wouldn't be able to go on much longer. The misery of the journey was not the problem, though it didn't help. The jungle, too, had been miserable. No, Liander was ill. His body shook and quaked in the saddle, his hands were weak on the reins. He thought he had hidden it from Liana well enough.

It was the cut. The arm had ached with the wound, which was expected, but the ache had not faded. He didn't think it was poison. No, Liander suspected that the wound had simply gone sour. His body was tired from their travels, exhausted from lack of food and good rest, and it had failed to heal. Infection was a danger even amongst the well-rested and able. Had he not been young and vital, Liander expected he would have succumbed already.

He did not want to die.

Ahead Liana pressed forward. He needed to live, to protect her. She had lost so much. Going forward alone would be a terrible thing, no matter that she seemed to have new hope for the future since the jungle. He wanted to see Herkunsland again, to sleep in a bed, to be warm. He wanted to see his sister on the throne, and perhaps at peace, and he wanted to meet his wife, whoever she might be, and he wanted to meet his children. They were simple wants. Liander had no room for anything else.

Liana had stopped moving forward. He didn't realize until she grabbed the reins, making the gelding toss his head. The motion jostled Liander in the saddle. He realized his head was spinning with exhaustion when that nearly made him fall from his seat.

"We'll stop here," Liana said. Liander focused his eyes, looked around. A copse of pines with heavy, weighted branches was before them. Perhaps underneath there would be some dry ground, some shelter from the endless snow.

"Liander," Liana said. "Are you listening?"

"What?" he asked, his voice croaking.

"I am going first to break a path. Wait here, until I find a good place." Her voice sounded matter of fact, not threadbare. He envied her that. She turned and marched away in the snow. Liander leaned forward over the horse's neck, pressing his cheek against its mane. The strands of it were coarse and wet, the fur beneath at least warmer than the air.

"Who travels a mountain range in winter and expects to survive?" he asked the dark gelding. His feet were numb in their boots. Perhaps he would get down and stomp around, try to get some warmth back into his legs.

When he slid down from the gelding, he jostled his arm. The pain made him moan.

His feet hit the snow, and Liander stumbled. The gelding whickered nervously, shifting away from him. The prince found himself sitting in the snow. His teeth chattered in his head compulsively, but he wasn't sure he felt cold. He wasn't sure he felt anything.

I'm delirious, he thought, feeling his head list in the unsupporting air.

Suddenly Liana was standing above him, saying his name. He looked up at her. His eyelids were heavy. The air no longer felt cold.

"Get on your horse," Liana said, her gold eyes boring into his. He struggled to do as she asked, his limbs unresponsive. He felt her hands touch him like fire, and almost shied away. They reminded him that he was cold. The cold made him want to lean back into them. He climbed instead, obeying instructions with some tiny core of sanity. His body curled around the saddle, his face once more in the horse's mane. He felt the gelding step forward tentatively, setting the world to rocking.

Then they were in the trees, and Liana was lifting him down, staggering under his weight. There was a fire going, and pine needles blanketed the floor of the glade, soft and dry. The air was warmer than it had any right to be. Liana shoved some warm thing in this hands. He sat, shivering, distantly aware as she moved to the horses.

Time jumped. Liana returned. He cried out when she put a hand on his arm.

"Take your jacket off," she demanded. The warmth was removed from his hands, and he almost cried out again to see it go. His jacket and hood and shirt were peeled away. Cool air brushed his skin painfully, then hands like living flame. He did make a sound then. The dressing caught on the wound as it was peeled back.

"Herkun," Liana breathed. Liander opened his eyes with a force of will, and looked at the wound. It was yellow and weeping, and red lines of infection ran up from it.

"Liander, why didn't you say something?" There was fear in her voice. She left for a time, wrapping him in one of their spare blankets. He sat there, shivering again, cold again, glad to feel cold. She was digging in the packs, he could hear that. Then she crossed back to the fire. There was a knife in her hand, one they used for skinning things, sharp and small. She held it in the fire until the metal was scorched, then removed it. She turned to him as it cooled.

"This will hurt," she said. He nodded.

"I understand."

It did hurt. The knife sliced into the old wound, lancing it open. Pus spilled out, and then blood as Liana massaged and squeezed. He thought the blood was good, but the pain was too great for him to tell for sure. The inflamed skin screamed with agony. Liander kept still only by dent of will and exhaustion, shouting wordlessly, hot tears gathering in his eyes.

Then she came back with the water, still hot from the fire. She poured it over his arm, flushing the wound. That was nearly too much. He blacked out for a time, losing everything but the sensation of heat and agony.

"I don't know what to do after that," Liana was saying. "Liander, can you hear me? I think we should wrap it again. We need something clean, something new." She dug in their supplies, pulled forth the last of their small supply of bandages, wrapped his arm. He slipped into sleep almost before she had helped him put his clothes back on.

They stayed in that copse of trees for four days while he recovered, four days that they could not afford. Liana cut evergreen boughs and made windbreaks around the clearing. She built the fire high. Outside, the endless winds and gusting snow continued, but inside their shelter it was almost warm. Liander knew this abstractly, but still he wound himself in their blankets and shivered uncontrollably. Liana forced him to undress every morning and evening to change his bandages, cleaning the old ones in boiling water. Water was the one thing they didn't lack, courtesy of the snow melt.

Food was another thing.

They used the grain from the horse feed to cook a slurry that cramped his stomach but at least left him feeling full. There was still some dried meat, fruit and nuts from Gino's stores, but not enough to feed them both if it was all they were eating. Liana gave him most of the fruit, insisting that he needed it more. He couldn't argue. His sister was gaunt, but still functioning. Liander was not functioning. Liander could barely stand to go relieve himself without feeling the whole world moving under him.

Four days of sleep helped with this. The reduction of the infection helped. The wound was still tender and reddened, but the pus was mostly gone and Liander knew that was good.

"We have to keep moving," he said to Liana at the end of the fourth day. "I'll stay on the horse." He ignored the worry in her eyes, and curled back up to sleep on his pallet of pine boughs.

They kept moving.

Liander had cause to be grateful that the days had grown shorter. It meant that he had to stay in the saddle for less time. The weather had worsened, storms blowing across the mountains in rapid succession. The horse underneath him plodded forward with head bowed, its skin shivering. They had slung a thin blanket across its back, held roughly in place by the saddle, and wrapped its ankles in the same fur muffs that both he and Liana wore. A few times it balked, and Liana walked back from where she broke a path for it and spoke soothingly. Liander often found himself leaning over the poor gelding's neck, trying to share between them what body heat he could. It was not an entirely altruistic gesture. Even with his extra furs and the blankets wrapped around him, he could never get warm, and the numbing, dull ache of cold became a constant companion.

Liana found a cave a few nights later, and they all hustled in, the horses in the doorway to block the wind that managed to come in regardless. Liander sat and shivered while his sister busied herself unpacking food and building a fire with wood she had collected the night before at their last campsite, carried on the pony's back to dry as best it could. Exhaustion pulled at him. He felt worthless.

"Better if you left me," he told her through chattering teeth.

"Don't be a cad," she said back. Her head was turned away,

her focus on the fire as she breathed it into life. She pulled her gloves off and held her hands, white with cold, over the flames. Then she rubbed them together briskly and pulled at the pack that held their food, taking out their single pot and the grain she had apportioned to them. The horses had already been fed, their hooves checked and balls of ice removed. None of this had been Liander's doing.

"I don't want you to die here because of me." Liander forced the words out. His shivering had abated somewhat with the warmth of the fire, but he was still cold, and bone-weary.

Liana pulled something out of the bag. He heard the rustling as she unfolded their map and spread it over the cave floor. "Look here, Liander," she said calmly. "I think this is where we are. If we can make it over one more ridge, it is all downhill. Straight into the desert. We're nearly there."

Liander snorted. "At least we can die warm."

She looked up, her eyes glinting in the firelight. They were as hot as the flames. "We are not going to die," she said.

Liander wished he were sure.

28 THE SEER

The Shadows found her in the tunnels, but only after she had walked for all that day and most of the night.

Nicola wandered the lengths of them surrounded by fragmenting visions. It was like climbing steps when the distance between each step kept changing. Her feet were sure enough, but her mind jumped and scattered. The earth trembled, and though she did not fear these ancient tunnels collapsing, her visions jumped and jittered with each shake.

Each inch of this castle was rich with history. She saw men laying stone, in her mind's eye, though she knew the stone was beneath her feet. She saw kings pass, and men like knots of shadow, too, and knew them all a dream. But that did not make it any less real.

The past, Nicola thought, this is the past.

The future was there, too. She knew this. There were futures upon futures here, but they were not so firm. Where the past hung clear as crystal, the future danced like smoke. That, at least, was familiar, though she had never seen quite so many futures so vividly at once.

As she wandered, Nicola thought about the possibility of madness. Yet madness did not come to her. Instead, she floated on the sea of her visions and did not drown.

After a time, the visions stilled. After a time, the earth was calm again.

When she came upon a Shadow at last, it was not by accident. Her feet had followed the spore of him through ages. There he stood, a shade that sheltered the world, waiting for her. Silently, she followed him.

The tunnels wound around them as they moved. Nicola sensed above them not the vastness of the castle halls, but small, less substantial structures, when she had energy to sense at all. She was exhausted - it had been a long walk through these depths, and the bucking, rolling earth had made that walk slow. She would have rested.

The Shadow, though, moved quickly, his feet sure in the

darkness. He did not carry a torch, but she supposed he did not need one. He was a creature of darkness, more so than she was. He moved with fluid abandon through the halls, and she, with her short legs, strove to keep pace. It was hard.

At last, he slowed in front of her, and Nicola pulled up short. Her visions told her when he opened the trapdoor above himself, and told her too what lay beyond - a shallow space between floor and hard packed earth that would, if she followed it out, lead her to open sky. It was night but not for long. Sleeping minds dotted the street, some even now awakening.

In one house, a man sat, awake despite his weariness. It was a soul whose taste she knew well, though she had met the man only the once.

Nicola climbed up and out, leaving the Shadow to make his way after. She was glad he did not crowd her as she wriggled forward in the cramped space, cradling the god's ashes in one hand. It seemed an eternity before the crawlspace spat her out. The ground beneath her hand was icy and slick with snow as she pressed herself up.

She paused then, in the alley, her senses overwhelmed.

The smell of smoke hit her first, and brought to her visions of the day's travails. Blood was there in that ruinous smell, and rot. The people of Herkun's City had worked hard to repair the damage the quakes had caused, but there was only so much that could be done so soon. Nicola did not feel that she herself was the cause of the quake, not exactly. But guilt niggled at her heart. She could not stop the gods from doing as they willed, she told herself.

The pain, the smells of death and ruin, told her she should have tried.

The Shadow emerged behind her. This alley smelled of food scraps and excrement under the odor of ash, but it was not overwhelming. These were lingering smells, the necessary parts of civilization, she thought. The cold of the night air dampened the scents. Nicola shivered.

"Come," the Shadow said, his dark voice breaking her revery.

She followed him as he led her to the back door of the building where Bertrun even now waited. She could sense him inside, awake already, though the day was young. Far to the east, she could feel dawn breaking.

The Shadow knocked on the door.

After a moment, someone answered.

The captain, Bertrun, stood, studying them for a moment before he ushered them inside. Nicola stepped into the warmth gratefully. Her livery was not meant for wearing in such cold. The Shadow followed her. She knew that she was in a kitchen, that beyond the sound of their feet had awoken the other inhabitant of the house, an older woman, that the coals in the oven were nearly burned out, that the house was old, old and well-loved. She knew all of these things instantly, in the way of her power, and the knowing was a strangeness after so long but a comfort nonetheless.

She turned, in the kitchen's relative warmth, to face Bertrun. The Shadow stood to one side, witnessing, silent.

"You made it out," Bertrun said.

"Yes."

"I didn't think, when I left you there, that you would," he told her, as if they were continuing a conversation that they had had yesterday, and not one interrupted almost two years ago. "I thought for sure Drummond would find some excuse to kill you."

"He tried." Nicola pressed her fingers to her face. "But it is hard to admit you fear a blind woman." The blindfold, stiff and dirty, was not thick enough to conceal the shape of her eyes from her searching fingers. She followed its length to the knot behind her head with one hand.

"I have been blind for nigh fifty years. It wasn't hard to pretend for two more." She sensed his confusion, his apprehension, and tried not to feel it too deeply. Nicola's fingers trembled as she undid her blindfold at last. The hated thing fell at her feet. She opened her eyes.

Bertrun's face was before her. It was the first face she had ever seen, besides the face of the god whose ashes she carried. He was standing close, and Nicola reached out her fingers to close the space between them. She could still sense his energy, the echo of his emotions, but it came distantly. When her fingers touched his skin, those emotions were louder, a jumbled addition to the thrum in her own chest.

She could see him.

He was dark, far darker than her paleness. Her fingers were white bars against his face. His skin was coppery where the green god's had been so dark it was almost blue. Each pore on his face stood out starkly to her. The loose curls of his hair, a reddish black streaked with gray, were a marvel. She had not known hair could look that way. His cheekbones were high, his jaw squared. His nose was a knife through the lines of his face.

He said nothing as she traced his features, touched his curls, matching the textures to the visual reality of him. Her fingertips grazed the colorless dips of old scars, and she peered until she could pick them out. Bertrun likely could not be called beautiful. Charismatic, she though, attractive perhaps, but his features were strong, a little unbalanced. Nicola noted this, and did not care. In that moment, he was the most beautiful thing she had ever seen. His scent seemed to compliment the clay tone of his skin, a pleasant, earthy musk. It was nothing like Drummond's. There were no sharp edges to it. And yet it was not like the green god's either.

The god had smelled of home.

Nicola dropped her hand to her side and stepped away from Bertrun. She had known when she had met him, so long ago, that he would be important to her. The awe lingering beneath her breastbone affirmed the knowing. His was the first human face she had seen with these eyes, eyes that were the gift of her lover. The seeing nearly took her breath away.

"I think I need to sit down," she told him. It was hard not to look at him, hard not to look at the complexity of his features, so she turned her eyes away from him and away from the Shadow, who loomed beside them. She staggered through the door into the dining room, where a chair was waiting, and sat in it, breathing deeply through her nose. Let her head dip, her eyes close, so she stared at nothing.

"Are you alright?" Bertrun asked. That was real concern in his voice, she knew. She could feel her awareness stretching around her, expanding, as if her long captivity had kept her bound inside as well as out. The world was vast, impossibly so, and yet the events here would shape all of it. Her head spun, and she leaned back in the chair heavily. She had not realized that she had closed her eyes until she opened them again at Bertrun's touch on her shoulder.

"Nicola?" he asked. She looked up into his earnest eyes. They were brown eyes, a light brown that caught the light clearly.

"I'm dizzy," she told him, though that word was inadequate. She was nearly lost.

Marie came out then, and Nicola knew her name and everything about her simply by hearing her approach. She, too, filled the seer's eyes with detail - curled white hair and blue-gray eyes, wrinkles that Nicola longed to trace with her fingers, skin near-translucent with age, painted pink and blue where veins passed beneath. Nicola shut her eyes again. It was like looking with the green god's vision, but not the same. It was engrossing, and limited, and so detailed. With the water clamoring inside her too, telling her past and future and elsewhere, it was too much.

"Who is this?" Marie asked. Bertrun shrugged helplessly. She could not keep them out with her eyes closed.

But Nicola had no time for her weakness. She touched her throat, where the locket should hang.

Bertrun was introducing her to Marie when Nicola opened her eyes again. She watched the way they leaned together, saw the tendrils of affection. Remembered her duty, and used it to ground her in the now while the future tried to grab her up and the present tried to drown her.

"Bertrun," she said, "I need help."

He looked at her, and Marie looked at her. Nicola met both of their eyes, but it was the Shadow who spoke.

"You mean to go back," he said, voice flat, hollow. Nicola looked at him then, at the way the past spread out from him like cinder and ashes, burned already to nearly nothing, though some of its shape remained. At the blankness of his face, and the small scar there that spoke of a story nearly lost. He was so much a thing of the fire that she could not see what he was, and it eased her.

"Yes," she said. "I mean to go back for him."

"Go back for who?" Bertrun demanded.

"A friend," Nicola told him. "He saved me, though I did him ill. I cannot leave him behind now."

Even now, across the city, she felt his pain, bones broken and flesh rended. She would not leave him to die when it was her fault. Her fault she had not been more powerful, more willing to hold onto the powers given her. Matthius needed her.

She pushed down the visions of him, focused on the now. She could not help him wrapped up in fear and violence.

"If you are caught -" Bertrun began.

"I will not be caught." Nicola put all of her authority in it, or what she imagined authority sounded like. Still, her head spun. Her moment of power sloshed back like a wave into the sea.

"You cannot go as you are," the Shadow said. "And it is a trip better made at night. I will go with you."

Nicola went still, then. The future clambered, telling her why the Shadow would come. She did not want to believe it.

"I won't let you take him," she said, and knew even as she said it that she could not stop the Shadow from anything.

There was silence.

"The Shadow's advice is usually sound," Bertrun said. "I'll give your friend shelter, but you must wait until tonight."

Nicola closed her eyes. The world reeled behind her eyelids. They were right. She reached, with her sight, reached to see if she would go too late, but the visions bucked until she thought she would be sick.

It would take her time, to be useful. She could feel the water calling her, calling her down into its vastness.

She could only hope that Matthius would hold on long enough for her to reach him. She could only hope she would not be too late.

29 THE KING

The fog was on him. It came sometimes during the day, a bitter exhaustion the result of sleeping on the bars of his cage, or, more commonly, not sleeping. Alexander kept hoping that someone would forget to lock him in, as they had the night of the first shake, but no such luck followed him. The guards were too afraid to leave him roaming the room, unsure if the demon would return. Alexander could hardly tell them why it wouldn't. It was too easy of a thing for his brother to use against him, and most people did not so easily believe in the hand of the gods on mortal lives.

Alexander hunched on his throne, feeling the chill of the large room in his too-thin limbs. The manacles at his ankles, hidden by a blanket over his lap, chafed. The blanket was heavy with brocade, but a blanket nonetheless. It made him look sickly, doddering. That was intentional. He did not mind the blanket. The manacles were unnecessary, but he couldn't fault them, even after weeks of perfect behavior. No one wanted to get their eyes plucked out by a madman. But they could not be seen, and so Alexander entered the room before anyone else each day that he was allowed to court, and took his seat, suffering to be chained. Drummond entered after the nobles assembled, announced with due pomp. The arrangement left Alexander so much scenery in his own courtroom. A figurehead, nothing more, a doddering old man with whitening hair and bird-bone limbs. He made sure to play the part.

It was far more interesting to be here than inside his high and lonely tower. Though the servants cowered in the hallways when he walked by and the nobles sneered behind their hands, at least there was something to look at besides a narrow sliver of sky and the angle of the sun. And he learned much at court.

Things had changed in his absence.

Drummond was seated before him, and guards arrayed along either wall. The throne room was long, making the high ceilings seem low with its length. Tapestries in red and gold covered the walls, and paintings of old kings. They were in the old style, and not to his taste. The artists of Perlen did better, giving depth to their subjects where Herkunsland's style had been flat and lifeless. His own portrait, painted when he was young and Liora was still alive, deviated from that tradition - or would, when it hung in these halls upon his death. The painter had been one of her less affluent relations, a boy who had taken up art rather than inherit lands or title. It was sometimes done, there, that a son could step aside, if his brother or sister was better suited to rule. A different world entirely from the one his children had lived in.

Nobles entered through the wide wooden doors at the other end of the chamber, filing women to one side, men to the other. Alexander studied the current group's faces through bleary eyes, fighting not to yawn. They were the same, more or less, as they had been the last few times. There was a fashion for high necks on the gowns, now, and for gloves and veils, no doubt product of the new emphasis on modesty and separation of lords and ladies. Where in his court all had mingled more or less freely, social constraints aside, there was now an aisle down the center of the room demarcated with rope. No chance for husbands and wives to stand together, for unmarried women to possibly meet their suitors in carefully chaperoned spaces. Just somber, murmuring men on one side and silent, faceless women on the other. Alexander wondered how many had thrown their lot in with his brother and now regretted it.

Before Drummond's seat, on the steps, stood a priest, ever watchful.

There were three high priests to Herkun in the temple, all golden-robed and well-fed. All of them had hated Liana, and Alexander had generally not been kind to those who were unkind to his daughter. This one was named Ermen. He had been the worst of them. It was unsurprising that he had thrown in his lot with Alexander's traitorous brother.

The priest held up his hands, calling invocation. His white and gold robes glinted overbright in the gloom of the hall. His voice droned.

"Herkun, god of light, dead and undying, immortal sun, Allfather, see us now in this, the hall of your hand on earth."

Alexander wondered how the hand of a god could be so easily

crippled.

He had not been to the temples where the priesthood was housed for nearly a year before the coup, and Alexander reflected that his annoyance with the priesthood and the ostentation of their ceremonies had likely cost him his throne. Herkun's temple took donations and burned offerings to the god, though it had started its existence as a place of contemplation more than any other use. It was believed that the smoke of burned offerings reached Herkun in the Heavens. Yet many of the donations received by the temple, which should have gone back into feeding the hungry, went instead to priests' pockets. Alexander had brought peace and prosperity to Herkunsland. In doing so, he had unsettled the balance of power the priesthood and many nobles maintained. A ruler who had luxuries when his citizens were impoverished did not deserve respect or title. Once the king had made this clear, many had been forced to divest themselves of the most egregious of their affluence or face disputes with their subjects in Alexander's court.

Now, his people suffered. He could hear it in every announcement that was made in this sham of a court. No farmers or merchants graced the throne room. Even lesser nobles hardly came forward. Instead the herald called lord after lord. Many of the names he knew. Just as many he did not, though those lords were often young enough that he expected he had known their fathers or uncles. Such was the nature of a coup. Faces changed, people died through betrayal or simply because they were too old to live through the times. Alexander had not been surprised at the new faces, but he had learned their names in the past weeks with the habit of long years spent as a politician. Now, bored and tired from poor sleep, he found his consciousness wondering.

Then the herald called the name of a master.

The king's children had had many tutors, but to hear Master Wrothfurt's name sent a spark of panic through him. Alexander's eyes found Wrothfurt's across the distance of the room. There was a moment of recognition, a scarcely seen hitch in his step that Alexander might have imagined. Alexander pulled his eyes away. It would not do to remind Drummond of their connection. He feigned indifference instead, returning to his exhausted, hunched position in the cradle of the throne.

"My Lord Regent," Wrothfurt said, bowing low, and then, smoothly, "Your Majesty."

Drummond did not glance at Alexander, but the priest Ermen did. Everyone who approached the throne was forced to recognize Alexander, for politeness if nothing else, but Wrothfurt's tone had been pointed. Alexander kept his posture neutral, though his gut tightened. Drummond said that the king was ill, so let them all believe it. Let the gauntness, the shocking silver of his hair, buy him this much at least. An ill king was not of interest to the ambitious.

But he might attract the righteous despite himself.

"You may rise," Drummond said after a pause. Wrothfurt rose, and waited.

"Speak your claim, Master," the priest commanded, his voice sneering on the man's title. Wrothfurt did not seem to notice. He looked at Drummond, ignoring the priest. At last, the Lord Regent nodded. Alexander could see the priest's face twisted in anger.

"My lord," Wrothfurt began. "I come before you today with a grave issue. As of the week past, the temple has banned the teaching of many classes at the Academy. They have also removed common born students from the rosters. The restriction of knowledge goes against the purpose of the Academy as established by the Sun Throne. The Academy is yours to govern. This cannot be the will of the Crown. With these restrictions, our students will be less able to contribute to our kingdom."

Alexander had been installed at the head of the court, a mad, sickly king, as a wall to bolster Drummond's reign. He knew this, just as Drummond and all assembled knew that, were Alexander still king in truth, he would uphold Wrothfurt's assertion without question. It was on Wrothfurt's face, in the set of Drummond's shoulders. It was in the silence of the hall before them, and the tension of the priest's jaw. Alexander felt rage, and wrestled it down. Forced his breath even, though he could not help the blush that crept to his cheeks.

He had known he was lost when he paid the price to save his children. How was it different, to see the Academy he had reformed undone? Nothing lasted after death.

He would rather have died.

"The temple does what it believes is best for our kingdom," Drummond said. "With the instability of our times, we must cut costs to the Crown and support the temple in its charities. It would do no good to educate commoners who will only starve."

Wrothfurt stared at Drummond, his expression nonplussed. Alexander longed to know what he was thinking.

"The Academy feeds its students, my lord," Wrothfurt said. His skin had flushed - shock giving way to anger. "Without that support, they become a burden on their families. You speak of educating people who will starve anyway, but that is not the case. By educating them, we feed them. We keep them from starving now, and they help us to solve our problems later."

"The Crown cannot afford to feed peasants who do not know their place," Drummond snapped. He lifted a hand, a clear gesture of dismissal. Wrothfurt did not move.

"If the Crown cannot afford to feed its people," he said clearly, "then why have a Crown?"

The air seemed to suck out of the room. Alexander could see Drummond's neck flush scarlet. His brother would call that treason. He wouldn't be wrong.

Alexander did the only thing he could think to do. He moaned, and collapsed to the floor.

The court erupted into worried murmurs. Some cried out in dismay. Alexander convulsed, grasping at his heart. His ankle chains rattled, audible even over the hubbub. He moaned louder to drown them out.

"Guards!" Drummond shouted. He was already hurrying up the steps of the dais, his expression holding fear. Alexander knew the moment that his brother realized his fakery, saw it in the way wrath transformed his features.

"Court is dismissed," Drummond roared, turning back to the crowd that seethed against the velvet ropes. "Guards!" Men poured from their posts on the walls, corralling the assembled nobles back through the great throne room doors.

The shouting died away as the guards cleared the room, but Alexander did not drop his pretense until Drummond grabbed him by his collar and shook him. His head struck the floor with the force of it. The king began to wheeze laughter. Drummond twisted his fist in Alexander's jacket until it was nearly strangling. He drew Alexander up, meeting his eyes with venom.

"If you do that again, I will make you regret it," Drummond hissed.

"Lord Regent," the priest said. His voice was scandalized.

"It was a trick, Ermen. No doubt we've lost that traitor in the chaos." He dropped Alexander, who gasped in a breath.

"Take my brother to the tower," Drummond bellowed to his guards. "And find Wrothfurt!"

30 THE CAPTAIN

Nicola's haunted eyes burned holes in his back as he left the safe house. It was strange having her there, when there had been only him and Marie before. She did not seem to think about what other people could see, and he'd had to tell her more than once over the morning not to peer so eagerly out of the windows, kept closely curtained to stop the prying eyes of neighbors and passersby. She had never seen the world before, he reminded himself. Not that such pretty reasons would stop them all from being executed if she were found.

Marie had given her some different clothing to wear, a plain off-white dress that hung on her, and promised to look after her. The seer wandered about the house like a sleepwalker, or sat still as a stone, her face wrinkled with what looked like pain. She neither ate nor drank. For all her frail perfection, for all that he felt protective of her, she made his skin crawl.

So Bertrun had left her with Marie to care for her and gone to where he was better suited. He had an appointment to meet his council.

The streets were still impassable in many places. The quakes had taken down houses and scattered them like children's blocks. Bertrun had done his share of work fighting the fires from the first. The second, though longer, had caught fewer abed and by surprise. The damage was still extensive, but no fires had spread. They had been lucky.

They might not be so lucky again. The seer had not said anything about the shaking that made any sense to Bertrun. All of her words seemed to come across a great distance, when she responded at all. No doubt she was exhausted.

No answers came from that quarter, but Bertrun had other worries. He followed the Shadows along the streets, his skin jittering in the insipid winter daylight. This location was not easily accessible from the tunnels. Not every spot was. Often the exits had been boarded up, paved over, or otherwise obscured. Bertrun had them marked on his maps with a slashed line, showing that something blocked easy use.

The Baroness, not aware of the network of tunnels in any detail, had picked this new location following the temple's movement against the Academy. The Shadows had supported it as a temporary spot. It was not ideal long-term. There was nowhere for them to run if they were found. Bertrun hoped the Shadows could find something better soon, or his little council would have to resort to communicating via letter and cipher. It was possible, but responses were slow, and there was always the chance the letter would not make it to the right recipient, Shadows or no Shadows. It was hard enough to ensure that each member received the meeting location and time.

Traffic was light in mid-morning. Bertrun walked between two Shadows, trusting that eyes would mostly slide off his companions and, therefore, himself. The scarred Shadow remained a staple in his escort. The other Shadow was short. His lack of height was his only memorable quality. They knew where they were going even if Bertrun did not.

This was the northern part of the city. His brother and Syria lived nearby. Bertrun knew the streets well. It was no surprise when they turned to the east, where the residences of merchants and more affluent tradesmen gave way to the households of the nobility. Not everyone chose to live in the castle when they visited the city.

The house they arrived at looked closed up. It was up a long avenue lined with trees now denuded of leaves, and the small yard was overgrown with clumps of near-feral bushes. The old stone was blackened with moss. Only the large glass windows showed how wealthy the family who owned it was - or had been, once. Bertrun thought it likely that this was a the home of a noble family that had fallen out of favor, someone perceived too loyal to Alexander to safely come back to the city now. The glass glinted with color in the gray morning light, reminder of happier times.

One Shadow took post on the front street. The other led Bertrun down the carriage drive, to a small servants' house which crouched behind the mansion itself.

He was not the first to arrive. His brother-in-law was leaning against the wall.

Bertrun stopped in the door, surprised. He had not expected

to see Rufus here. The man had been less than exuberant in supporting their cause, for all that his dominant trade routes ran to Perlin. He had always struck Bertrun as nervous, but he was a shrewd haggler and ran his business well, and Syria seemed to love him.

"Rufus," Bertrun said. "How are you? Is Syria well?" His sister was normally the one who attended these meetings, and her pregnancy may have kept her from the temple but it should not have kept her from this.

"She was feeling nauseous today," Rufus said, smiling thinly. He ran a long-fingered hand through his fine, gold-flecked brown hair. He was a pretty man, and knew it, one of his few significant flaws in Bertrun's opinion. "I decided I would wait til spring to make the run to Perlen."

"Understandable." Bertrun seated himself. The small room of the servants' kitchen contained a short table that would seat six. The chairs were in good repair, for all that they were dusty with disuse, and Bertrun's legs were tired from the walk. Rufus followed suit, sitting across the table from the captain.

"Who will join us today?" Rufus asked, just as there was a sound from outside. Bertrun looked to the Shadow, but the lack of alarm in his posture meant the arrival was expected.

It was Wrothfurt, followed closely by the baroness.

"You came together?" Bertrun asked. "It's dangerous to be seen together."

The master cast a guilty look to Masana, which she brushed away.

"It is dangerous to do anything," the baroness said. "Master Wrothfurt is my charge, for now." She stood, all decorum, until Master Wrothfurt scrambled to draw her a seat. Then she sat gravely.

"What news?"

Wrothfurt took his seat as well.

"Besides the news of your escapade in the court?" Rufus said, voice slightly peevish. Bertrun looked sharply at Wrothfurt and Masana. This time it was the baroness' turn to cast a glance at Wrothfurt.

"I had to try something," he said. "The Academy is too

important."

"What happened?" Bertrun demanded, and listened in horror as Wrothfurt detailed his petition to the court.

"They are looking for me now," the master said ruefully. "I daresay I will be executed if found."

"If they had caught you -" Bertrun began.

"They did not," Masana said firmly. "Though I believe we have King Alexander to thank for that more than any quick thinking on my part." The baroness folded her hands, pursing her lips.

"In any case, we should focus on what happens now. First the coronation, now the Academy? We should capitalize on the mistakes Drummond has made."

"Capitalize?" Rufus sputtered. "I thought we were waiting for Liana to come back."

"We've waited," Wrothfurt said, adding his voice to Masana's. "The country cannot take much more. The quakes alone have done too much damage. Part of the southern city is without water, where the cisterns have cracked. People are starving, still. This powder keg will blow with or without us. It must be with us, lest the burn fizzle and leave us worse off than before."

Bertrun sat back, exhaling deeply. The master's counsel had merit. He had seen the desperation hit its peak. If there was no hope, things would only get uglier. They had done their best to spread the rumor that Liana still lived, but nothing more than that. They had not known more. Now they did. Now they knew that Liana came west, thanks to the Shadows. It was one of the only things that Nicola had confirmed for him before he left, and he did not doubt the seer in this. Liana came west, from her exile over the Spine. If anyone could make the journey, it was a sun-crowned queen.

"I agree," Bertrun said, "but if we are to begin to marshal our forces more avidly, I will be the one doing the marshaling. I cannot keep allowing others to take all of the risk."

"You are the centerpiece -" Wrothfurt began.

"I am nothing of the sort, hiding away," Bertrun said. "The people need to see a face. They cannot see Liana's. Mine will have to do, for now."

There was silence, as the table absorbed his announcement.

"Very well," Wrothfurt said at last. "I have contacts amongst the students. I will find a place for you to speak to them."

"I can help," Rufus said quickly.

Bertrun eyed his brother-in-law, then shook his head.

"Not with this," he said. "But we will need more than one of these meetings around the city. If there is another group amongst the merchants you think amenable, I will meet with them, too. It will be a start."

Rufus nodded, clenching his long fingers tight together. Bertrun admired his bravery in the face of what was obviously fear.

They talked a little longer then, but they all knew there was nothing more to say. There were protocols, if it became too dangerous to meet. There was speculation as to when Liana would arrive. But as of now, all of that was planning against a day not yet here. What they could do, now, was to begin recruiting in earnest. The time for listening and learning was over.

The time for action had come.

They left, as always, one after the other, spaced apart so that they would arouse less suspicion. Bertrun went last, this time. It was only after the others left that he realized he had not told them that Nicola had come to live with him. Some careful whisper of conscience had stilled his tongue.

If Drummond wanted Wrothfurt, how much more must he want the seer who had served him so long? Better none of his compatriots knew her location. What they did not know they could not be made to give up.

With that grim thought, Bertrun took himself back out into the street.

31 THE PRINCESS

Liana roused Liander, willed some heat into him. There were dark circles under his eyes and his skin was pale. She had never been happier for her powers over fire, for the heat that lived under her skin.

It was hard to leave the cave, but the series of storms that had passed over them for the last several days had at last abated. The air outside was still, deathly so, and bitter cold. But still air was better than wind, and they were running out of food rapidly. They would have to press on. Liana only hoped that she had read the map aright, and that they were truly nearing the edge of this mountain range. Once they reached the desert...well, it may not be better than the ice, in truth. A hot way to die, instead of a cold one. She reminded herself of this because too much hope left you as dead as too little. They would need to be ready, if they could be.

The new snow pressed down upon the layers of old snow. It was up to her waist now, though she only sunk in to her knees most places. Liana had a hatchet, gift from her erstwhile assassin. Before this last snow, she had used it to cut the ice. Now the ice was over a foot down. She had nothing else but her body.

Happily, her body was warm, unnaturally so. The feverish heat that rose from her eased her passage. She couldn't keep that heat up forever - whatever was inside her that channeled Herkun's fire grew tired eventually. But the days in this high valley were short, the light that reached them cut by the clouds and the peaks that rose to either side. By the time they got moving in the mornings, they only had a few hours left to travel before they must begin looking for a likely place to camp. It was a slow pace, even with the horses to carry Liander and their supplies. She worried about it, when she had the energy. They were so close, in terms of distance.

They were so far, in terms of time.

She knew that her brother thought she would move faster without him. It was true they had lost some days resting because of his foolishness in not caring for his wound, and they needed every day they had. But the horses moved at the pace Liana could slog a path clear. That would not speed up, with or without Liander. It was sickness and despair that made him talk of dying. If only she could point to something, a landmark, something to prove that their travails were nearly over. The white, though, was never ending. The mountains were a strange, jagged monotony. They had only estimates of their passage extrapolated from a map stolen from a dead murderer.

That would have to be good enough. There was no use speculating about it. There was nothing else to be done. She pressed on into the snow, leading the horse forward, while Liander shivered and tried to stay upright and the pony plodded along behind them.

When the ground beneath her started descending, Liana thought that it was simply a hollow, a dip that would soon level off. Instead, it continued. She found herself leaning back into the grade, taking longer steps. Ahead, the valley they passed through bent. When they rounded that curve, a new sight greeted them.

In the clear air, beyond the blinding whiteness of the mountain range, they could see a smear of reddish brown stretching to the horizon far below them. Liana gasped despite herself.

"Liander," she said. Her twin didn't respond. She looked back, and saw him dozing in the saddle. A hand on his calf woke him.

"What is it?" he muttered.

"Liander, look," Liana said. He raised his head. She saw the moment that he understood what they were seeing.

"The desert," he said. His voice was choked with emotion. "Liana, that's the desert."

She smiled. She could feel the tightness of her skin over her cheeks, the ache in the cold. "We're so close, brother. Hold on for me, just a little longer."

The pass soon curved, and they lost sight of the desert. That night they made camp with light hearts, and Liana pulled out the map as soon as she was able. The notes and directions it contained showed that they should be heading generally downhill from now on, though Liana thought there might be some moments of climbing. The downhill would help them to go faster.

The further down they got, the less snow there would be. It would not be easy, with the scant rations that remained to both them and the horse and pony. Liana thought they had enough for a week, if they stretched their supplies.

It took them ten days to hike out of the mountains.

She had been nearly right in her assessment. They had six days of food, light fare that it was, before they ran out completely. By that time, they had moved into lighter snow. Liana was able to ride for part of the day, and the pace of the horse was faster despite the sometimes tricky footing. They drank snowmelt until their bellies hurt with the cold.

On the eighth day, Liana shot a rabbit.

She was not the best with a bow. Liander was better, but his arm was still unusable. The wound had not healed, though it was no longer so infected as to imperil his life. Likely it was the cold, and the exhaustion and poor food. So they made camp earlier than usual and she strung the bow, careful of it in the cold, dry air. Then she moved along the stream they had camped beside, running mostly clear. There were little sprigs of hearty winter greens beside it. Liana stepped softly, straining her ears in the quiet. When the rabbit saw her, it froze in panic. She shot it before she had time to feel pity.

They ate the thing barely cooked, cracked the bones and sucked the marrow. They were still hungry, but at least they would live another day.

On the ninth day, they had descended far enough that most of the snow was gone. Dead winter grass stuck up from the ground, and scraggly, thorny bushes. The horse and the pony tore at the spare forage. Liana was able to bring down some kind of pheasant that she didn't recognize. It was light eating, but it kept them from gnawing on their saddle leather. Liander looked more gaunt than ever. Liana allowed herself to contemplate that she might lose him.

On the tenth day, they reached the desert.

It was winter, so the dry air was mild. Liana realized that she had stopped feeling the cold at all, though Liander still shivered. It was not warm air, not the heat she had expected. She could tell the nights would have a bite.

The sun, at least, was stronger here, and the heat of that body made her sweat despite the moderate temperature of the air. Even Liander's shivers abated as it rose into the sky.

Liana had packed their water-skins with snowmelt the day before, and now she made sure that they rationed this, too. Their stomachs snarled with emptiness. At first, there was scrub and occasionally hillocks of grass in the gravelly earth for the horse and pony to forage on. They were both nearly as gaunt as Liander, she saw, looking over them critically. She hoped that there would be more for them to eat soon, that they might find some soul in the desert who would feed all four of them. She knew better than to hope.

The dryness made her lips crack, left her mouth tacky with longing for water. Liana held off, plotting the deceptively monotonous skyline. The desert stretched on forever, with no real sign of life. The mountains were a heavy, piercing weight behind them. She turned back to look at them once. They seemed to stretch until they blocked out the sky.

Liander got off the horse and walked some. The poor animal did not look as if it could carry him much farther. The pony looked like it had fared better, though Liana suspected that was because the mare's thick fur hid her bones.

That night, they camped beneath the endless desert stars. They seemed closer even than they had appeared in the harsh, clear air of the mountains. Liana kept watch as Liander slept, not tired despite the long days of toil that were behind her. Her body thrummed as if in concert with those stars. For the first time in a long time, she allowed herself to think of her son. He was out there, somewhere.

She would not die. Liander would not die. They would make it through this together. They would find her son, and take back her kingdom. She would do whatever was necessary.

In the morning, she did the horse a kindness and slit his throat.

32 THE SEER

They flitted through the darkness below ground, a Shadow and a pale flame of a woman drifting like a ghost. Nicola did not question her steps, but she did not reach for the vision in the water, either. Visions might drive her mad, if she looked too long.

She had pulled the earth and water inside her into alignment, but the earth still fought to buck her control. The earth did not want her to go back for Matthius. The water knew it was necessary. The water had given a promise.

The water saw many things the earth could not.

It was the first time that Nicola understood that her lover might have been less powerful than her. Have been, because he was not here and she was, her power growing every day and no longer so easy to control.

Neither of them could escape the machinations of the elder gods. Herkun and Herka both made what power she could summon look childish. Even their lowest servants, the Shadows and the darker things that were made by Herka's curse, were a danger to her.

They would not always be. She could feel that certainty in her belly, and it scared her.

She felt it when they passed beneath the castle, the weight of the old stone above. The Shadow knew the tunnels well, and he led them closer to Matthius with ease, guessing rightly that her former guard was held in the dungeons. Those rooms were on level with the tunnels, underground where no sun reached. The darkness was complete, but darkness had never stopped her. Nicola had never known these halls by light. Their twists and turns were a map as familiar to her as her own mind, and she took them accordingly, driving towards her goal with speed. Running was foreign. Her body was not made for it. It labored at the exercise, at the quickness of her movements. It would not fail her yet, maybe not ever. She ignored the burning in her lungs. Her muscles trembled, insistent.

She ignored that, too.

When they came at last to the edge of the secret passages,

Nicola put her hand to the door before them, stretching out her senses. The hall beyond was empty. Her earlier panic, her earlier pain, was gone.

The door opened at her touch, pivoting away to reveal a wall of stone and a sconce, flickering with fire. The movement of the flame mesmerized her for a moment before she blinked and rubbed at her still-new eyes.

They were in the dungeons.

The empty hall echoed slightly with her soft footsteps. She remembered the sound well. She and Matthius had come here to see Corvin, after the master had almost killed her. Everything about the place made her skin crawl.

Guards came through these halls periodically. In Alexander's time, they had been rigidly frequent, those patrols. Under Drummond's rule, the guards only came to feed the prisoners and take out their used dishes and refuse buckets. The Shadow was not sure when they would come through next.

But that was why he was with her. The Shadow stepped past her, his sword drawn. Nicola envied the man his ability to move others' eyes from him, to blend in with his surroundings. Even now, knowing that they were both intruders, her mind insisted that he belonged. It was unsettling. Nicola followed him down the corridor, extending her senses behind her.

If they caught her here, Drummond would not kill her quickly.

Matthius' cell was only the third one down. The door was thick wood, the grate small and blocked by a sliding metal cover. The Shadow let her close the distance without argument. She slid the cover back, hearing it grate. Her heart beat loudly in her ears at the sound. She looked through the bars.

Matthius was inside. She knew him by his shoulders, which were wide, by his long legs splayed out before him. That was all she recognized.

His face was purpled with bruises, swollen so that he looked inhuman. His sword hand was gone. There was blood in his hair, making it a dark, brownish red. It was her first view of him with her own eyes, and she wanted to take it back.

Nicola held herself still, held her breath in until she knew her voice wouldn't shake. Then she called his name.

He didn't answer. She stepped away from the door.

The Shadow handed her his sword. She took it woodenly. He put a key in the door, turned it. The tumblers clicked together. The door swung inward. No doubt the Shadows had keys to all sorts of things, she thought inanely. They had so many secrets, Herkun's own as they were. She took a shuddering breath.

Then she stepped inside the cell. Matthius awoke when she touched him with her hands.

"Nicola," he said. His lips could barely shape her name. Drool coated his chin.

"I'm here," she said.

"Not me," he mumbled. "Not me. Save her. Save them."

"Matthius." She took his remaining hand, heart sinking. The fingers were broken. The water was welling in her, blocking out thought. Not him, he said. But she was here, and the water demanded that she be here.

She pressed her palms into his hand. He groaned. She heard the Shadow pull the door closed behind her, trying to block the sound from escaping. There was no room in her for worry.

One by one, she pulled his bones back together.

The snapping of the sounds rang through her. Nicola felt the desire to gag well up, felt it quelled. There was no time for it. Matthius wailed beneath her hands.

"Hurry," the Shadow hissed. Nicola reached for Matthius' legs. A bone was broken there, too. She pulled.

The jagged edges popped back into place and knit. Matthius screamed.

Distantly, she heard raised voices in the corridor. The Shadow stepped out. Nicola moved her hands, though Matthius was pleading with her, his hand pushing at her weakly.

"Almost," she told him. "Shh, almost." Her hands settled on his face.

The bruises melted away, as if his skin were fluid. The water flared. The world behind her eyes was blue.

Nicola fell back. Her mouth tasted of copper, her breath came too quickly. The dim cell spun.

Matthius stood, dragged her to her feet. She staggered.

Nothing came without a price. Nicola felt fatigue seep into

her, blackening the edges of her vision, thickening as the moments passed. In the corridor, she heard the clash of swords.

"We have to leave," she panted, more to herself than to Matthius. She took a step to the open doorway.

"You shouldn't have come," her guard told her, but he followed. His steps were just as halting as hers. They would not be of much help to the Shadow.

Happily, he did not seem to need it. The sound of fighting halted. Nicola rounded the edge of the cell door to see the Shadow cleaning his blade, slumped forms beyond him. When he returned it to its sheath, she almost forgot that it was there.

"Come," he said. "They will notice soon."

They had already noticed. Nicola's inner sight showed her that clearly. She moved, staggering towards the hidden doorway, pressing it open.

The three of them vanished from the corridor, into the hidden bowels of the castle.

33 THE PRINCE

Their pony led them to a spring, hardly more than a shallow puddle, on their third or fourth day in the desert. Liander had long since lost count of the days, one blurring into another, a wavering fever dream. His arm ached. Liana seemed to think this was good. Now that they were out of the mountains, he was able to keep it uncovered more often, but there was no water to use to clean it. They had run out of water quickly, and the horse and pony had been desperately thirsty. Then Liana had killed the horse, and that had been in many ways a relief.

Liander had helped redistribute their almost nonexistent supplies while she butchered the gelding, and kept the pony from running off. He did all this as if immersed in honey.

Threading thin slices of horse meat on twine with fumbling fingers, they had spread the line between a scraggly, stunted tree and the hobbled pony's tackle. The poor bay mare, having survived many trials, seemed too exhausted to protest further, despite the blood. It had taken both of them to drag the horse's body away from camp. They had no idea what creatures might be drawn to it out here in the open wasteland. Liana said they would travel at dusk, through the cold desert night, and leave potential predators behind. The harsh winter light dried their carefully hung strips. Liander slept, an exhausted sleep without dreams.

He awoke as the sun set. The sandy, flat-seeming horizon revealed crags and dips in the slanting, golden light. The whole landscape felt washed out and strange, and the air held a chill.

"How do you feel?" Liana asked him, her golden eyes on the white orb of the setting sun. They, too, must travel west. Liander shrugged, the motion pulling at the wound in his arm. It still wept pus.

"Not dead yet," he said lightly. His voice was gravelly in the twilight. Liana cast him an unreadable look.

They settled their new provisions on the pony and set to walking. Liander tried not to think of how the gelding had carried him faithfully through the Spine, and failed. He ate a strip of meat anyway.

They walked through a good portion of the night. Liander's feet were like stones on his ankles by the time his sister finally let them halt and make camp in the dark. Exhausted, he fell into his blankets almost immediately, leaving Liana to do the things that needed doing.

In the morning, late morning, the panting pony pulled against her lead as they set out. Liander watched as Liana pulled back, trying to force the mare onwards.

"Let her go," he said, surprising himself. "She's pulling north."

Liana dropped the rope in disgust. "She's pulling to pull," she said, her cracked lips splitting with the words. But she followed the pony when it began its meandering walk north through brambles and brush. By midday, they had reached a watering hole, nothing more than a shallow, seeping depression in the sand and rock.

They strained the muddy water through a piece of cloth into their water-skins and into their mouths. The brackish liquid tasted like life. Liander drank until he thought his belly would burst, then moved aside for the mare. When the pony finished her turn, there was no more water to be had.

"It may be days yet before we find water again," Liana said, looking, as always, west.

"I hope she makes it," Liander said. His sister glanced at him, surprised. He shrugged. It was true. He liked the mare. He didn't want to eat her.

They moved west, and sometimes north, when the sun in their eyes made west blinding. Herkunsland was north, but Liana sought the desert folk now. He was not entirely sure why, but he had little energy left to contemplate it. Their water-skins were small - they had not needed larger before. They emptied quickly. His wound was not worsening, but it was not getting better either. It sapped his strength. His skin peeled beneath the endless sun, reddened and sore even in the winter light. His legs burned with strain. The horse meat was less than filling, and hardly lasted them days. Even Liana seemed exhausted, her bones standing out beneath the skin of her face. The streak of white in her hair had grown more pronounced. Eighteen was too young for her to look so weathered.

They came upon the camp of a sudden. One moment the desert expanded before them, eating up their meandering steps. The next, a horse called out. They topped a rise they had not realized they were climbing, and there was a man and a woman.

And Liander knew the woman.

He blinked, opened his dry mouth and then closed it. Surely this was a mirage. It was Liana who broke the silence, his practical sister who was either too tired or too calculating to be stunned.

"Jessa," she said. "What are you doing here?"

"Waiting for you," their friend said. There was something wrong with her voice. It lacked the vibrancy he remembered. Her face was still, blank. Jessa had never not had some sort of emotion, some sort of expression. Liander swayed on his feet, trying to bring the blurring world back into focus.

"Jessa?" he said.

She spared a glance for him. Just one, but in it was a shadow of the girl he had loved. Only a shadow.

"What did you do?" he asked. Liana looked at him sharply, then looked at Jessa again. She was frowning, as if trying to recognize something. He saw her touch her breastbone. Jessa stood up, stepped forward.

"I have become your Shadow, Liana," their friend said. "So that you will not burn up the world."

"I don't..." Liana said. He looked at her, tearing his eyes away from Jessa. She was staring into the distance blankly, her golden eyes seeing something he could not.

Then she fell. He lunged to catch her, crying out as her weight landed on his wounded arm. His knees hit the gravelly sand. The pony whickered in alarm.

"Liana!" he called, but she didn't stir. Her exhausted, thin face was quiet, too pale. At least her chest rose and fell with her breath. Liander felt his own breath hiss out in relief.

The man with Jessa stood at last. Liander looked up into his brown face. A member of the desert tribes, the ones Liana had been searching for.

"Do not worry for your sister," the man said. "She has merely burned too hot for too long. The Shadow keeps that fire calm, lets her sleep." He knelt, some distance away. Liander thought the man was trying not to spook him, and snorted in derision. As if he could be calm at this point. His heart was pounding so loud that he could feel the vibration in his toes. He staunchly did not look at Jessa, knowing that would not help to keep him level-headed.

"Who are you?" he asked instead. With Liana in his arms, there was no way he could reach his sword, but there was nowhere they could run to in any case.

"I am Kabrim of the Ashir, second brother to Sayala. We are here to give you shelter. Fear no harm from us, Prince."

Liander struggled to remember what he knew of the desert tribes. They had elaborate and foreign social customs organized around smaller familial clans, and lived by movement, breeding beautiful horses like his Silberlief and trading spices and tea, metalwork and glass from their small cities. Those cities were said to be beautiful, too. He could not remember what second brother meant, could not at the moment parse what anything meant. His brain was swollen with fatigue, listless with want of food and water, and the adrenaline that had kept him moving was rapidly dwindling away.

"You are nothing more than skin and bones," Kabrim said. "Let me feed you, and your sister sleep. We will rest here tonight, and you may ask of me anything you wish. In the morning, I will take you to my tribe."

Liander looked down at the sleeping face of his twin. She was cool to his touch, and he realized that he thought that only because she had been so hot for so long. He might also be running a fever.

"Alright," he said, his dry throat cracking the words. There was no other choice to make.

34 THE PRINCESS

Liana picked her way through the camp quietly. Firelight flickered, the steady inhalation and exhalation of coals about to expire. She could feel it, distantly. The intoxicating immediacy was gone, but the fire was still there, filling up that place inside her. It was a place that would otherwise be teaming with darkness.

When Jessa had placed her curse, Liana had feared she would never feel the fire again. That sudden dislocation, the dimming of the world, had shocked her so badly that she had lost hold of herself. Blackness as profound as death had rolled over her. She had not been quick enough to fight it.

She would not be so unprepared this time.

Her soft steps took her past Liander and the strange desert man. She spared little thought for them. Her quarry was beyond the fire's ring, small though it was. In the desert, one did not need a large fire to light the night. Any flame could be visible for miles. This one was situated in a hollow, a dip in the earth that cradled it, hid it from prying eyes. Once she stepped outside that cradle, only darkness greeted her.

Liana was no stranger to this type of darkness. The weight of the night should have held terrors for her, perhaps. But she had learned that the moon's arm was longer than the night stretched, even nights like tonight where no moon hung in the sky. Her hand tightened on the knife she held. The knife would free her of this new enemy, just as her sword had freed her from Jei. She would not be bound, be made less. No forces would move her fate but her own.

Wind sighed through the scrubby bushes that pocked the desert sand. Liana stretched her ears to listen. Her beating heart, the wind's sigh, something that might have been a mouse moving in the darkness, these all reached her. With no moon, only the stars lit her way, but they were brilliant here. It was enough light to see by.

She caught Jessa's shape in the near blackness.

The outline was enough. The girl, once her friend, was changed. She would sense it if Liana crept too close, and so Liana ceased to creep. She gathered her muscles instead, and leapt.

Her knife caught the starlight, and for a moment she exulted.

Jessa moved with a speed that rendered her invisible in the blackness. Liana felt a hard grip on her wrist, pressure at her hip, and then she was sailing, her momentum carrying her forward through the night air. Sand and gravel caught her, digging into the thin, tattered fabric at her shoulder. Her bones jolted. Skin tore. Liana gritted her teeth around around the pain and fought her way back to her feet. Jessa had not moved.

That made Liana angry.

She rushed Jessa again, her movements sloppy with rage. Jessa side-stepped easily. Almost, it seemed as if Liana's one-time friend had blinked out of focus and blinked back in again. Liana spun, trying to track Jessa, certain she would attack. Her breath came harsh and fast in her throat. Her hair prickled on her arms.

"I will not hurt you," Jessa said, her voice still dry, still strange. And then, "Liana, it's still me."

That voice was the voice of the girl she had known, had played with as a child. Jessa had taught her to climb trees. Liana remembered the exhilaration of the high branches, the brightness of it. The freedom in knowing that there was someone else like her, even if she were only a groomsman's daughter and not a princess. Her hands trembled, then tightened on her knife.

"Release me from your curse, then," the princess said harshly. "Give me back the fire."

The fire kept her safe. The fire was the only way she could see her son, had been the only way she'd ever known him. The distance hurt like a hole in her.

"Liana, can you not feel how the fire in you burns the world?" Jessa said. "I must bind it. I must keep you and Herkunsland safe."

"Herkunsland can burn," Liana growled. The words surprised her because they were true. Herkunsland had cast her out. Herkunsland did not want a queen. Let it burn as Ma'alu's children had burned, if only she could see her son again.

"But it does not have to," Jessa told her. "It does not have to, Liana."

"That is for me to decide, not you. The time may come when

you can bind the fire from me, but it is not now. If you stand in my way, I will do all in my power to end you, no matter what you were to me and my brother." The words nearly choked her, but there was steel in her voice when it rang in the night air. The anger was clarifying into a thing with a hard, high edge. "You are for me or against me, Jessa."

There was silence, then. The desert night moved and sighed around them. Her anger made each moment perfectly clear, made the weight of Jessa's attention take substance. Almost, she could hear Jessa communing with whatever strangeness inhabited her.

"As you wish, Sun-crowned," Jessa said. There was no inflection in her voice. It was dry and dead as the desert sand.

Liana lifted a hand, then forced it back to her side. She had what she wanted. Her heart should not ache for it.

Then the light flooded her. Her knees wobbled, but Liana spread her arms, embracing the warmth. The fire in the hollow flared, and she heard Liander yelp.

"Thank you," she said, the words slipping out of her. How could they expect her to live without this? It was impossible. "Thank you."

Jessa did not answer. When Liana looked, she realized that the girl was already gone.

35 THE SEER

Nicola crouched in the tunnels beneath the castle and waited for her strength to return.

The cool, damp air wrapped around her, held her close. She relaxed into it gratefully, trying to ignore the sounds of soldiers, faint through the wall of the castle corridor to her left, and the harsh panting of Matthius to her right. He did not seem to like the dark. That same dark was now, to her, a balm. Nicola sucked in lightless, damp air, feeling its coolness in her lungs. Feeling the blue inside her condense once more into something with weight.

When it was done she reached out with whatever part of her was connected to the water. Nicola still felt exhausted, but that exhaustion was waning. It was as if her soul was a still pool. Her frantic efforts to save Matthius had splashed some of the water out, but now it trickled back slowly. She did not regret her actions. Even now Matthius' mind, his energy, was a familiar presence beside her. Sensing him in the darkness, she reached for his hand. He jerked away at the contact, and then reached back. His large, calloused fingers gripped with a strength just shy of crushing.

"The Voice will return soon," she whispered, and then remembered that not all knew the Voice's title. "The Shadow." The darkness seemed to quiver at her words. Nicola shifted uneasily despite herself. She had never before feared the dark, when she'd had no choice but to live in it. Now she found herself missing the vibrancy of colors. The green inside her gave a pulse, as if in comfort. She had almost forgotten that it was there, so focused had she been on the depletion of the water's buoyant power.

But the green was there, and while Nicola couldn't use it the way that the water answered to her, she could at least seek direction from it. It was not agitated, resting calmly in her belly. Despite the heavy weight of Matthius fear and her own anxiety, the green stayed solid and warm. She held onto that feeling. Gradually, the voices of the soldiers receded. They had not been able to find the entrance to this tunnel, at least.

They were not safe yet. There were many ways to access the

tunnels, ways that Drummond knew. No doubt he would be pacing even now, his wide shoulders tense with anger. She could almost smell him, the musk of his rage thick and cloying. It made a knot form in her stomach that had nothing to do with strange powers, and everything to do with fear.

There was a faint sound beside her. The Shadow melted out of the darkness, his heat and presence suddenly filling the small tunnel.

"Matthius," she whispered. "It's time to go."

They crept through the tunnels without the benefit of their eyes. Matthius did not protest, and Nicola knew that, despite his fear, he was cognizant of the implications of light in this small, dark space. Light would blind them more surely to the dangers that sought them than darkness would. In the dark, they could see their enemies coming. Nicola's senses stretched out, her steps sure enough for both of them. Light and its lack made little difference to her in knowing where she was, and she guided Matthius after the Shadow. That man's gray aura hung before her like smoke.

Matthius' was brighter, streaked all through with gold.

She pondered that relative brightness. It was not a burning gold like the sun-crowned kings carried in their veins, but a faint, warm luminescence. It appeared for many of Herkunsland's citizens, a common thread through them, and in the auras of the desert folk as well, though their gold was different still. There was a lot of thinking to do as the Shadow led them through the darkness. Her steps and her senses took some of her attention, but the going was tedious. They were forced to rest often, for Matthius' sake. Her healing had kept him alive, but he still hurt. And his thoughts, she grew to realize, were troubled. It was a level of upset not due to the darkness or their relative vulnerability as escapees. Something that drifted just under the surface of his mind, colored his whole self with poisonous worry.

It took her some time to realize why, and when she did she nearly cursed aloud, an expletive she had learned from Drummond.

"Matthius," she said. Her soft voice carried in the tunnel. "What will happen to your family?"

There was no answer, but the tightened squeeze of his hand,

the sharp breath, told her all she needed to know.

"Voice -"

"We must escape first, seer," the Shadow said, his voice low. "Then, if we are not too late."

Nicola swallowed. Matthius stumbled behind her like a man drugged. It was exhaustion, made more weighty with despair. Now that she had a name for it, she could almost taste it on her tongue it was so thick from him.

She did not look into the future to see what the outcome would be. She did not want to know, and the future was hard to see clearly with her heart pounding in her throat. Instead, Nicola moved faster, pushing her will into Matthius. There was a chance that she could do something for them, if she got there in time. The Shadow, sensing her urgency, stepped more quickly as well.

They made it out of the tunnels and into the streets. She was surprised to find that it was dark.

They moved through the back alleys and unlit roads of the city. Nicola could feel her energy draining away, realized that she was in fact feeding Matthius some part of her essence. The water, its power, seemed limitless with this small trickle its only drain. Her body seemed light, white skin glowing in the moonlight.

There was a moon, she realized. It was a small sliver. Its light rippled on her like a hand across her skin. Tonight it seemed to feed her. Its light made the shadows longer, and yet Nicola felt that her feet quickened still further under its touch. She did not know where she was going - but Matthius knew, and she used the certainty of his heart like a compass. The Shadow was no longer leading. Nicola led them now, her steps as sure as the stars.

They arrived at a house. All of the lamps were off, inside and out.

Nicola could sense darkness on the home immediately. She stopped, only then feeling the way her breath gasped in her chest. Fear radiated through the street. For a moment, she felt rage.

She let it go, let it fall from her like it needed to. Anger was something she could do nothing with, not now. Nicola stepped forward, studying the clean lines of the building. The Shadow moved, as if he might protest.

"This is ours to do," she said, her voice quiet. It felt like it should be heavy, loud. Matthius followed her without speaking at all. They stepped onto the front stoop, and Matthius, next to her now, put his hand to the door. It swung open.

He met her eyes, for just a moment. She saw the moment of surprise, saw the blame follow, and the rage. She understood that this was all her doing. She could never atone.

The light of the moon revealed two crumpled forms on the floor. Nicola did not have to reach with her other sight to know that they were the bodies of a woman, and a child.

Matthius knelt, and howled his grief to the night.

36 THE CAPTAIN

Nicola returned not long after nightfall. Bertrun, who had been pacing for much of the day, threw open the back door at her knock before Marie could reach it. She had stayed up with him, infected by his worry, and sat now drinking a tisane at the dining room table as he ushered Nicola, the scarred Shadow, and their new companion inside.

He was a big man, taller than Bertrun by a foot at least, with wide shoulders and eyes that spoke of horror. Yellow bruises mottled his skin, and he was missing a hand. He did not move like the hand had been gone for long, but the wound looked clean.

Marie stood hurriedly as the group made their way in, going to fetch them drinks from the kitchen. Bertrun pulled a seat for the stranger, who sat woodenly. Nicola stood, arms wrapped around herself. The Shadow stood as well, against the wall.

"This is Matthius," Nicola said at last.

The man flinched at her voice. Bertrun saw her face twist at it, saw tears well in her green eyes.

Bertrun was not happy with Nicola for bringing this strange man to their hideaway, nor, for that matter, for putting herself in danger, for all that he had agreed to it. But whatever had happened to this man had been payment for her safety. He understood the obligation.

"Matthius," he said. The man looked up at him. Such a gaze, as if he had watched the whole of his world burned to ash. Bertrun suppressed a shudder, meeting those eyes. "Are you loyal?"

The man's face twisted. His eyes closed, as if he were seeing something elsewhere.

"You would crush him," Matthius said. "The Lord Regent. You would make him pay?"

"Matthius," Nicola said, "you don't -"

"Enough." His voice was ragged and edged. Nicola drew back. He reached into his pocket, pulled something glimmering free. Tossed it to the ground at her feet. It was a necklace, Bertrun saw. Nicola bent to pick it up, her shoulders hunched. She curled around it as if wounded.

It was the Shadow who broke the silence.

"There are many ways to serve, if your intent is pure enough." Bertrun started, looking at him.

"No," Nicola said, "you can't, he isn't -"

"What do you mean?" Matthius said. He looked at the Shadow then, truly looked at him. "You're -"

He stopped, took a breath. Held up the stump of his wrist.

"I'll not be a swordsman again," he said.

"You will," the Shadow said. There was no hesitancy in his voice. "The fire would see to it. All it asks is your loyalty."

"That is not all it asks," Nicola said. "That is not -"

"Enough!" Matthius said, standing all at once. He was a big man. The chair flew away from him. Nicola flinched, cringing from a blow that did not come, and Bertrun saw in that motion the echo of two years spent at Drummond's beck and call and felt shame course through him.

Matthius saw it as well, he thought. Even as angry as the man was, he did not take another step towards her. He waited until she brought her hands down, until she looked up at him with a face that was trying not to twist into tears.

"You have lied to me enough. You have manipulated my life enough. I am not yours to command."

Her lips trembled. She was so pale already, but Bertrun saw her swallow, saw the pain whiten her face further. She had gone back for this man.

Something had happened, between her going to rescue him and his coming here. They had been gone for a long time, far after dark had settled outside. Some ill will had come between them in that time, on this man's part at least.

Nicola took a deep, shuddering breath. Then she turned, and walked up the stairs. No doubt she would find the bed Marie had made for her. She was an oracle, after all.

Bertrun still felt guilty, letting her go.

He turned towards the Shadow. "What do you mean, giving the fire his loyalty? What does that mean?"

"He means to ask me if I am called," Matthius said. His good hand brushed his stump. "If I am called to the fire, and to vengeance."

He stepped forward then, and knelt.

"If the fire means Drummond will burn," he said, head bowed, "then I will pay whatever price."

The Shadow reached down, gripped Matthius shoulder.

"I am not your king," the Shadow said. "Nor your queen. I am not the fire you will serve." He helped to lift Matthius to his feet. The big man lumbered up with surprising grace.

"Come," the Shadow said to him. They began to walk back into the kitchen. Marie met Bertrun's gaze, her eyes wide. She had re-emerged with drinks, but there was now no one to take them. The Shadow and Matthius pushed past her.

"Wait!" Bertrun said.

The Shadow paused, looking back.

"Take me with you," he said. "I would see him."

The Shadow nodded, once. Then he resumed walking. With a muttered goodbye to Marie, Bertrun hurried after them.

Bertrun thought on the choices that led a decent man to support a devil as he followed Matthius through the tunnels. It was not power, certainly. A castle guard had only a little power over others, unlike the street patrol. Duty, perhaps, would be the deciding factor in taking such a post. Duty to home and family, at first, and then duty to one's occupation. It was an uncomfortably familiar motivation, that sense of obligation. It moved him even now, as he walked in the darkness lit only by a small candle, a shield of copper casting the light before him instead of into his eyes, lighting up the stone halls. There was a whole other castle, a whole other city, down here. He had walked these corridors, and had the Shadows walk them, until he had a map of many of them, and sketched those maps out until they were memorized. The ones to the castle he knew best. He traced those lines in his head, and thought of the fate that obligation brought to those who succumbed to it.

He knew when they passed under the castle's walls. The air, always damp, began to cool and the moisture of condensation fed patches of colorless moss. Even moss could not thrive in such a lightless environment. The stones joined so smoothly that it still baffled him. Nothing constructed now fit quite so neatly.

Stonework had fallen out of favor in newer construction, and much of the knowledge concerning it was lost in the process. Working wood was far more fashionable, mostly because it was so much easier to shape and stone became cold in the winter. This stone belonged to another age.

Bertrun blew out his candle, letting the Shadow take the lead. The man always seemed to know where he was going, even in the dark. He could hear Matthius' labored breath as he dropped behind.

Soon, they turned off of the paths Bertrun knew. Their corridor dipped, descended to new depths. Bertrun felt Matthius' panic becoming infectious. He did not know if even he could find a way back, and these passages were labyrinthine.

The light crept up on him, concerned as he was with its absence. He rubbed at his eyes, blinked and rubbed them again.

"There's light," he said. Matthius grunted behind him. It seemed as if the frantic nature of his breathing lessened, but it was hard to tell for sure.

The light grew as they walked, the Shadow's outline becoming clear as he led them forward. It became brighter and brighter, at first flickering and then far too vibrant to be considered flickering at all. He saw the Shadow as a stark relief against it. It revealed the walls, the moss now growing freely, green as if it grew under the sun itself. Bertrun felt the heat then, heat that he had been ignoring. Sweat began to bead on his face. He wiped it away, feeling a deep sense of disturbance at the light. It was too bright. Too strong. What would he see, when he at last stood before it?

The answer was inferno.

At first he was so taken aback by the raging flame that he did not see the other forms already in the chamber. His heart pounded before it, old panics resurfacing.

"By Jassas," he said. The flames flared, and he flinched back.

"Be careful of the names you use," the Shadow said. He was blackness against the shape of the fire, almost unnaturally so, his features obscured. Bertrun stared at him, and then finally registered the presence of the other Shadows, spaced behind him along some predetermined interval. There were gaps, of course. There were only four of them, with Jessa to the south.

"This is what you are," he said, his voice hoarse with fear. "You are the jackals." He had dreamed of them, before, long ago when the castle had burned in Drummond's rebellion. He had dreamed and not known. Still he remembered the heat, the sensations of that dream, as Jassas' jackals had torn out his heart and swallowed it whole.

A shudder shook him, shook the whole of him. He took a step back, and bumped into Matthius.

The man was staring at the fire as if it were the most beautiful thing that he had ever seen. Bertrun followed that gaze.

In the heart of the fire was a man. When he stepped forward, Bertrun saw that that man was his king.

"Who is called to the fire?" the scarred Shadow said.

Bertrun bit his tongue, stepped aside. Alexander watched from the heart of the flames, but he could not read the king's expression. Was this the secret to the king's sanity? Jessa had become a Shadow, had walked into the flame.

Matthius stepped forward now. Bertrun clenched his fist, though he longed to reach out and hold the man back. It wasn't his choice, though every iota of his being screamed protest. He was not a creature of the fire.

"The flames rise," the Voice said, "will you stand in their way?"

"I will stand, as the god of fire and light has bidden," Matthius said. His voice was rote. This was ritual. Bertrun felt his breath seize in his chest as the fire seemed to grow.

"Then come, and join us in our circle," the Voice said. "The price is steep to cross the threshold."

He stepped back. Matthius stepped forward, his back straight and sure.

"I will pay the price the fire asks," he said. There was no question. He stepped past the Shadows.

The fire consumed him, and Bertrun's king watched on.

37 THE KING

The Shadow came for him again in the dull days while Drummond pouted and postured about letting him out of his tower. They both knew that his brother would let him out again eventually. Drummond didn't have a head for ruling. He was desperate.

But it would take time for his brother to recognize that, and Alexander was bored in that time. There was nothing to do in the tower. He had convinced his guard, poor soul, to bring him a book with breakfast. The man still acted like Alexander would bite him. He wasn't wrong, so Alexander tried not to begrudge him of it. There was still blood in the mortar of the stones at his feet.

There was still a curse inside the king.

But it was a curse in remission, for now. He fingered the knucklebone in his pocket, then patted it. It was a new pocket, in a new coat. They'd finally realized he should probably have regular changes of clothes if he was going to play king again. There had even been a barber in to cut his hair and trim his beard and nails. It was how he knew his brother had not wizened up. He was angry, and uncertain, but he was still planning on using Alexander in some fashion. Using a king was hard business. It tended to cut two ways.

He found, in those days waiting, that he did not much wish his brother ill. He still remembered their childhood together fondly. But he thought of his daughter, of her fire. Liana was his heir, and he had always known she would make a good queen. Yes, she was not unlike Drummond in some ways, but she was compassionate, too. He was sure of her, believed in her, hoped for her, even with his fate in the grip of a goddess that he did not worship. Gods had their reasons. Liana was Herkun's, not Herka's. She belonged here.

So he enjoyed his new luxury - changes of clothes and relative cleanliness, sleep, food, all things he had taken for granted not so long ago. He waited.

The Voice opened the door to his room when the moon was not yet risen. Alexander had suspected when the guard did not

168

come to lock him into his cage that he might receive a visitor. He had been lying on his bed, stomach flipping this way and that, fingers nervously touching the knucklebone to remind himself that it was there. It was still easier to be locked up at night. It felt safe.

He sat up when the door swung inward. He and the Voice met eyes wordlessly, and Alexander remembered that day, so long ago, when a boy with a scar on his cheek had pledged him service, and walked into the fire.

"Who is it this time?" he asked solemnly. The Voice shook his head, and motioned for the king to follow.

Once more he followed the Shadow down the stairs of his tower, out the abandoned corridor, torches along its length burning low. There were still people up and about, Alexander felt sure, but whomever might be awake at this hour had not ventured to this part of the castle. They passed unmolested, and once more down into the dark of the hidden passageways.

Alexander knew what was coming this time. Still, he was surprised when he saw the light so soon, and surprised too when that light and heat did not more quickly result in the chamber that held his ancestor's bones. When they did at last reach Sermund's tomb, he understood why.

The inferno had grown.

It was almost to the Shadows now, where they stood, already gathered. He could feel something inside him calling out for the fire, longing for it. He wanted its embrace.

He stepped past the circle of Shadows, into the flames.

They moved through him, this time. What had been comforting before was like ecstasy, and like ecstasy it was, nearly, painful. The king swallowed, fingers reaching for the knucklebone out of habit. He had to pull his hand away. Though he no longer feared the fire, Alexander found the bone too hot to touch. He wondered that it did not burn away his clothes. Whatever divine blessing protected him, however, held.

He turned, then, at last, and looked out, waiting for those who came supplicant. Two men entered as he watched. One stepped forward towards the flame. Alexander did not know his name, but he had seen this man before - behind Nicola, when his curse had nearly claimed her. It surprised him, that this man should give himself to the flames.

But the test was only his to administer, not to judge.

Alexander let the flames pass through him, into the man who would be Shadow.

The man locked his knees, muscles knotting in pain. His whole body seemed to shudder, all at once. Then again. For a moment, Alexander feared.

But the fire left him, and returned to its home, and he was not rendered ash. He was still, on the outside, a man.

The inside, that was a different matter. On the inside, he was Shadow.

The flame around him convulsed back. It still encompassed Alexander, but it was not so raging, not so wild. He wondered at its strength. In all his life, he had never seen the flames so large. It was terrifying, and wonderful. He had to fight the joy in his blood, fight to leave the flame's embrace.

When he did at last, the new Shadow was waiting. And someone else.

Alexander almost didn't recognize the captain. He had lost muscle, and his face was lined. There were scars on his palms and a small speckling of burns on his face. His curly black hair was graying.

The king stopped, feeling his tongue turn to wood in his mouth.

He did not want to give Bertrun to the fire.

"Your Majesty," the captain said, bowing. "I..." His voice caught and he cleared his throat. "I wanted to see you. To see that you were well."

To see, Alexander realized, if the rumors were true.

It made his words harsher than he meant them to be.

"Captain," he said, "you have seen me."

The new Shadow stepped forward then, cutting off any attempt he might have made to soften his words.

"Sun-crowned," he said, kneeling. Alexander noticed for the first time that he was missing a hand.

"Welcome to my service," Alexander said, his voice soft. He wanted to ask this man what his name had been, what had driven him to this. He knew the Voice would know, would remember, but it felt important that he remember the people who had sacrificed themselves for him, too. Yet the Shadow had made his choice, to give up who and what he had been. Alexander also wanted to respect that. He placed his hand on the man's head, in benediction.

When the Voice appeared, he did not protest being led back to his tower. He stopped, though, before the captain. Reached out, and brushed the man's cheek, where the burns had marked it. Remembered, too, this sacrifice.

Then he followed the Voice back into captivity.

38 THE SEER

She had made a mistake. She hadn't seen the outcomes, and she had made a mistake, and now Matthius, the only person who had every shown Nicola true kindness, would not even look at her. She thought of the cold of his house, of the dead that had greeted them inside. If she could go back, if only she could go back and undo it.

Nicola sat on her bed. The box that held the god's ashes open in her numb fingers. The room was dark. Darkness pressed against her eyes, comforting. She was used to darkness.

It was the light she could not see past. It was the light and the green in her belly, too, twisting the future ahead, blinding her. Her fingers buried themselves in the black sand, in all that remained of the flesh of the green god who had never given her his name.

Matthius sat downstairs and gave himself to the fire. She knew that was what the Shadow would ask of him. His soul, given to the flames to become ash and smoke and cinders. He would serve to protect the world from Herkun's fire the same way that burning a copse of trees in the summer could save it from forest fires in the dry fall, clearing out the brush, creating a place where flames could not pass. It was a necessary service, and the Shadows had been depleted. With Jessa's addition, they were five. But two more were needed, two more to form the ring of them.

She could not wait for two more. She could not make such a mistake again. And she did not want Matthius to be one of those two. Perhaps that was a foregone conclusion, but if she could just see surely she could find a path forward that didn't end up with Matthius a Shadow.

Her breath sighed in and out of her. She pushed her sight, the inner sight, outward. The future beckoned, each route of it coated in fire and golden brightness.

She remembered the field, then, and almost it appeared. It took effort to push it away, to push past it. She felt the light clutch her close. Heat came, impossible heat, the pressure of Sermund's golden eyes, burning in her. This heat crawled up her insides, along her veins. She felt the green inside her buck and scream.

Her heart clenched with fear, and for a moment Nicola reeled back.

The water rose up and pressed into every nook of her.

Nicola had not realized that she had summoned it, but now she sank down into it gratefully. The fire above flickered, faded. The light here was a soft refraction, and then it was nothing at all. All stilled. Blessed cold moved through her, numbing her loneliness, her grief. She forgot, in that moment, why she had come at all.

Her feet were on dry land, and the water hung above her, a canopy of dark motion. Her skin glowed in a soft light that seemed to come up from the ground. Nicola stood, waiting. Water whispered and lapped at the shore in the gloom, in time with her breath.

"My love."

The voice came from everywhere and nowhere. She dug her toes into the black sand beneath her feet, its luminous darkness. There was a knot in her throat, as if she might weep.

"I have missed you," he said, but she still could not see him, still could not see his face. She turned, peering into the darkness, stretching out all of her senses. For a moment, the vision flickered. For a moment, she remembered urgency, remembered that he was already gone, but then he spoke again, pulled her back.

"Listen, my love. There is little time.

"I must soon be born."

"Be born?" Nicola said. Her voice was barely a whisper. The water above trembled with it, even so.

Her lover, his voice rich and weighty even in death, kept speaking. "My mother comes north even now, as I promised you so long ago. My love, deliver me."

All at once Nicola understood that he would leave her. Emotion took her with the suddenness of dreams. A sound came out of her, a keening. The waves, soft and soothing before, pounded and shook.

She could not be alone again. He had said that he would not leave her.

"I will never leave you," he said now. "I do not forget my

promises. Trust me."

Nicola could not.

She fled into the darkness, away from the island of obsidian sand, away from the inevitability of loss. The water drew her up, cradled her, and she wrapped it around herself, leaving the memory of her lover behind. Her grief was as wide in her chest as an ocean, and Nicola wondered at it. She had been alone for so long that being alone should not trouble her, but trouble her it did. He would leave her. He had promised.

She had also made a promise.

Nicola wrapped the water tight around her and ascended. The light met her, as it had before, but she did not seek to escape it now. She climbed into it, the heat seeking her and sliding away. The water insulated her. It was the part of herself she needed to resist the heat and light of Herkun and his cold, bright bride. She stretched the water between her hands, a lens of the smoothest glass, and looked out into another world.

There was fire, but she had known that.

The future spread forward like the branches of a river. Each fork grew smaller, more attenuated, until she could not make out its nature in the distance. But the nearest branches were large, and visible. She could see war down every branch, death and fire. Nicola shied away from the chaos in them, attempted to peer down into the minor depths for one thread, one presence in the jumble. Matthius must be here. He would stay with her, he would help her.

She found him at last, already moving along his course. The castle loomed before him, and the flames at its heart. It had, even at this remove, already become a part of him. There was no escape.

Nicola felt the grief a second time, no less painful than the first. The pressing ache of solitude caught in her throat like a needle. The visions spun from her grasp. Her breath stuttered.

Far away, in the depths of the castle, a man walked alone into flame.

The fire consumed him as she watched.

Nicola lay on her bed and shuddered with tears that fell like cold glass beads in her hair. It was dark and she was alone. The green in her was a heavy weight, a stone in her belly that she could not cough up.

They would leave her. They all left her.

It took some time for the tears to run their course, for the grief that had been building in her for fifty years to finally press its way out of her like sickness. She gasped in its aftermath, her throat sore, her body aching. Crying was the hardest thing, it seemed, that she had ever done. Yet she felt washed clean.

She had survived every leaving. She would continue to survive. Nicola did not need to look forward into the future to know that. The water in her shifted, rose and fell with her breathing. Water could not be broken. It hung in the air, moved through the earth. It was everywhere in this world, and she soon would be everywhere. She would meet a thousand beautiful souls, and they would likely all leave her not because of the leaving, but because of her staying.

Nicola tried not to feel it a curse. It was impossible.

39 THE CAPTAIN

The king had Shadows. Bertrun had always known this. He had worked with the Shadows, and had never questioned their origin.

Matthius was another issue. Matthius was not just anyone. He was a man, a guard like Bertrun had been. He had paid everything to the crown, had lost his son and his wife. Nicola had told him what had awaited them when they had gone to Matthius' house - a place ransacked, home only of the dead. Bertrun could not help but think of his brother, of his sister, of the pain of losing them. He could not bear the thought.

But then to walk into the fire?

The captain still had nightmares, sometimes, of his journey through the castle. In these dreams, the flames were alive. They hunted him like jackals, herded him forward with long tongues of fire. He awoke from these dreams sweating, certain that he had been spared intentionally - and temporarily. It was only a matter of time before the flames would claim him once more. Before they would consume him.

It was a grim retrospective, to realize what he had never before known about his king. King Alexander had raised him up. Bertrun was still grateful - even if that gratitude were twisting and turning in his stomach. Still he believed in the righteousness of the sun-crowned.

But how many men had died in that hidden pyre for a crown that held no regard for them? For Alexander had not known Matthius. He had looked at him, and been sorrowful, but he had not known him.

He had barely spared Bertrun himself a glance. One glance with those sun-soaked eyes, flames reflected therein. One touch upon his cheek.

Then gone, gone into the darkness of his captivity once more, where Bertrun could not free him.

The captain had thought he understood service. He was mistaken. Matthius' induction proved this. He had not understood service at all. He was, in this moment, with Matthius walking through the streets beside him, glad of it.

The streets at this time of day were not particularly busy. Matthius and Bertrun walked together, two men, both less than memorable in winter cloaks, their breath fogging even in the late afternoon. It was easy to walk abreast without the normal foot traffic, easy to chance glances at Matthius' face. Harder not to. The man was already blurring in Bertrun's vision, becoming less and less exceptional. Only his height and broad shoulders stood out - a big man, but big was all you would remember to tell if asked. The color of his eyes, the cast to his face, were all lost to the flames. It made Bertrun uneasy, but he had cause to trust the Shadows, even if Nicola would no longer come down to see them.

In truth, the seer was more disturbing. She did not eat, she did not drink. She lay on the bed and stared at the ceiling, and when she deigned to she told him of her visions. Bertrun suspected what she related to him was incomplete. The look on her face when she did speak to him, like she was trying to parse too many threads, all cutting to hold, made him uneasy. It was good incentive for leaving the house, even if leaving her like that made guilt curl in his stomach.

There was work to do.

The Shadows said Liana journeyed towards them. Nicola agreed, when he had dared to ask her, but would say no more. That meant that Bertrun must ramp up his recruiting, against the hope that the princess could use the people themselves to unseat Drummond. Alexander would be no help in rallying support for their resistance, and Bertrun couldn't help but flash back to the moment when he had attacked Nicola, weeks ago. There were rumors that he had done worse. The king was no longer fit, and seemed content with it.

But his daughter was young. Drummond was a tyrant. Someone had to lead them out from under him, someone with the golden eyes of a king.

Today, Bertrun and Matthius would take their first foray into the streets. Commoners had been banned from the Academy by the clergy, with the ban supported by the Lord Regent. Protesting that ban had cost Master Wrothfurt his position, but he still had connections to the students he had taught and to the other masters. He had put together this meeting today through those connections. It was in a part of the city near the Academy, in a tavern owned by a sympathizer called the Green Goat.

They came up on the Goat well before the appointed time. Matthius paused with Bertrun to loiter at the corner, an easy smile on his features where before there had been only blankness. Bertrun was not so relaxed, but he stood with Matthius as the other Shadows who had been tailing them scouted the place.

When they had given the all-clear through some method Bertrun could not perceive, Matthius placed a hand on his shoulder, urging him to walk again. The captain swallowed down nerves, tilting his cap to cover his eyes. There was sunlight still, sharp and slanting, a good excuse to tilt it even lower.

They entered the Goat with little fanfare, and did not stop as they walked towards the back, except to nod at the innkeeper behind the bar. A door in the back wall led them to a small room, with a door on the alley behind. Anyone really watching would wonder at it, but the plan was that no one would really be watching. Bertrun hoped that the plan was a good one. At the moment, he had little faith in anything.

The students were already there.

They were a varied sort. Young, eyes hollow with shock or bright with rage. They were here because their futures had been taken from them. Bertrun understood the feeling, but how much sharper must it be when you were young? When you had thought you had your whole life in front of you, only to find all of your chances cut down?

The Academy only took men for most official classes, but they had educated women in sums and such necessary skills to manage a household or a business. The small crowd in this room was mostly made up of those women. It surprised him, that so many had chanced the streets. With their hoods down, their faces gave them away, but most of them were wearing thick winter clothes and trousers, not skirts. Two years ago, Bertrun would have been surprised and a little uncomfortable to see women in men's clothing. For all his blood, he had been born and raised in Herkunsland. This was his home, and its biases his own, too. This afternoon, he felt that it was only practical. Women were forbidden taverns, now, and traveling as a woman alone on the streets was not always safe with Drummond's guards sharing the roads. He wished them whatever would make them safe.

Matthius closed the door behind them and stood before it. Bertrun studied the assembled. They didn't speak. They were used to lecture halls and waited patiently for him to study each of them.

"You are here because the Academy has been barred to you," he said. "Your rightful place taken. Just as it was taken from me. Just as it was taken from our Queen." The assembled shifted. Their discipline broke.

"Who are you?" demanded one. A boy, to Bertrun's eyes. Most of the men in the room were boys, barely old enough to grow beards. This one was one of the few people in the room not of common stock, based upon his fine cloak. The weave of the cloth was too tight, though he probably thought the dark gray color nondescript. He was standing close to another boy whose cloth was not so fine, though the cut of his jacket was just as fashionable as the nobleman's. A seamstress' child, perhaps, or his retainer. They brushed elbows with a casual familiarity that spoke of long friendship.

"My name is Bertrun," the captain said. "You may have heard it."

"You were meant to be a traitor," said an older woman, older being relative in this room. "And dead."

"If a traitor calls you traitor, whom do you serve?" Bertrun said, lightly. "I survived, and Drummond is a liar. Does it surprise any of you?" He waited. There was no response. They were listening.

"Queen Liana escaped the castle," he told them. "The night of the fire, she was spirited away by the gods. Even now she returns to her kingdom, to claim it."

"What's to stop her from being another Lord Drummond," someone called from the back.

"She is Alexander's daughter," Bertrun said, "and the God's own marked heir. Which is all very well and good, to you, who do not know her. But I have met those who knew the princess, and her brother. They were wise beyond their years. And the queen is brave - I saw her wounds when she fled. Wounds cut into her flesh by traitors."

Bertrun paused. They were not sold. Well, he had never been a good speaker.

"You must make up your own mind about whom you would serve."

"Things were better under Alexander," a woman called. There were murmurs of agreement.

"What do we do?" the noble's boy asked.

"Do?" Bertrun said. "Prepare a way. Spread her name. Wait, for when the time is right and you receive word that she needs us."

He might have said more. Might have told them to designate networks, given them a map for the future that would settle their hearts.

There was a shout from the common area outside their door. Matthius' head came up.

"We must leave," he said.

It was the first time Bertrun had heard him speak in days, and his voice was blowing ash and bone. The captain shuddered, frozen, but Matthius had already grabbed his arm and hustled him out the alley door. It happened so fast. He heard the children - they were not adults yet, not old enough for this - begin to shout, several spilling out after him. Heard the door crash in.

His legs remembered what it was to run.

40 THE PRINCESS

They had been traveling for days with their new companions, if traveling more comfortably. Liana felt the renewed energy that regular food and drink and sleep gave. How long since she had had fruit, had regular access to fresh water? The pony, which Liander still insisted on leading along, seemed better as well, though it would take more than a few days to put enough weight on it that it looked like anything but a skeleton walking. She supposed the same held true for her brother and for herself. It was hard not to contrast herself to Jessa, to her firm curves and smooth, uncracked skin.

Then again, she had never been beautiful. She was better suited to fierceness. If she was a corpse walking, at least she still walked.

Kabrim had proven a capable guide through the desert. He spoke a great deal to Liander, of course, who seemed glad to have someone to talk to besides Liana. The princess, for her part, listened to his endless chatter when it seemed useful and otherwise spent her days watching the horizon. The sun burned hot in her, and hot above them. It was comforting.

Jessa had tried to take it away.

Liana thought of Jessa's words, turned them over in her head. Did the fire burn? It had never seemed to harm her. But she remembered how the village had burned, and all of Ma'alu's children with it. When it had happened, there had been only satisfaction, a grim feeling that lit her up like daylight. Now, as they traveled through the desert following Kabrim to his people, she forced herself to think on the implications. She had once banished fire. Now she called it. It was not the power of a woman, nor of a king. The warmth it gave her, the way it fed her - Jessa seemed to imply that such warmth would harm others, would harm Herkunsland.

The thought sat uneasily in her. Herkunsland had been her home, once.

Its people, though, had run her out. They had rendered her exiled, and likely murdered her father. She had not the strength to ask Jessa of his fate, not yet. Liander had also remained silent on the subject. Neither of them wanted to hear the words. But if Jessa were a Shadow, and she had come to Liana, then it seemed likely that there was no king to serve.

Her father would have done what was best for Herkunsland, she knew. No doubt even her own death would not have stopped him from doing what was best. It shouldn't have stung, but it did.

This fire was hers. It had freed her, and it was the only thing that might lead her to her son, the son that she now knew that Herka had taken. Each time the heat of it flared inside her, she knew that he lived. Without it, how would she keep herself from falling back into madness?

Her horse, a beautiful desert-bred gelding, tossed his head, shaking Liana from her reverie. Liana patted his neck absently. Then a shift in the desert wind brought her what the horse had already heard. Harnesses jingled ahead, and voices echoed over the scrubby dunes.

Kabrim let out a shout and kicked his horse into a canter. The gelding whinnied, seeking to follow. Liana pulled it back, even as Liander shot past her, following Kabrim. He had seemed to regain some of his old spirit along with his health. It would be useful. She would need their help, after all, and Liander was charismatic where she was hard.

"You will win them," Jessa said from beside her. Liana cast the other woman a narrowed glance. "You are the heir to Herkun's throne. That means more to the southerners than you think it does."

"You're chatty today," Liana said. Jessa merely smiled, a tight-lipped thing that didn't reach her eyes. Her horse kept pace with Liana's even when Liana pushed them into a trot, hoping to leave Jessa behind.

The camp emerged with the same suddenness with which all things seemed to appear in this desert. A shift in the land revealed it like a trick pulled by a mummer in a city square. One minute, it was vanished. The next, it appeared. Tents striped in reds, golds and blues greeted her, their proud peaks topped with banners that likely meant something but which to Liana's eyes were incomprehensible. Horses called greeting, and goats tumbled about in a haphazard way. One or two dogs darted among them, yapping with high voices. Liana reigned in sharply, overwhelmed by the sounds. People were coming out of the tents, their dusky skin darkened with desert sun, their leather vests and long, loose robes strange to her eyes. They called out to Kabrim in a dialect of the desert tongues she didn't recognize. She caught her hand grasping towards a necklace that wasn't there, and felt her stomach lurch.

Straightening her back, she pressed the gelding forward.

Her hair had grown long in the desert, and it swung around her face as the horse kicked forward, obscuring her view. Between one moment and the next, the chattering voices had left off. Liana lifted her head in alarm, pulling back on her gelding again. Only the animals pierced the silence. The humans all looked at her.

Liana took a deep breath. Liander was looking around as if confused, but he said nothing. Jessa had reigned in behind her. She waited out the silence, fighting not to reach for the fire that welled in her at her unease.

Then a woman stepped forward, shattering the stillness.

"I am Sayala," she said. She had on a red leather vest over a white robe like the others, but the collar of her vest was decorated with a ring of strange white shells. Liana stared at them for a moment, those seashells so far from the sea. The woman's face was wide, her cheekbones high. Her nose was sharp, as were her deep brown eyes. She couldn't be more than a few years older than Liana herself. Liana pressed her lips firmly together, and forced herself to dismount. The gelding sidled beneath her, feeling her nervousness. She dropped the reins to the ground, trusting the horse to stay where it was, and stepped forward to meet Sayala.

"I am Liana," she said. A simple greeting. She wondered if she should say more.

"The Ashir welcome you, Liana," Sayala said. She paused, expectant. Her eyes shifted to Liander, and back to her.

"This is my brother, Liander," Liana said. It was a guess, but it seemed correct. "We are of Herkunsland. I believe you have met Jessa."

Sayala nodded. "The huntsman is known to us." She stepped

back, gestured with her hands.

"Come, Liana of Herkunsland. Let us have tea together. Your brother will be made comfortable." With that Sayala turned and walked to the largest tent. Its flag, Liana noticed, was a deep red.

Red suited her better than white, at least. She followed Sayala inside. Jessa followed her as well, which Liana ignored.

Inside it was dark. Sayala seated herself on the pillows and deep carpets that lined the floor. Liana's boots tracked sand in despite her best efforts.

"Sit, sit," Sayala said, gesturing broadly. Liana sat, crossing her legs uncomfortably. Her clothing, stiff and worn nearly to nothing, chafed at the backs of her knees. She felt incredibly dirty, sitting there in front of the Ashir's leader. This woman was, undeniably, the leader. Liana turned the thought over in her mind. No one had ever felt it necessary for her to learn much of the desert folk. They were trading partners, yes, but widely seen as uncultured, with their floating clans and lack of solid cities. More importantly, they were not a threat. Nor was the desert something anyone thought to claim besides them. Herkunsland was relatively cool, a trick of the wind off the sea the masters thought. They said the hot desert climes did not agree with a Herkunslander's constitution.

Liana felt herself amused at the thought. The desert was hot, certainly. Liander's skin was patched with sunburn and heat rash. But Liana herself found the heat pleasant.

Then again, Liana suspected that she was as unlike most of her countrymen as she was unlike the woman before her.

"Tell me, Liana, of your journey," Sayala said. Her voice was even, her brown eyes steady. Liana cocked her head, studying the woman. Why did she think she was nervous? Certainly Sayala gave no sign. Yet Liana felt as if she could taste the nervousness on her tongue. She would have shaken it off, before. Caution lived more fully in her now.

"Tell me what you know," Liana said instead. "Allow me to fill in the gaps."

The pause was there. Liana felt her mouth firm in a grim line. Her eyes cut to Jessa.

"You have surmised that the huntsman came to us first,"

Sayala said, following Liana's glance. "She told us of your exile, which we knew not the nature of. Many rumors say you are dead. None speak of the fire in you." The woman took a deep breath. "You are a sign of the second coming."

There, that was the source of the nervousness.

"What is the second coming?" Liana asked.

"Our legends say that Jassas will come again to burn the world," Sayala said quietly.

"This is Herkun's other name," Jessa said. "The southerners call him Jassas, god of fire." Liana waved off the explanation. Her old guard, Bastas - and that name was bitter still - had told her of Jassas. A god of fire, who had scorched the desert clean so that only the southerners could live in it. The desert folk like the Ashir.

"It is not another name," Sayala said, shaking her head. "Even a thing of light may have two sides. Your Herkun is a thing of peaceful days and fond memories. Jassas is something else."

"He is fire," Liana said. She thought of the heat inside her, the rage. The need to punish those who had wronged her. The whole of the moon village had burned, and she had felt no remorse. "I see."

Sayala looked at her sharply, then nodded. "I believe you do."

Liana took a breath. Jessa had said something similar. That the Shadows ringed the light of Herkun, protected the world from it. Light and heat were never long separated.

She remembered, then, the words of her son when she had first known him in her womb. *Then do I make the shadows?* Her stomach twisted reflexively, as if in longing for him. It made her next words harsh.

"You have not answered my question."

It was Sayala's turn to look grim. "The huntsman said that you have suffered much. She gave me few details except to say that you had birthed a son."

Liana bared her teeth, feeling pain clench in her middle. How had Jessa known that gem?

"Then she will have told you that he was dead before he drew breath," she growled.

It was a lie. She was sure it was a lie. But she said it with all of the conviction that she had felt for so long.

Sayala looked, if anything, more alarmed. "I see," she said.

"I doubt you do," Liana said, the words forcing themselves past her lips.

"Peace, Liana," Jessa said.

"Peace?" Liana laughed. "Never, until all my enemies have fallen. Do you think I forget what awaits me to the north?"

"That is a thing worth discussing," Sayala said. "We have news of your uncle."

"Tell me then," Liana said.

"He has declared himself Lord Regent, and your father unfit."

"My father lives?" Liana demanded. She had been so sure he was dead.

"He is not himself," Jessa said, voice holding a hint of emotion at last. "You should not treat him as such."

"You did not tell me," Liana said. Her voice was hard, even. She was proud it did not betray the beating of her heart. Jessa shifted beside her.

"You did not let me tell you."

Liana made a sound in her throat, half growl. She and Jessa would have words after this, Shadow or no Shadow.

"Continue," she said to Sayala.

At that moment a young boy entered bearing tea in ornate glasses. Glass was an expensive thing in Herkunsland, and unheard of to the east. Liana could not help staring at it.

"Let me offer you refreshments," Sayala said. "You are weary, and there is much to tell."

Liana nodded.

"Well enough," she said, "but you must tell me everything."

41 THE PRINCE

The camp of the Ashir was a place that reminded him uncomfortably of the village of Ma'alu's children.

Liander could not say what it was that made him feel so. Perhaps it was the comfortable way everyone seemed to know everyone else, or the shouts of the children. Certainly the brightly colored tents were not evocative of the well-constructed huts of the Ma-peli'a. Nor were the people themselves particularly similar. The village people had run tall and slender, with skin as pale as the moon and hair as dark as the space between stars. These people were shorter, tending to broad shoulders, with skin a sandy brown like the desert they inhabited. If their hair and eyes were dark, they were an earthly darkness.

Still, he felt the sense of it prickle across his skin. As if he stood in a village of ghosts.

Kabrim took him to a tent that was, it seemed, his own. It was a small tent. Kabrim explained that it was the tent of a bachelor, and technically belonged to the tribe. When he married, he would live in his wife's tent.

"You don't own anything?" Liander asked, surprised. Kabrim shrugged, lounging on the pillows scattered across the carpeted floor.

"I own my horse," he said. Liander blinked. Kabrim was not unlike himself. Liander owned his weapons and his horse, but would have been sent to a foreign court. There he would have inherited land, but it would not have come with him.

For the first time in a long time, Liander thought of his mother. How she had left Perlen, the only home she had ever known, with almost nothing - gowns, surely, perhaps some tapestries or favorite small possessions. How she had come to a foreign court to become wife to a man she had met once.

Their paths would not have been dissimilar, if Liander's life had gone as planned. He, his mother, Kabrim - they were all things to be bartered.

"You are having dark thoughts," Kabrim said.

Liander forced a laugh. "Pay no mind to me, friend. I am still weak from my travels."

It was not a lie. Kabrim looked at him like it was, but did not press the point.

"Let us get you some tea," he said instead. He leaned to the opening of the tent, calling out a request. One of the children came in some moments later with a kettle that steamed and smelled of a woody, flowery substance, beautiful glasses, and tiny flaky cakes. Liander was always hungry now, and he set to the cakes with alacrity. The tea was a bit more foreign, but he found that he liked it after all. It tasted bright and strange in his mouth. The glasses were etched with swirling patterns, and the liquid made them nearly too hot to touch.

They whiled away a leisurely time, Kabrim telling him about life in the desert and not asking hard questions. It was refreshing to talk to someone not his sister. It was also nice not to have to travel, at least for a day or two. Kabrim assured him that their stopping place was not a permanent one, as the water source here was not large enough for them, a small upwelling that pooled in a bit of rock and little else.

"We were only waiting here at the request of the huntsman," he said. "Tomorrow, we will move on to a real oasis, and you can see how my people really live."

"An oasis?" Liander asked. Kabrim had called Jessa huntsman before. Liander refused to ask what the term meant. She had hardly spoken to him since he had first seen her, and her changed nature made him surprisingly comfortable with that distance.

He did not want to understand what she had done to herself.

"It's a place where water is plentiful," Kabrim said, bringing him back to the moment. "We have permanent settlements there."

"I thought the desert folk had few cities," Liander said, surprised. It was what the masters taught, in any case. Kabrim laughed.

"They're not like your cities, anyway," Kabrim said, shuddering exaggeratedly. "Who would want to live there?"

Liander snorted. He had felt the same, sometimes. Now all he wanted was a bath. He rubbed his hands along his dirty, sweat-stained clothing. Kabrim noticed. He clapped Liander on his shoulder, avoiding his still sore arm.

"Don't worry, princeling. We have baths." Liander sighed in relief.

There was a sound outside the tent. Kabrim called a greeting, and one of the children ventured in. Liander was sure that it was not the same child as before, but beyond that he could not tell either gender or anything else.

"Sayala asks after the prince," the child said. Liander thought, on hearing her speak, that she was a girl. She was not in a dress, but Liander thought that whether or not you were wearing a dress meant very little amongst the Ashir.

"We'll join her in a moment," Kabrim said. To Liander he added, "Finish your tea. I think you will need it."

"Is your sister so fearsome?" Liander asked as the child ducked out of the tent again.

"Perhaps not so fearsome as yours," Kabrim grinned.

It was hard to force himself to move again. The tent was comfortable, and even with the sweet cakes and fortifying beverage his body was tired. Liander had hoped to sleep a while. Instead, he let Kabrim help him up and made his slow way to the large, red-flagged tent.

Inside sat Liana, and Jessa. Liander allowed his eyes to slide over his former lover, looking instead at the third woman.

She was short, like most of the Ashir were, with long dark hair bound back in a braid and round, brown eyes surrounded by creases, as if she smiled often. She was not smiling now. Her back was straight, her body rounded, throwing Liana's bony form into stark relief. With the white stripe in Liana's hair, she looked far older than this woman, though they both exhibited steel. Liander bowed greeting.

"Sit, sit," Sayala said. Kabrim crossed to sit by her side, so Liander sat by his sister's. The opposite side to Jessa, but that was, he assured himself, expected.

There was a pause, and Sayala looked long at Liana. "Are you sure?" she asked. "Your brother is weak."

"He will not be weak forever," Liana said. "I am sure."

"Very well." Sayala nodded, then turned to him. "Kabrim will guide you to the oasis. A healer lives there, and water is plentiful. You will rest and heal under his guidance."

"I -" he began.

"Do not argue, Liander," Liana said quietly. "I need your help in this. The nearest oasis is towards the sea. When you are better, you and Kabrim will continue on with some of the Ashir as escort. You will go to Perlen."

"To Perlen?" he asked. It was hard to obey her command, but he would not gainsay her in front of Sayala. He had made that mistake before. Their arguments were for in private.

"You were always meant to go to Perlen," Liana said tiredly. She turned to look at him, her golden eyes lacking their usual spark. "You must plead with our uncle for aid. Perlenian ships would provide a solid addition to our forces."

"You mean to take back Herkunsland by force," Liander said.

"I see no other option."

"What will you do, while I head to the sea?" he asked, unable to keep the hurt from his voice. Liana's mouth firmed.

"I head north. The rest of the Ashir move north with me, and any desert folk who might offer aid. We will take the trading city of Southmark and establish ourselves there, gathering allies. When you have secured Perlen's aid, you must send a messenger to me with all speed. We will hit Herkunsland on two sides, and I will have my uncle's head." She turned back to Sayala as she said this. The Ashir nodded.

"We will help you," she said. "If only you keep your fire in check."

"My fire is for my enemies, not my friends," Liana said.

Liander wondered if his sister understood that fire often burned indiscriminately. The memory of the village's destruction came upon him hard then. He reached out and placed a hand on her arm. Liana's skin was as hot as the sun.

42 THE CAPTAIN

The Shadows coursed around him, and he remembered his nightmares.

Bertrun ran through the city streets. Shouting continued behind him. He heard a woman cry out in pain, heard a man shout in anger. Glass shattered. Somewhere, flames began to roar. He could feel the sound in his bones.

Why was it always fire? Why did this always end in fire?

The Shadow in front of him ducked around a corner, and Bertrun followed. In a group, they should be easier to spot, but the people that they did pass appeared not to see them. Their eyes slid over Bertrun's companions, and because those companions surrounded him they slid over Bertrun as well. They were simply Shadows in the night.

Besides, there were other things to concern themselves with.

It was like kicking an ant hill. The guards came from seemingly nowhere, manifesting in their livery, swords drawn. And the people, the people Bertrun was, he hoped, fighting to save?

They came, too.

They had no swords. Some of them carried torches or pots and pans. They boiled out of their houses, the fear and helplessness that had been growing for weeks manifesting once more into rage. It wasn't everyone. Many of the common folk Bertrun saw emerging were concerned about the fires, the shouting. They came out to protect their homes, or their businesses, or both. Fire was not an easy thing in this packed city, and they remembered the fires from the quakes too well. They were attuned to the sounds, and to the bell that even now clanged alarm. But the ones who came out for other reasons? They had been waiting for this moment.

Now that it was on them, they took it.

If he'd had the breath, Bertrun might have tried to call them back. He might have argued that it was too soon. Liana was not come. There was nothing to do on these streets tonight except die.

He had no breath. What air he could get burned in his lungs.

Bertrun was no longer a young man, and he had not had reason or method to practice his running. It was not something his body remembered how to do in anything but the vaguest sense. He felt as if his heart were going to burst.

The Shadows seemed to realize it. They twisted down another side street, forcing him along. One had a hand on his elbow, pulling him to a walk. That same Shadow kept him moving when he would have folded over and retched with fatigue.

They shoved him into a cubby. It was dark here, and they were blacker outlines in that darkness, blocking him from sight. For a time, they were still.

He heard the shouting swell. A shape ran past the mouth of the small alley they hid in, and another followed it. A sword flashed. Bertrun heard a scream.

He almost started forward then, to do what he didn't know. The Shadows held him back.

The street quieted.

After a time, the Shadows led him forward again.

In the darkness and the panic of their flight, Bertrun had lost any idea of where he was in the city. Once he had known these streets like the back of his hand, but it had been a long time since he had come to visit the Academy aboveground, and they had run far. There was no guarantee they were still on streets he knew. So he was unsurprised when the Shadows split up, three ranging ahead, two near him.

One was the scarred Shadow, the one that spoke to him most often. It was the first time Bertrun had seen the man tonight.

"That was close," he said. Feeling the need to say something, to break the quiet of the street. The scarred Shadow nodded acknowledgement, movement almost imperceptible in the darkness. The street lights here had gone out with no one to tend them, and Bertrun's eyes strained to make out those impassive features.

"I want to help." It was foolish to keep talking. The men around him were ghosts and he was alone. But the fear was an animal in his belly, and the grief, too. He had to distract himself. There was nothing he could have done.

Yet he had caused all this.

The Shadows on either side of him stopped. The scarred Shadow spoke.

"Tomorrow, you can repair. Tonight, you must survive," he said.

Bertrun nodded, and followed him without further protest.

Finding a tunnel entrance was easy. Passage back took longer. By the time he had reached Marie's house, the temple bells were chiming deep night in the distance. No sun would come for hours yet, but the darkest part of the night had commenced. He let himself into the backdoor. The kitchen fire was banked in the oven, and the warmth after his long walk through the cold of the tunnels was welcome.

Marie threw open the door to the dining room as he was warming his hands.

"Bertrun," she cried, "you're alive! When I heard about riots at the Academy..." She rushed into the kitchen, pulling open cupboards. "You must be starving, and chilled to the bone."

He leaned against a counter, trying to stay out of her way as she ladled a bowl of stew from the pot on top of the oven, handing it to him with a slice of bread and butter.

"Take this into the dining room and I'll build up the fire," she said.

Bertrun did as he was told, thinking of the people in that room, barely adults. Thinking of the mothers like Marie who would wonder where they had gone when they did not come home tonight. Knowing she had thought him lost.

He spoon the lukewarm soup into his mouth, tore into the buttered bread. It should have tasted like ashes, like guilt and grief. Instead, he tasted life. He was so grateful, for this food. Marie finished adding wood to the fire, and crossed to sit with him.

"I'm sorry that I worried you," he told her. She put an old, strong hand in his.

"I knew what I was getting into," she said, but there were tears in the corners of her eyes.

Bertrun squeezed her hand, and took another bite of his soup. Tomorrow, he would go back to fighting.

Tonight, he lived. He was home.

43 THE PRINCE

There was a feast before he left. They held it out under the stars, with burning fires over which goats were roasted. Liander was reminded uncomfortably of Et'zela. If his sister saw the similarity, she gave no sign.

He sat beside her at the feast, and tried not to be overwhelmed by the sheer amount of people around him. It had been months since he had seen a human face besides Liana's, at least before Jessa and Kabrim found them. It was strange to see so many faces now, and none of them known. The firelight, the sounds of music, the laughter and dancing - all of these overwhelmed him. They seemed to overwhelm Liana as well, for she stood and wandered away as the party dragged on. Liander followed her into the shadows between tents.

They had not spoken much since Liana had bid him north, and now he did not know what to say. They walked together in silence, leaving the camp behind. The stars speckled the sky with wild abandon. The desert swallowed sound. It was easy to feel that they were once more alone, lost in its vastness, but Liander did not fear being lost. Liana could sense the fires behind them. Using her gifts no longer troubled him.

No, he had other worries where his twin was concerned. Chief among them her Shadow, who seemed to have left them alone tonight. That was probably for the best, as neither twin quite knew what to do with her. The Shadows had been ubiquitous as his father's companions, men of no words and strange presence. To think of Jessa as one of them, to see her act like one of them, made his skin crawl. Then again, changes like that had made him unsettled before, and he had regretted his prejudice. He could only hope that this situation were similar.

"You know why I'm sending you," Liana said, breaking his thoughts. He nodded in the darkness, then realized she could not see him.

"I know," he said. "It was logical, when I stopped to think about it." Logical, but not welcome.

"Not easy," she said, as if echoing his sentiment. "I don't like to send you where I can't see you."

"I don't like to be sent where I can't watch over you, either," he said lightly. "Liana, we must defeat our uncle one way or another. We cannot do it without Perlen."

"I know that," she said. He knew she did. He had only said it to reassure her.

Silence reigned in the night. He counted his breath, stared up at the stars beside her. When she spoke again, it startled him.

"There's something I must tell you, Liander," she said. Her voice was quiet, pained. "The gods have heavy hands in this. You know that She took us east, to that...place." Liana breathed out, hard. Took a deep breath. "I think...Liander, I think She kept him. I think She kept my son."

Her voice was broken on the words. It took him a moment, distracted by the sound, to register her meaning.

"Liana," he began.

"I know," she said. "I saw it. I remember. But that water, the water of the lake, it wasn't just a place for graves. It was a portal. It's how we got there." She seemed as if she might continue, but then stopped. Liander swallowed.

"Have you told anyone else?" he asked. "Tell no one, Liana. No one at home even knows about him, and that's a bargaining chip for you. Once we have Herkunsland -"

"Once we have killed our uncle, you mean," Liana said. Her voice was hard, almost antagonistic. Liander felt his stomach twist.

"Once we have Herkunsland," he said, calming her, "we can find out. We can find a way."

Did he believe the words he said to his sister? Liander didn't know. It was possible that she was right. It was also possible that this was the lingering effect of her madness, some rationalization that she had made that let her continue forward. It didn't matter. She believed. If he did not support her in that belief - he thought of fire, and he shuddered. A sane Liana was better than the creature that had destroyed the village.

"Yes," she said. "When we have Herkunsland." But she did not look at him, and he could not see her face in the darkness.

Liander hoped he had chosen well.

The next evening, he set off for the oasis with an escort of five, including Kabrim. It was a spot of green to the west and south, and on their path to the coast. There was a trade city there called Ileas, a stopping point for ships coming up from the south. Liander had never heard of anything south of the deserts, but Kabrim assured him the world was vaster than he had ever dreamed. The port of Ileas would have ships.

Liander had never been anywhere by ship. The only country worth visiting by sea was Perlen, at least as far as those in Herkunsland knew. The desert was seen to be a wasteland. He was beginning to realize that was far from the truth. The nobles of Herkunsland had been backwards in more ways than one. He didn't know why he was surprised.

They stayed at the oasis for several days. Brick and stone building sprouted between thick, green foliage fed by water from the deep earth. Liander was allowed to eat as much as he wanted and do absolutely nothing. His wound scabbed over and began to heal in truth. Some small amount of extra flesh came back to his limbs, and energy with it. He spent his evening walking beneath the foreign trees. Kabrim told him that they produced dates and oranges and all sorts of strange fruit that Liander had only ever seen packed in sugar or salt. He tasted all of these fruits. Some he liked more than others. The cooking of the desert folk was simple and flavorful, and he found it no hardship to eat several meals a day. His constant hunger faded.

There was, as promised, a healer at the oasis, an older man in bright blue robes with a beard nearly down to his knees and a hood on his head. Kabrim assured Liander that the robes meant he knew what he was doing, despite the beard. Liander's own beard had grown in shaggy and reddish-blond, and he was more than happy to shave it in the ample waters the oasis provided. The healer said that Liander's clean face helped him to see his bones, and pressed long fingers into his flesh, feeling for what Liander did not know.

"Travel lightly and you will continue to recover," the man said at last, and Liander knew it was time once more to go.

He and Kabrim and their small escort, some four men of the Ashir, continued south and west. They traveled, as the healer had said, lightly, stopping frequently to replenish their stores at smaller oases. Liander observed no barter system at these locations. Travelers were allowed to take what they needed, though Kabrim always left something in return. The desert, Kabrim told him, was too harsh to deny aid to anyone.

At night, as they rode, Liander looked up at the sky. The stars were impossible, so many of them that it nearly blotted out the blackness between. He pondered those stars, and the fate that had moved him to this point. He pondered the distance between him and his sister, growing larger every day. He kept turning to her, expecting to see her somewhere beside him, or perhaps riding ahead. But she was far behind, and traveling north into uncertainty.

They had never been so far apart before.

He grew to know the names of his companions, them being so few. Kabrim led them, but the other men deferred to him as one might defer to a respected elder brother. It was a bond of love more than rank, and Liander watched it enviously. There was Ifan, who said he had a grandmother from Herkunsland who had run away from her father and his ideas of what a woman was good at, and Ashul who took care of the Quet'le-Ma pony that Liander had insisted on bringing along. Dun-mar was darker than the others, his curls tighter, a quiet man Liander's other companions treated with deference. Kabrim said that he would likely become a healer and never take a wife. Hafir was the oldest, a second son with no need to marry except for love, but they were all young. Their swords were curved but sharp, their horses spirited, and even with the pony and Liander holding them back, they made good time.

So it was that, on the the last dawn of days that ran together in dream and nights of laughter and celestial brilliance, they came at last to the sea.

Liander smelled it first, and didn't know quite what he smelled. The air took on a heaviness, and a salted tang. There was a constant breeze that made his hair rise and blew the sweat from his face. The horses pricked up their ears and moved forward. The pony, grown thin and lethargic, lifted its head and made better time. The heat was too much for it, just as it had been in the stifling jungles. He should have sent the poor mare with Liana.

Then again, Liana cared little for horses. She was not cruel, but Liander did not trust the pony's chances with her. And this way he had at least one companion who knew what he had been through to get here, even if that companion couldn't speak in words.

The ground changed as they neared the sea. It had been a thing of rolling hills and scrub, but now they climbed shifting dunes, large and imposing. Kabrim said that it was the northern edge of a much harsher desert, a spit of it that they must cross to finish their journey. The horses were not well made for such terrain, with their small hooves, and so the men got down and walked. It took only seconds for Liander's calves to burn protest at the uneven footing.

The sky was lightening in the east just as they crested one of the taller dunes. Liander looked out over the rolling sand, then on to a horizon limned in orange light. The space between where the sand ended and the light began was a mobile blackness.

"Is that the sea?" he asked Kabrim in the desert tongue.

"Yes," he said. Then he clapped Liander on the shoulder and they started down the dune.

They did not make camp at dawn, but continued on in the steadily rising heat. The sun here was relentless. Liander was glad for the loose traveling robes he had been offered, which protected his body, and the equally lightweight scarf for his head and face. The garments had seemed strange to him before, but after days in the dry of the desert he found them much more comfortable than his own clothing had been. His sunburns had mostly faded, except around his eyes, and the sand and wind had nowhere to chafe. Still, even in the robe the heat and weight of the sun's rays became oppressive. They were soon exhausted with it. But they did not have long to travel, and the dunes became small enough that they were able to mount once more. Before noon they had reached the edges of the small city of Ileas.

It was a thing made all of stone and brightly colored awnings, perched right at the edges of a gently curved bay filled with small ships. Trees grew up in its embrace, and birds darted out over the sea and then back to the white walls. Liander thought it was the most beautiful city he had ever seen. Ifan whooped and set his horse to a canter. The other horses pulled forward after him of their own volition, spilling them down the small dune on which they had been perched and onto the stone road that lead to the main gate, or what Liander assumed was a gate. There was a low wall on the landward side of the city that, he suspected, protected the city's buildings from the encroaching dunes. It did not look defensive, and there were no defenses on the harbor itself. Liander supposed there was no need for additional defenses beyond the ones nature had provided. It would be hard to march an army across the desert.

The stone road rose underneath his horse's hooves, a blessed staccato after the endless sand. He found himself whooping along with Ifan as the horse bunched its great muscles beneath him, as fast as the wind.

They slowed as they reached the first of the white stone houses. People were still moving in the streets, despite the late hour and the gradually building heat, not quite dispelled by the ocean wind. The men of the Ashir formed tight about him, though they waved greetings from time to time. One or two of them had apparently traveled this way before. It was a small comfort, but Liander found he needed little comfort here. The smell of orange blossoms mixed with the salt air, tantalizing. It was so beautiful that it put him off his guard.

He was too busy looking at the buildings and the birds and the trees and flowers. He did not see the group in their path until the Ashir pulled up around him.

Liander turned, then, to look. Activity on the street had slowed, and the men around him were dismounting. There were men and women arrayed across the street, their bright clothing patterned with sewn metal armor, their skin the darkest he had ever seen. Liander nearly drew his sword, hand firm on the pommel. Then he saw her.

She was all in blue. It was a blue so deep that it was almost black, but it was obviously blue, when contrasted against her skin. That skin was nearly dark as pitch. She was like a void in the air, broken by the blueness of her robe and the brightness of her eyes and teeth. Her hair was a gray-white corona, close cropped to her head. Without that hair, he would have thought her a statue, she stood so regal and still.

"Prince Liander," she said in the desert tongue, her accent musical. He found himself dismounting without thought, following the lead of his companions. Whomever she was, she was obviously someone of note.

"My lady," he said, the courtly grace sounding strange in the southerner's language. He did not take his eyes from her. She was arresting, but his travels had also made him cautious of strangeness. She smiled widely at his greeting.

"Please come with me," she said then. Liander swallowed around a knot in his throat, but the Ashir stood, postures easy. They followed without question.

Liander, at last, did the same.

44 THE PRINCESS

Liana rode, and tried not to think about what she was leaving behind her.

Liander had still been ill when she had ordered him away. Sayala promised that there were healers in the oases, men who would make sure that he was fit for his journey. He had certainly survived worse than traveling over the desert by horseback while with her. She had not protected him from the danger of the assassin, nor from the infection in his wound. Even the frail protection of her heat had barely kept him from losing digits in the cold. She was lucky he was alive at all.

But there was no safety anywhere.

Jessa rode by her side. Liana had almost become used to her there. It was not a comfortable thing, but it was no longer so glaringly uncomfortable. Her friend - for she had once been a friend, even if Liana no longer thought she could have friends - had made herself a Shadow. She had, to all appearances, done it in order to act as Liana's protector and escort. If Liana could not trust her enough to appreciate the gesture, she no longer faulted her for it either. If Jessa were to be believed, she could help curb the more terrible bits of Liana's nature. There was power in having that option.

Not that she fully trusted Jessa's discretion. That was the rub. There was no way to be rid of her but to kill her, though, and Liana was not quite ready to go so far, not anymore. Even if she thought she could manage the deed.

So Jessa rode by her side in the long caravan of people which made up the Ashir, moving through mornings and evenings, sleeping through the roughest parts of the day and stopping to rest during the cold part of the night. Liana felt neither cold nor heat, but she disliked traveling under the moon. It waxed above her now, its cold light growing stronger each night, like an eye opening slowly. It made her skin itch.

Sayala said that they had legends of Herka, too. Kahara was a jealous mother who did not want to quit the earth and leave it to her children. She ate her daughter and her son fled in fear. She was also a welcome respite from the fiery god of fire, bringing cooling winds and darkness to the earth.

"Nothing is entirely good, nor entirely evil," Sayala said, her gaze on the distant horizon to the north. There was still nothing there but sand.

Liana gritted her teeth. She knew what evil was.

Evil was the moon.

Still, she rode underneath it. Each night she moved north, and the moon followed her in the sky, steadily growing brighter. The caravan was slow, with all of the livestock needing to stop and graze on the thorny desert plants. Even so they made it to an oasis before the moon was full. She was grateful to spend the nights of its brightest light in her tent, hidden away from it. The days she spent absorbing the heat of the sun and contemplating not her brother to the south, but her father to the north.

Almost, it seemed she could feel him there. It was a small, small light, almost lost against her own brightness. Sometimes it would nearly flicker out, and she would think that she had imagined it. But then Liana would wake up and it would be there again, at the edge of her awareness.

Jessa had told her that he still lived, but that he suffered. Was that suffering what caused the light to wax and wane? Liana did not know.

She wanted to see her father. She wanted to pass the leading of the kingdom off to him and leave it behind. It would be so much easier. Her pregnancy, the loss of the child, whether he lived or not, these things left her, in the eyes of Herkunsland, unfit to rule. Liana knew this. Once it was discovered that she had had a child, they would murder her on her throne. Or perhaps the assassin would come when she refused to marry. With her father in power, perhaps she could disappear. It was a foolish notion. Alexander was no longer a young man. He would die, and she would be forced to inherit. Such a solution was no solution at all. It only prolonged the inevitable.

She wanted so badly to escape the fate of a queen.

She didn't know what else she could ever be.

Their stay at the oasis ended. Liana resumed her ride north, the Ashir her escort.

It took them another half turning of the moon to reach the trading city at the north of the desert. It was a strange place, with stone walls in a ring the color of pale rose. Most of the people who moved in and out of its bounds were desert folk, but many were relatively pale like her, their hair and skin noticeably lighter than that of the Ashir and their countrymen, if the desert could be called a country. It was not a city of Herkunsland, but only because it was a touch too deep into the desert for Herkunslanders to live comfortably. Her father had never stationed a full garrison here. There had been no need.

There would be, soon. Liana would change history.

But not tonight. It was darkening, but not dark yet. Sayala rode up beside her, her horse prancing in excitement.

"My queen," she said, and Liana breathed deeply at being addressed so. It still startled her. She was not ready to be queen.

She would have to be ready.

"Sayala," she replied to the headwoman of the Ashir.

"It is likely no one will recognize you as you are, but just in case, I recommend you wear your veil wrapped tight," Sayala said. They had all worn veils in the desert, elaborate things, but they would not hide Liana's eyes. She said as much. Sayala shrugged.

"It will be enough, I think," she said, "just don't look up."

It was hard to ride into a strange city trusting those around her not to give her away. Jessa rode at her side, watching. Liana at least trusted Jessa not to get her killed. She reminded herself of that, her stare burning into her horse's neck. The gelding jittered under her, his hide flicking with nerves. Liana inhaled, fought to keep herself relaxed. It would not do to make the horse too upset, and he would sense her emotions if she could not contain them.

They passed into the city, and she saw little of it. The darkness became more complete and lanterns were lit. The streets came alive as the air cooled, bustling with even more people. The buildings were all of stone or brick, and glass hung in the windows, enough glass to make Liana's gut twist. It was expensive stuff in Herkunsland, and even more expensive in Perlen. She supposed that it made sense that it would be cheaper here, where it was made. Still, the many-colored panes could not have been that affordable. This was a merchant's city, and a rich one.

In the middle of the city was a great plaza. The earth here was so flat that Liana had not seen it before, and so did not know to expect it. The walls around her simply opened up, fell away to leave them in open space. She risked looking up.

The plaza was huge, and it was filled with pens. Most of them were empty now, but a few held livestock. The Ashir herded their goats and spare horses into one of those pens, then left a handful of young men to guard it. Liana had noticed that, while the Ashir seemed matriarchal, they did not keep their men bound up in fripperies as her country kept its women. It was simply that the Ashir valued the role women could play as mothers and mediators and traders more than they valued men's swords. Not that Liana doubted Sayala's prowess with a weapon, if the time came for it.

The remainder of their group journeyed to a large building a few blocks away from the plaza. Liana and Jessa followed. Sayala had said that the Ashir had a place in the city, and when she rapped on the scrolled wooden door, one of a pair, it opened readily. An old woman was standing there.

"My daughter," she said, her face creasing along a thousand, ancient lines, and embraced Sayala. "Welcome back from the sands."

"Mother," Sayala said. She pulled herself free of the embrace, her hands on the small crone's elbows. "There is someone with me I wish for you to meet."

"Come in, out of the night," said the old woman. She stepped aside. The second door was opened and the Ashir began piling into the house, scattering so quickly that it seemed as if they vanished entirely. Liana entered last, and the open, airy space that greeted her was empty, except for Sayala and her mother. She heard Jessa step in behind her and close the door as she met the old woman's eyes.

"Oh, Sayala, who have you brought to me in my last days?" the old woman whispered.

"Mother, I present to you Liana, Queen of Herkunsland."

Liana unwound her veil, then, feeling that it was rude to continue concealing her face. The old woman crossed to stand in front of her, studying her features.

"My name is Nia," she said finally. Her eyes had been brown

once, but now were nearly white with age. She turned that rheumy gaze to Jessa.

"Huntsman," she said, bowing her head. Jessa nodded back.

"It is a pleasure to meet you, grandmother," Liana said. "I thank you for your hospitality."

Nia turned her brittle, boney visage back to Liana, studying her. "You are going to war, then."

Liana blinked her golden eyes once, slowly. "I am going to war," she agreed.

"Of such things are prophecies and legends made." Nia smiled wryly. "Come, fire-touched, and rest for tonight. War is always waiting."

Bemused, Liana followed.

45 THE PRINCE

Her name was Priete, and she was a priestess.

The power she wielded was effortless. Liander felt it brush against him every time he saw her in her indigo robes. There were others with her, all staying in an airy building by the sea, its stones white and glittering. This was not their home, but another trading city of the desert folk. He had not realized that the desert folk had so many cities.

The Ashir called them the water people. They called themselves Erobians, in his tongue, after their empire to the south.

At first he had not believed there could be a whole empire of which his masters had never taught him. The Erobians had been amused by his ignorance. They had known of Herkunsland for at least a century, through trading with the desert tribes. They even visited Perlen occasionally. Priete could speak his language as easily as she spoke the trade tongue.

Their association with water in the Ashir's language had disturbed Liander at first. Water as a power had not been kind to him, nor to his twin. The Erobians worshipped a goddess of water, and Ma'alu's children had associated water with the moon. But Priete said their goddess was a different creature entirely. Ma'alu was cold, calculating. The goddess of these people, he learned, was kind, or so they believed. She had also not yet been born.

"Our legends are elaborate," Priete said to him, sitting on a balcony above the harbor. It was the morning after their arrival. Liander was glad to rest and let his body recover from the journey. He had even had a bath, and sat now wrapped in a thin robe. It should have made him self-conscious, that robe. Priete, however, was simultaneously the most and least intimidating woman that he had encountered. He felt more self-conscious for being in her presence at all than for his state of dress. The Erobians seemed to wear little better than robes or loose shifts most of the time in any case. She had invited them to stay, and provided them clothing, baths, and, now, breakfast. Who was he to argue with what clothing she thought appropriate?

"We have come here to meet you, Prince, because those who read the blackest waters have dreamed the same dream. There is an awakening. Gods will walk. The Ashir know it." Priete here nodded to Kabrim, who had come with Liander to this strange, informal meeting. Kabrim had a plate of hand foods and was biting down on a small, pickled fish. He waved at the reference to his clan, and Priete smiled. "We are two very different people, but we share many things that your people do not."

"Somehow, I feel that your gods are very different from ours," Liander said. His hands had clenched at the mention of deities, and he loosened them. "The hand of fate has not been gentle on me and mine."

"No," Priete said, "gods rarely use their chosen gently. But some are kinder than others." She smiled, an enigmatic thing. A breeze rustled the sheer curtains of the wide, open windows, smelling of the sea. "Have you heard of the earthen god?"

It was an innocuous question, coming in the desert's trading tongue. They did not, to Liander's knowledge, share the beliefs of the Perlenians, his mother's folk. He swallowed. He had been told by the priests who led the hours of worship in his father's court that those beliefs were false. There was no god in the earth. Yet Liander had seen strangenesses that those same priests would scoff at. He rubbed at his chin, feeling the cleanness of skin that had not been well shaven for days. He was half-Perlenian himself. Perhaps he should give more credence to the traditions of his cousins.

"I have heard of the earthen god," he said. "Though I do not know what they call him."

"He is nameless, in the Perlenian tradition," Priete said. "My people call him Tetep. He is a very old god, as old as the earth itself. But he too is unborn. He has never walked in flesh. Until now." Priete leaned forward. "I tell you this so that you know why we come. Our offer of help is genuine. We will not betray you as the moon folk did."

Liander stiffened. "You -" He began. He did not know how he intended to finish the sentence, but Priete cut him off.

"I dream. I see," she said. "I know, and I do not judge."

Liander sat back, head whirling. If she was telling the truth, he could not let her near Liana, near anyone. His sister would kill her for speaking of her dishonor. He would do it, if he had to.

The realization made him sick. She had been only kind. But if she threatened his sister, he would do what he must.

"I am no threat," Priete said calmly. "My god does not demand intrigue, and favors secrets."

"That seems a contradiction," Liander said, his words tight.

"It is," she said, smiling. "Listen to my offer, and decide for yourself."

Liander took a deep breath, settling back. Then he nodded.

"Good." Priete settled back, too. Kabrim shifted beside him, and Liander realized that the Ashir man had been ready to stand as well. It troubled him that he did not know for sure which of them Kabrim would have stepped in to defend if Liander had become aggressive with Priete. He didn't know which of them he wanted Kabrim to defend, if it came down to it.

"My people are a seafaring one. We have traveled far, even to Perlen. We explore for exploration's sake, so we cannot help you with a fleet. But the ship that I have brought will take you to Perlen, that you may bring an army south. This is the aid we offer."

"And in return?" Liander asked. It was a small enough bit of aid. Free passage to Perlen would help them when they would have otherwise had to rely on the relative wealth of the Ashir. That wealth was limited to what they could safely carry. It would not be easy to buy passage out of this port, though Sayala had sent them with trade goods and gold.

"In return, you will send word with me to your sister. She will accept me into her retinue as she journeys north. My dreams call me to the halls of your ancestors, son of Herkunsland. I cannot deny them."

Liander pressed his mouth into a thin line. Priete did not ask for much, except access to his twin. Others had used that access for ill.

"How many will travel with you?" he demanded.

"I will go alone," she said. Her expression was sad. "I mean no harm to your sister. I will be no threat. When my task is done, I will return to the sea. My people will meet me there, to bring me home."

Liander opened his mouth to ask what task. Then he closed it. She had said her god appreciated secrets. He thought that this was one of the secrets she would keep close.

"Swear on your god. Swear on Tetep that you mean Liana no harm."

Priete nodded solemnly. "I swear on Tetep, on the unborn, on the born but not yet awake. I swear on the waters and the sands. I mean no harm to the children of the sun, nor any of their line."

Liander looked to Kabrim.

"It is a heavy oath," the Ashir said.

"Then I accept your honesty," Liander told Priete, hoping he chose aright. "We will travel north on your ships."

46 THE CAPTAIN

Bertrun was exhausted. His eyes hung in his his head like stones, rough and heavy. His hair smelled of smoke. He looked no different than the other patrons sitting in this dark tavern, soot-covered and with bruised eyes. Half of the city must have burned, he thought, staring dully into his mug. There had been no water in the cracked southern cisterns to stop the fires this time. How many dead? Was it worth it?

A shape slid into the chair across from his, and Bertrun looked up. Maldun sat there. It took a moment for him to recognize his brother, so dull were his thoughts. Maldun had arranged this meeting with the Shadow he had contact with. Bertrun had known he would be here. Yet exhaustion hung so heavily on him that for a moment, his brother's dear face was a stranger's.

"You've returned, then," the captain said at last, setting his mug on the table. The beer wasn't worth the additional lassitude it would bring. He set his palms to the tabletop and leaned back into his chair, feeling his bones ache with the need for rest.

"You look half dead, brother," Maldun said.

"I feel it." Bertrun shook his head. He had left Marie to go fight fires from the most recent riot sometime yesterday. The Academy was closed, the area of the city under heavy patrol that did not stop new citizens from chanting in the streets nearly daily. Those halls had served too many. Bertrun knew that he was not the only one of their group who had been out in the mire - Lisa had intended to take food to the injured, with a Shadow to guard her. No doubt Maldun would be livid to know. His brother stopped in for a drink, now, before he had officially returned to the city, riding in just ahead of his caravan. He was dressed in traveling clothes, nothing which shouted wealth. He had had the foresight to let his beard grow in, though only for a day or two. A smear of soot added to his disguise. They could not be too careful.

"What news?" he asked his brother tiredly. "I'll likely not be able to see you again before you leave." The streets were crawling with soldiers, some fresh conscripts with less sense than a turnip.

"I passed Jessa on the way north," Maldun said. "She said the princess had made it to the desert, to send you word. I almost didn't know her, Bertrun." There was a question in his voice that Bertrun didn't have the strength to answer, not after two days of fighting fires set by rioters and perpetuated by Drummond's mismanagement. Not after seeing his king mad and frothing, and a seer's depthless eyes, and a man walk into fire. His hands ached, the skin of the palms tight and nerveless, as they had been since that first fire, on the night that changed everything. He thought that the whole world might end with fire.

"Anything else?" Bertrun asked when it became   clear that Maldun would not continue without a reply. His brother's face twisted, and for a moment Bertrun thought he would protest. Then he exhaled roughly.

"Bertrun, I spoke to one of our cousins among the Beshem." Maldun paused. Bertrun knew that he had kept in touch with their parents' tribe. Their mother had left the Beshem as a second daughter looking to improve her fortune. There was no bad blood between his family and the tribe that had given rise to them. Yet Bertrun himself had only ever met his grandmother, a singular woman. Her stories had given him nightmares of jackals and an inferno that swallowed worlds.

"The Beshem say that Jassas has been reborn." Bertrun blinked, looking at Maldun. His brother's words made no sense. Jassas was a desert superstition, a god. Gods did not walk among men, whatever the legends said.

Yet Bertrun thought of the Shadows, of the words he had said to them and the king's golden gaze, of the seer even and her visions. He thought of the eternal fire below the castle, the unseasonable weather, the heat of spring like a weight though there were still many days of winter remaining. If those strange souls existed, did not gods also exist? Had not the gods laid their hand upon those things?

"Jassas," Bertrun said. "Jassas is a god of fire and retribution."

"Yes," Maldun said. "Brother, it troubles me. The tribes gather in Southmark. More trickle in every day. None of the Herkunslanders seem to have noticed yet. I came back because I had traded all my goods. There was no way to stay without arousing suspicion. But something is happening among the tribes, and if Jessa is right about Liana crossing into the desert..." Maldun paused. "I won't be in the city long, Bertrun."

"What of Lisa?"

"I will take her with me," Maldun said, his voice low with pain. His eyes travelled over the despondent men in the tavern, over their burns and lowered heads. "I fear this city is to become a battleground."

Bertrun did not correct his brother. This city was already a battleground. All of Herkunland had been battling itself since Liana had vanished. The violence was now out in the open. The people merely gave back what had been given to them.

"Stay off the street this evening. Stay home with Lisa," Bertrun said. He stood, putting coins on the table. "When you leave, I will have cargo for you."

Maldun went to stand as well, and Bertrun pressed him back into his seat.

"It was good to see you, brother," he said, squeezing Maldun's shoulder. He did not add that he hoped it was not the last time they saw one another. If Maldun had not realized yet how this war might end, Bertrun would not inform him. Let his brother have what peace of mind he could keep.

Bertrun had battles to fight.

These riots had accelerated his plans. The Shadows had extracted Nicola. Drummond was beginning to become desperate. The king was alive, and his daughter rumored to live as well. The protesters knew this. Vandalism and looting were what the starving did. Rebellion was for those who saw a way out of their trap. Drummond's troops were still fed, and there was food still for those with money. It was a stalemate, of sorts. With no one to rally behind, many accepted their oppression.

Liana was coming, even now. A queen was coming who would set fire to this powder keg of a city. The immolation that followed would either destroy Herkunsland or cleanse it.

As he walked down the smokey streets of Herkun's City, Bertrun hoped that he and his could survive that fire, whether Herkunsland did or no.

47 THE SEER

It was a strangeness, to leave Herkun's City, and to leave it with eyes.

Nicola rode on a wagon with Lisa, Maldun's wife. She wore a dress that was a little too long, one of Lisa's own, and her locket. She kept a bag beside her that held a change of underthings and the green god's ashes. It was more than she had ever had to her name before, yet it felt like nothing in the vastness of the caravan's length.

A stranger drove the wagon, one of Maldun's men, and Lisa and Nicola sat on a bench behind him, where they could see the road and take air. Behind them was a furnished cabin, a clever thing with pull-out beds where they could sleep on the long road south, away from the men that accompanied them.

Maldun was going to the desert once more. He was taking Nicola, and Lisa, with him.

The city was overwhelming, people moving to and fro with focused intention. Their intentions Nicola could handle - she had occupied space in the castle, after all, where as many people ducked back and forth on their various errands and routines. It was the movement that blurred her eyes, even after weeks of sight. Even before she had left, the sight of Marie or Bertrun had sometimes been too much to contemplate. She had closed her eyes to process the newness, and forgotten to open them again.

Here, in this bumping, jittering wagon, it was even harder.

"Are you alright?" Lisa asked. Maldun's wife was dainty, and nearly as pale as Nicola was. When the seer looked at her with her sight, she could see the recent sickness that had marked her, but when she looked at her with her eyes, Lisa looked well enough. She rode in the wagon with Nicola, though, and would for the whole journey, out of respect for her frailty. Nicola saw that she and Maldun loved each other deeply, and would have no children, and that it would always be a grief for Lisa, who loved children, and that was too much. She exhaled, trying to banish the visions of the future.

It was hard enough to parse the act of seeing, much less see someone and overlay their whole history upon that sight.

"I'm fine," she said, belatedly answering Lisa's question. Tried to smile, as she had seen others do. Lisa did not seem convinced by it. Nicola let the expression fall from her face.

"The city is very busy," she said instead, gazing out.

She could sense Lisa's nerves, and the moment she decided to cover them with conversation.

"It's not usually so quiet, actually," Lisa said. "The riots and the shakes, see where that building is all ashes? There has been a lot of damage." She pointed, and Nicola watched her thin, long fingers, letting the flow of words pass her by.

There would be more quakes, and more riots. The city would be more cinder than not, when things were done. Nicola watched the houses, the once-bright paints of some now stained with grime, watched the flow of dirty, pale people through the streets, saw hunger, saw fear.

Before she had left, she had told Bertrun that it would get worse before it would get better. He had looked at her. Then he had asked her what she saw for his future. She had studied his face, seen the tracks of fire and betrayal, of loss.

They were the same tracks she saw now, on this city, on these people.

"Nicola?" Lisa asked, breaking her reverie.

"I'm sorry," she said. "I was just daydreaming."

They came to the gate that would let them out of the city. Nicola sat calmly in her blue dress, with her hair pinned behind a kerchief that Lisa had given her. She was to be Lisa's maid on this trip, and it was no trouble to look the part. When the soldiers asked them to step out of the wagon, she helped Lisa to step down and stood behind her, eyes downcast. They passed by her, and Lisa, too. Maldun passed some coins to the man with the most rank, Lisa and Nicola resumed their places on the wagon, and the long train of the caravan passed through the city gates.

Nicola had not passed outside of those gates for fifty years. She clutched her parents' locket. When last she had come through this place, she thought that there had not been so many houses, so many people built up against the walls, but she had been blind in truth, then. She could not separate her own memories from the history of what she saw around her.

"This is Gold Town," Lisa, said, breaking her concentration. "It is not a kind place. Many of the children the temple feeds come from here, or used to, before." She stopped on the before sharply, as if she would have said more. Nicola understood. Even outside the gates it wasn't safe to speak ill of the Lord Regent. One never knew who might be listening. There were more hungry people inside the city now than there had ever been in this ill-seeming town under Alexander. It smelled, a sharp, bitter odor, and as Nicola watched some poor soul dumped their slop into the muddy road. A pig soon appeared to root in the mess.

Drummond would burn this place, when the armies came to his door. Nicola could see it, the taste of charred flesh in her throat, the black smoke rising as the crows circled. She could see Gold Town's end.

She closed her eyes, reached into her bag. There was one more thing she had brought.

The blindfold she pulled from its depths was white linen, as her old one had been. She had begged it from Marie, when the visions became too strong.

"I think I will go lie down," she said, the length of it gripped in her hand like a lifeline. Lisa looked at her, and nodded.

"We will pass into the countryside soon enough," she said. Nicola nodded acknowledgement.

Lisa was kind. When the time came to go north again, Nicola would fight to have her left amongst the desert folk. She did not think she would have to fight hard. Maldun knew that his wife did not deserve war.

Nicola did.

She went to rest in the wagon, binding her eyes so the darkness was absolute.

It was not hard, now, to sink down inside of herself, to sink beneath the water.

Black sand touched her feet, and she lay herself down in the coolness of it, listening to the waves lap the shore of this place that was not a place. There was a melancholy to it. She wondered if there always would be.

"I do not know if I am strong enough," she told her god-

lover. A touch brushed her cheek, then was gone.
 She stayed there anyway.

48 THE KING

Alexander thought he heard a whisper in his ear. It woke him from a sound sleep, or as sound as he managed on the bars of the cage. He'd demanded a cushion to sit on within its confines, and the guards had at last complied. It was long enough that he could fit most of his body on it at night, but still not as comfortable as a bed. After so long without any sleep to speak of, he hardly minded.

Awakened, Alexander peered around the room, bleary-eyed. It was after dawn, but before his guards would enter with his morning meal. He could not say, exactly, what had moved him to awake so early. The sun had climbed over the horizon, and he had felt that in his dreams, as he felt the sun every moment now. He could point his finger in its direction without looking, like a bird finding north.

Now, however, something else hung behind his breastbone, a feeling lost in sleep and the sensation of the sun's rising. Something moved towards him across the vast expanse of the world, close. His eyes opened where they had drifted closed. His brow furrowed. Alexander did not like knowing things without knowing the why of them, and he knuckled his chest in unease, sitting up. The knucklebone fell out of his pocket as he did so. He reached for it.

The door opened. Alexander slipped his hand into his pocket, hoping the guard had not seen. It was impossible to read if the man had noticed the motion. His eyes were flat, his face closed. It was the face of a man looking at something inhuman.

Alexander waited until the guard had set the food on the small table, and come to unlock his cell. His nervousness made him stand too fast, and the guard gripped his sword.

"I mean no harm," Alexander said, hands raised.

The guard said nothing, merely studied him with those cold eyes, fearful and dismissive all at once. Then he left, locking the door to the room behind him.

Alexander went to eat, and tried to put the incident out of his mind.

Throughout the day, the sense of presence did not leave him. It was familiar, he thought, and could not say why he thought it. When he was collected for court, his hair brushed and a circlet placed on his head - symbolic of his kingship, such as it was - Alexander went happily, glad for something to take his mind from the feeling, like a missing tooth beneath the tongue. He had talked Drummond back into allowing him to appear at last. His brother did not always call him, but he called him more often than not, parading Alexander as if to prove his magnanimity. Several days of the routine had passed without incident. Court was tedious and at times agonizing, but it was something more than the confines of the tower. It would keep Alexander from straining after the feeling that plagued him.

As always, they brought him in first. Nobles filed in, gray, stern faces, men to the right side, women to the left. There were less of them than there had been - several had left the city, he thought, as soon as the roads became passable, or sent their wives and heirs away. Alexander had heard whispers, when his guards thought he wasn't listening, that the riots had only become worse. People rioted over hunger and fear of death, his father had told him once, and Alexander thought it likely that his people rioted for both.

It was not warm in the throne room, though it could become stifling in the summers. Spring had not yet established a firm foothold despite early warm days that had burned too hot, but now there was rain enough to mean it was coming. During the cold and rainy days of winter's waning, Alexander listened to the monotonous drone on his roof and thought of stolen days in bed with Liora, a lifetime ago. They had been precious few.

His brother entered, Ermen in tow, and was seated. Court began.

There were few enough petitioners. Alexander had watched his brother hand down unjust judgements. He would not be quick to take his chances here either. So he was surprised when a man approached with clear, sharp eyes and the long, braided hair of a rural holding. It took Alexander a moment to place his colors. A minor lordling, from one of the southeastern holdings that abutted the Spine. Older than Alexander, he stood with a slight stoop, but his eyes were fierce. The Spine as a mountain range made the Rib seem tame. No one had ever crossed it that the king knew of, except perhaps the desert folk far to the south. It was impassable from anywhere in Herkunsland. This lordling would have to be fierce to hold land there, where the snows and storms came rolling down from the east.

"Lord Albert of Evenshold," said the herald, and the lord came to a stop.

"My Lord Regent," he said, bowing. "Your Majesty."

Drummond made an impatient gesture, and the old lord rose.

"State your case," Ermen said, voice snide. Alexander felt his eyelids flicker in annoyance. The priest could never be cordial to those he considered lesser.

"We have had floods," Lord Albert told him, his words short and clipped. A no nonsense man, which Alexander approved of in this environ. "Several of my villages are gone. The people who survive have nothing. We would ask the Sun Crown for help to rebuild."

There was a pause, as the room waited for a genuflection that never came. Drummond shifted, and Alexander knew the shift was temper, kept bottled.

"You have not made your tithe," Ermen told him, obviously relishing the news. "The crown owes you no assistance. When you have produced it, you may approach once more." He made a shooing gesture with his hand, obviously expecting Lord Albert to withdraw at his words.

Albert did not move.

"Evenshold fought beside your father in the war with Perlen," he said, his words directed to Drummond. "We have tithed gladly, except when hardship keeps us from it. This year was one such.

"There have been floods," he continued, speaking slowly, his words measured. "There are no tithes. There were no crops, and what we kept from that meager harvest is gone now. My people are starving, and they will freeze or sicken to death without shelter."

"If they are starving, what need have they for shelter?" Drummond said, speaking at last. Alexander blinked. "They will die in any case, and I will waste valuable soldiers that could be used elsewhere."

His brother was mad. Madder than Alexander had ever been.

Albert had turned red, his face nearly the color of Alexander's coat. The lord took a deep breath, then looked up. His eyes caught on Alexander. The king shook his head, a barely perceptible movement. Albert smiled.

"I would hear the king's own words on this issue," Lord Albert said.

"My brother is unwell -"

"And yet he sits his throne." Albert's words hung in the air, a challenge. The court had gone silent, and still. Alexander sighed heavily.

Drummond would punish him for this. His hand spasmed, longing to touch the knucklebone, longing for the reassurance.

"Lord Albert has cause to claim the crown's support. We will rebuild his people's homes. He may waive his tithe for last season's harvest." He paused, wishing he did not have to rush such momentous words. "Any natural disaster is the province of the Sun Crown. We are Herkun's hand on earth, and He expresses his displeasure only from Our actions."

The court stirred. He heard the murmurs stretching back into the room. Their king spoke, their king was not mad, he was not sick. Why then did Drummond keep him locked up? Why then did he not rule? Herkun's displeasure still struck this land, and why was that?

"As my brother says," Drummond said. His voice held a warning. "We will send aid."

His words were almost lost in the shuffle of bodies in the long room. He had to raise it to be heard when he spoke again. "Court is dismissed. There will be no more petitions today."

The milling continued, the confusion, the whispers.

"Get out!" the Lord Regent shouted. Guards stepped from the walls. There were yelps as nobles were corralled towards the doors.

Lord Albert of Evenshold bowed deeply, his eyes never leaving Alexander's. Then he turned and walked into the press of bodies.

The room emptied quickly, with the guards' help. Drummond

was standing stiffly before his chair, fists clinched. Alexander had not bothered to stand. He was still shackled. There was nowhere he could go. He waited until the heavy doors were closed and his brother had turned to stalk up the stairs to him.

"You were not to speak!" he shouted.

"You are the one who sat me on my throne, brother," Alexander said calmly, gripping the arms of his seat. "And you were wrong. Your reputation is in tatters. If you had helped him freely, it would have helped you as well."

"I will have every lord from here to the Rib coming to me begging for aid now," Drummond growled.

"We shall have to kill the lord," Ermen said.

Alexander looked at him, brow furrowed.

"Are you stupid?" he asked. "You will kill a nobleman the Lord Regent disagreed with before the whole court?"

Ermen did not meet his eyes, but his cheeks went red.

"Alexander is right," Drummond told the priest. "No one would believe it an accident, no matter how convincing. It was too public."

"You listen to his lies, to Her lies, and believe you still walk a righteous path?" the high priest said.

Alexander laughed.

It was a long laugh, his own laugh, but Drummond still flinched.

"You, priest, think this is the sound of Her creature?" Alexander leaned forward in his throne, forced the man to meet his gaze. "You have never seen one of Her creatures, then."

Ermen went pale. Drummond shook himself.

"Guards, remove my brother to his tower."

"Sleep well, Ermen," Alexander said as the guards undid his shackles and bound his hands. "You are just as much Her tool as I. No one escapes the hand of the gods."

"I am Herkun's own!" the man howled. Alexander laughed again, an ugly sound.

"Who belongs to Herkun more than I?" he asked.

The priest had no answer.

49 THE CAPTAIN

The riots had not ended, not really. They had died down for a time, but each morning saw graffiti scratched or painted on the walls, guards beaten and left for dead in the alleys, and, more than all of these, new arrests. Bertrun thought that the jails must surely be full. He did not know where they were putting all of the people, though rumors said many of them were found dead in their cells.

They couldn't kill the whole city. He reminded himself of this.

The council could not meet with the chaos. Bertrun had conferred with the Shadows, and the Shadows had conferred with the other members. Wrothfurt had been in hiding already, and had managed to stay that way despite participating actively in the activity near the Academy. Many of those who had come to meet Bertrun before were Wrothfurt's old students. The captain wondered how many of them yet lived.

The south, where the Academy was, was crawling with soldiers and guards alike. But the north of the city, that was bare of patrols. The neighborhoods he moved towards now were home to soap and candle makers, and butcheries. Many of these people were still doing decent business. Meat, at least, would remain in supply a while yet, until it became so expensive that only the nobles could afford it. Candles and soap, though, the common folk could no longer afford much of at all. They were luxuries that belonged in better times.

The soap makers sold to nobles and to the temple. The clergy, at least, had money. That was how the Shadows had found these people, through Syria and her connections there.

Religion could be a curse or a blessing. It would depend on Bertrun's words.

They emerged from the tunnels in an alley, crawling from the space beneath an old carriage house. The houses in this part of the city sat on enough land to fit small storage buildings and other extra structures. This one had stood for long enough that the mortar holding its stone walls together was crumbling. No doubt the wood floor had been a more recent addition. The wooden door that hid this entrance was not set up to open with a floor only two feet above it. They had cut a large hole in the floorboards to allow it to swing open, the clutter of a building full of near-useless items hiding it from view. Not for the first time, Bertrun wondered how a city could forget the maze that spread beneath it, and how doors obviously untouched for generations could remain whole and functioning for so long. It was unnatural. Bertrun was heartily tired of the mysteries of the unnatural.

It was a clear, early spring day, the air brisk and the sky a deep blue that tugged at the heart. Bertrun squinted in the brightness of the alley, wishing it was overcast. The transition from dark to day was too much for his eyes and left him nearly blind, but his vision did clear. The alley revealed was not so dirty as he had expected. Trash pickers and soil collectors must still be working this place, unlike the alleys in other parts of the city. Bertrun followed the Shadows as they walked along, until they came to a door.

It was an unlovely door, obviously used for access to the alley and little else, set in an old wooden fence that had seen better days. Beyond it towered a house, shutters drawn tight.

Matthius was beside him, as he often was these days. He was wearing a sword that the gaze slid off of on his right hip, so that it might be drawn by his left hand. He had not been a swordsman who could fight with his left hand, before the flames took him, and Bertrun worried now that he was still not a man who would fight well with his left hand. He tried not to think about it, tried to trust the scarred Shadow that seemed to lead them. Surely he knew what he was doing, assigning Matthius as a bodyguard.

Bertrun himself was without a sword at all. He had no magic to keep him from being noticed with one.

Matthius threw out a hand to restrain Bertrun when he went to pull the cord that would flip the catch on the door to their destination. He and the other Shadow stood in tense silence, and Bertrun froze too, his earlier calm, such as it had been, gone.

There was a moment that stretched like an indrawn breath.

The shorter Shadow nodded once, sharply, and scrambled up the building on the other side of the narrow alley, almost quicker than Bertrun could follow with his eyes. He was so busy ogling that climb that when Matthius began to pull him back down the alley he was unprepared. Neither Shadow had said a word. For a moment, it seemed as if they might escape whatever threat awaited them cleanly.

A sudden whistling broke the quiet. A crossbow bolt buried itself in the ground behind him. Bertrun shouted despite himself, a guttural sound, breaking the silence. It did not matter. The door in the garden wall behind him burst open, spilling a double handful of shouting soldiers into the alley. Bertrun started running, then. Matthius dropped behind him.

How had they known where they were? Both times, they had known. It was too close together, too much coincidence. Bertrun's feet pounded against the paving stones. What had seemed a short distance before stretched. His heart was already in his throat.

A bolt took someone in the throat behind him. Bertrun had heard that particular thunk and gurgle before, when he had patrolled these streets. Crossbows were expensive, and restricted, but some criminals still managed to acquire them. There was no point in looking back. He put more weight into his strides, as if he could outrun them by sheer force of will. Another thunk, and a tumbling scream from behind him. The Shadow, he realized. The Shadow had a crossbow as well.

He had almost reached the carriage house. Bertrun felt his breath tearing at his throat. His pulse pounded in his head, in his chest. He shouted in rage or agony, he knew not which. Bertrun dove into the open door, bouncing off of the gathered detritus of others' lives. The breath went out of him as he collided with something hip-height and invisible in the gloom. Where before the light had blinded him, now the dark did. Bertrun panted desperately, pawing forward in the darkness. The door to the tunnels was closed. He would have to open it. But first he would have to find it. He searched for a darker depth in the darkness, the faint outline of the hole in the floor under his feet. There was a clash of swords behind him.

His eyes adjusted at last, revealing a pit of blackness only feet away. Bertrun lunged for it as well as he could, pushing aside the objects in his way. The door was below his hands then, and he stood in the cut hole, the cluttered, abandoned carriage house around him, and lifted. Adrenaline gave him strength. The door flew wide on its ancient hinges. Bertrun began to climb into the pit revealed.

They had left the lamps somewhere down here. Bertrun crouched, fumbling at the damp stone floor, then realized that he had no way to light it. Matthius had been carrying the striker, and the Shadow could not be counted on to join him. The door to the tunnels still stood open above him. He heard the sound of sword on sword, his hand gripping for a blade that he had not had for years now. There was shouting, and then silence.

Bertrun sat in that silence a few moments more, working up his courage, listening. There was no further sound from above. Every nerve screamed to run headlong down the passage, but Bertrun knew that would net him little better than starvation, his last moments spent wandering the blackness, lost. Still, there was no time. They might find him here, but more importantly, someone had known to ambush him. Someone had cared to lay this trap. Enough people had seen his face now that there must be more than a suspicion that he was alive. It was only a matter of time before they found Marie's house, one way or another. He had not been so careful as he could have been. He had to warn her, and Syria. At the thought of his sister being discovered, Bertrun's blood went cold.

He stood. His stretching hands sketched the walls around him, fingers grazing smooth stone. With a deep breath, he stepped forward into the dark.

He knew the way home, the route memorized hours before this failed escapade. He could still see the slate in his mind's eye, marking the path he would take. He just had to follow it.

It was a long, silent walk.

In the darkness, Bertrun worried. He worried for his brother to the south, perhaps even now meeting his queen at last. He worried for Nicola, who had seemed so scared and alone. He worried for Syria, his sister, and for the child she carried; for Wrothfurt, who could not stand to sit idly by; even for his king, whatever else Alexander had become.

But he worried most for Marie, and for the maps in his rooms.

Could they have tracked him to his home, even now? No doubt if they knew for sure they would have cornered him there, but they must be close, to have set this ambush.

How had they found him?

It took him a long time to make it back to what he thought was a familiar entrance, but make it back he did. Bertrun felt along the walls for handholds, pulled himself up. The door above opened into the crawlspace below the bakery, the scent of sugar clear to him even down here. He pulled himself out onto the cold stone of the alley and ducked past the boxes stacked to conceal the entrance. There was already a Shadow waiting by the door, one that Bertrun rarely saw. He had thought all of the Shadows with him in the ambush, but he had forgotten that Matthius' addition meant there were five of the men, not four. Bertrun hurried to him.

"Are they coming here?" Bertrun demanded. The Shadow met his eyes, nodded. Bertrun felt his heart skip a beat. He stepped past the man and threw open the door.

Marie was kneading dough. She jumped when he entered.

"Marie," he said as she squeaked, floury hand to her heart, "they've found us."

Her face went pale.

Bertrun pushed past her, ran to his room. The maps he and the Shadows had painstakingly made were sitting on the desk by his bed. He gathered them hurriedly, shoved them in a nearby bag. There was nothing else here he owned but his cloak. Bertrun grabbed that, too, and hurtled back down the stairs.

He had made it to the dining room when a pounding struck the door.

Marie emerged from the kitchen, wiping her hands clean on her apron. Her expression was set, determined. Bertrun moved to her quickly, tried to turn her around the way she had come. She shook free of his grip.

"Come on," he said urgently, keeping his voice low, "there's no time."

"I'm staying," she said. "Now go."

She stepped past him, gripping his shoulder once. Bertrun turned to argue, to pull her back.

A hand grabbed his arm, pulling him into the kitchen. The Shadow closed the door behind him just as the front door opened. He heard the rumble of the soldiers' voices as the Shadow met his gaze.

Bertrun closed his eyes, gripping his bag of maps close. Then he followed the Shadow out the back door.

50 THE KING

Smoke hung in the air even here, high in his cell. Alexander, king of a burned city in name, prisoner in truth, stood on the table, looking down on what he could see of the world through the narrow slit of his window.

Most of the fire was ashes now, but his window looked out on the temple, and the Academy. He could see the worst of the damage, a black stain across his city's face.

The king was old, and tired still, and he could not hold the position for long. His calves ached, and his table wobbled, and he was forced to step down, the weight of his aching heart dragging him towards the floor quickly enough that his knees almost buckled with the motion. Alexander swayed, and sat on the bed. He wished, in that moment, for Liora, for his wife long dead and entombed. Their marriage had been brief. It had taken her three years to conceive, and the birth had killed her. Only three years and a little more to memorize her smile and her eyes, but he had tried. He had tried, even with the politics of running a country to keep him otherwise occupied. It had been a dynastic marriage, but he had loved her. It had nearly ended him, to have been the one to have killed her with that love.

And now his kingdom, too, was dying. If Liana did not come, if she did not survive, if Herka had broken her or killed her outright and all of his faith was a lie - but no. Drummond believed that Liana lived.

Alexander must also believe. Belief was all he had left, in this high tower.

He put his head in his hands, and tried to weep, tried to let go of some of the grief that was hardening behind his heart. No tears would come. The smell of smoke, the bright burning light of the sky, these things kept him company. No salt tears, no release. The ghosts of his city would not let him go so easily. Yet what more could he do? He had fought the curse that bound him, fought to regain some of himself, and succeeded in that, for now. He had fought his brother, too, in more subtle ways. It had seemed like he was helping.

Perhaps there was never any way that his city, that his country would come out of this unscathed. Perhaps it had always been inevitable, this fire. This ending, this fracturing, this war. He could do nothing to put an end to it. But his daughter could.

The door opened.

Alexander was not facing it. He turned, thinking that his guard had come early with the evening meal. It was not his guard who greeted him.

It was his brother, and a girl.

Alexander found himself on his feet, horror quickly replacing grief.

"You said -" he began, hating the vulnerability in his voice.

"Shut up." Drummond stepped inside, the girl along with him, her mouth pinched with pain.

"You promised that there would be no more -"

"I don't have to keep promises to you," Drummond said. "You are a demon in my brother's skin -"

"You are a monster! You have taken everything -"

"And you are the one who cursed yourself for a pair of Perlenian curs. This is your fault. You're breaking the kingdom -"

"You are breaking it!" Alexander said. "You are the one who is breaking everything. It was always you, Drummond, always. We were brothers!"

"You are no brother of mine," Drummond told him, voice hard. Alexander felt his breath catch. "I said I would try things your way, as long as you were useful. You've ceased to be of use." He pulled the girl forward.

She was blonde. It was a surprising color for a Herkunslander her age, though she could not have been more than seventeen. Her eyes were wide and brown and terrified. Her clothing was rough spun enough that she was probably not even a castle servant. Just some poor girl, plucked off the street to die at Alexander's hands.

Except she wouldn't die. His brother would know his secret, the secret of the knucklebone in his pocket. And when he figured it out, Alexander would be ended.

"Make me an heir," Drummond said, and closed the door, leaving the girl inside.

Alexander gave her credit. She didn't scream when the door slammed behind her. Nor did she start crying, though she was obviously afraid. They stared at each other, and Alexander reflected that his own wide-eyed, desperate gaze was not so different from hers. He exhaled, and smoothed his features into something more comforting.

He did not want to comfort. He wanted to rage. But she did not deserve that.

"What's your name?" he asked.

"Anna," she said. Her voice was not strong, but it didn't shake either. "Are you going to kill me?"

No honorifics, he realized. Alexander gave a half-smile despite himself.

"Not if I can help it," he told her.

Then he walked to his cage, and shut himself inside, hoping against hope that he could keep his word. The knucklebone hung in his pocket, burning.

51 THE CAPTAIN

Marie was who he thought of as he moved, panting, through the dark. Marie, who had chosen to be left behind. Bertrun had shared a home with her for nearly a year now - and she had made it a home, despite all of his melancholy. And he had left her to stall the soldiers. He had left her, a sacrifice.

He wanted to believe that when the guards had come that they had not questioned the empty rooms upstairs. He wanted to believe that they had pitied an old woman and left her alone. That her staying as a distraction, as a stopgap, had not cost her her life.

But there was a reason that Marie no longer attended any of the meetings of the rebellion, no longer took part in it at all. Maldun was lost as soon as Bertrun was found, but Maldun had left already, along with his wife. Lost as well was Syria, though she was a woman and married into another household. Rufus was a well-respected member of the community who had never, to Marie's knowledge, helped their cause, so she might yet escape if Bertrun could warn her fast enough. None of the others were known to Marie. Nicola was safe, extracted. Jessa was far to the south. Wrothfurt's name was already black, but his whereabouts were unknown.

Marie could only give them what they might already suspect. That was by design. He had always known that she could be taken.

His fists ached from clutching tightly, his jaw from the steady clenching and unclenching he did between rapid breaths. The thumping of his feet was a cacophony in the tunnels around him, and the dim light of the torch the Shadow carried lit little. There was nothing but the running and his regret, nothing but his rage, and only one place to go.

He had to get to Syria, and get her out. He had to save his sister.

He ran as if Jassas' own jackals were at his heels.

His breath was tight in his chest by the time they came to their destination. There was a wooden ladder before them, worn and warped. The scarred Shadow touched Bertrun's shoulder, forcing him to stop when he would have thrown himself up it. He leaned on his knees, catching his breath.

"This may be a trap," the Shadow said.

Bertrun jerked his head up, meeting the Shadow's eyes. The man looked old to him, as if he had aged years on their run. As if Bertrun could truly see him for the first time. He met Bertrun's eyes and he said, "We can't go with you."

The captain sucked in a breath. Let it out slowly as he stood.

"I understand," he said.

"We will be waiting," the Shadow told him.

Bertrun climbed the ladder.

At the top, a door waited. Bertrun pushed his palm into the wood, pressed up. It was hard from this angle, but the door lifted enough for him to throw his shoulder into it. He climbed the ladder, pressed up with his legs, until the door rose enough that he could press his way up and out. He closed it behind him softly.

He was behind a garden wall.

It took effort to scale. Bertrun pulled himself up and over ungracefully. The house behind was dark, but it was Syria's house. He had been in these gardens before in better times. They were not so elaborate as a noble's garden, and he crossed through the shrubs and herbs in a few quick steps. At the back door, he did not knock, but lifted the latch, quiet as a knife.

The house beyond was not so asleep as it seemed. He heard voices from upstairs. Syria's and a man he hoped was Rufus. Bertrun listened for someone else, but heard nothing.

Syria's servants were day workers, as Maldun's had been. The house was not so grandiose as to require live-in help. With all of the lights off, they must be gone for the night. Yet if Rufus and Syria were awake, what had awakened them?

Bertrun felt his skin prickle.

"Syria," he heard Rufus say clearly. They had come to the top of the stairs, and Bertrun stared up from his place in the shadows of the dining hall door, where he had come to rest. Syria's rounded form blocked her husband's, a shadow before his candle flame.

"Keep my name from your mouth." His sister's voice as low, a snarl he had never heard from her lips. She turned, grasping the railing.

"Where are you going?" Rufus shouted. "I did this for you! For our baby!"

Syria whirled to face him again.

"This? This child? You gave us up for a baby that might not even survive its birth? And what kind of world will it live in with him on the throne? No." Syria turned away from her husband. Bertrun heard her feet on the stairs.

"You can lie to yourself, but you'll not lie to me, Rufus," Syria said. Her voice was closer. Bertrun drew back as she came into view, a darker shape in the dimness.

"Where are you going?"

"I'll not share your bed tonight."

"It's not safe to go out," Rufus said, voice high with fear. Syria did not dignify his statement with an answer.

She turned into the door on the other side of the hall. He heard her rummage in the dimness, and there was a flare of light from the spill in her hand. She touched it to the candle in its sconce by the door, only then looking up.

Bertrun met his sister's wide gaze, the breadth of the hallway between them.

She cast a hurried glance up the stairs, but Bertrun was sheltered by the doorway. Rufus could not see him.

"You have betrayed my family, Rufus, betrayed everything I love," she said then, clear and cold, her gaze on her husband. The round swell of her belly seemed to move in the flickering candlelight. "You have betrayed your country and your Queen. And I will remember it forever."

She turned then and left the hall, her back to Bertrun as she marched deeper into the house.

Rufus stood silently at the top of the stairs for a moment. Bertrun heard him curse, and the creaking of the floorboards as he walked away, taking his candlelight with him. The captain risked a peek out, to be sure that he had left.

Then he moved quickly across the hall to where Syria had gone.

She was waiting for him in the drawing room, a comfortable place where guests were entertained. She had built up the banked fire in the grate, and sat in front of it now on an ottoman, pulled as close as she could get to the still-small flames. Her nightgown was thin, and he realized the chill in the air now that his adrenaline was wearing low. He stepped quietly to a chest at the wall, pulled a knitted blanket from inside, and brought it to wrap around her shoulders. She accepted it without looking at him.

"Would you believe that I'm not surprised?" she asked. Her voice was soft, her face, in the firelight, still. He saw no tears on her cheeks. "I had asked myself when."

"You didn't say anything," Bertrun said, his own voice equally soft.

"I hoped that I was wrong." The fire crackled, flames beginning to climb. Ruddy light spilled into the room. Syria stood, her slippers scuffing the floor. She went to the mantel, and opened a box with quick, selective motions.

Inside, something glinted.

"I've kept this here, in plain sight. It's a puzzle box, like the Perlenians use. Rufus brought it to me when we were engaged." She turned the box. Gold coins spilled out in her hand, just a few. She slid them back inside. "Shall I teach you how to open it?"

"Syria," Bertrun began, then felt his voice die in his throat. There was nothing to say.

She closed the box and brought it to him, and he let her teach him how to find the smooth, small pegs amidst the carvings and depress them so that the box could be opened. Inside were several golden suns, the highest form of currency. Each one could buy him more food than he himself could need, even with prices as high as they were, and he stared at them. Surely he had had his own savings, before the coup, and the fire, but it felt so long ago. He could not remember the last time he had seen a sun.

"There is a priest whose help you will need. He waits for me each sixthday at dusk, at the smallest door to the temple complex where it comes close to the canal. The Shadows will know it." She looked at him then, a bitter smile on her face. "I don't think they'll ever look for you in the temple itself."

"Syria," he said, "come with me."

"You know I can't," she said, smile vanishing. "There's nowhere to go." He reached out to put a hand on her shoulder, and she took it.

"I believe that she will make a better world," Syria told him. "I can live here, until that world comes."

"Syria."

"He's my husband," she said, as if that explained everything. Bertrun supposed it did, for her. And she was right. There was nothing that he could do.

He took the box, and left her staring into the fire.

52 THE PRINCE

Water sloshed against the hull of the ship, tarred black so that it almost seemed to vanish beneath the dirty waves of the port. Liander gripped the thin railing, all that stood between him and the sea. The ribbed, folded sails of the ship flapped above his head in errant gusts of wind. It was the largest of five, larger than any ships Herkunsland could command, though built unlike them, and unlike Perlenian ships as well. It was foreign and the water was deep beneath him, though they had not yet set sail. This ship was still at dock. It would not stay that way for long. There was a breeze off the desert dunes. Soon, the *Nyantec* would cast off, and sail north.

Not for the first time, Liander wondered if he was making a mistake.

It would take a month to reach Perlen's harbors, they told him. This was no surprise. It would take nearly that to reach Liana in Southmark, and months more to traverse Herkunsland, assuming a blond man with a royal name would survive the trip. Another month north from the Rib would take him to the capital of Perlen, where his royal cousin waited. Four months then, if he were lucky. A sea voyage made far more sense. It was what Liana had asked of him, to barter passage by ship and sail north.

She had not asked for Priete. She would not look kindly on a priestess. His sister was suspicious of those touched by the gods, and with good reason. She had nearly killed Jessa, for all that she had tried to hide it from him. He could only hope that Jessa, even in her strangeness, might have a tempering effect in his absence. Liana was more stable than she had been, but his sister was a sharpened blade now. Her first instinct was to cut.

Kabrim had come up behind him while he stared into the sea, and now he placed a hand on Liander's shoulder.

"The priestess is here to see us off," he said in the language of the Ashir. Hafir, Ashul, and Ifan hovered behind him, their faces ranging from pensive to relaxed. No one shared Liander's fear, it seemed, which was just as well. He needed the Ashir men to be optimistic in the face of his uncertainty.

Liander nodded and followed Kabrim and his cousins to the ladder that led to the dock. They disembarked carefully, and walked down the stone pier to its base. Priete stood waiting. With her was Dun-Mar. Liander had known Dun-Mar would escort Priete, but saying goodbye to his friend still twisted his heart. He had said too many goodbyes that were final. The prince stepped forward last, kissing Dun-Mar's dark cheeks as the other Ashir had done. Dun-Mar was dressed all in the cerulean blue of the Erobians, the same blue, Liander now realized, that marked the men of the oases.

"Do not grieve me, prince," Dun-Mar said, smiling at Liander's distress. "I have at last been called to the water. The call may have never come without you." Liander nodded to his friend, though he did not truly understand what he spoke of. He understood that it was an honor to the Ashir, and that was enough.

"Do not fear for me," Priete said when he turned to bid her farewell. Liander swallowed. She was still intimidating, even with the deep indigo of her robes looped up over her face, hiding her features. Her presence was like a weight. "The fire is of no concern to me. Nor should it be to you, for now. You have other gods to worry over."

She gestured then, to her left, where another blue-robed figure stood. Liander had assumed that this third party was Priete's disciple, and perhaps she was. But by her gesture, the priestess made it clear that she had not brought the woman to accompany her into the desert.

"This is Elaiya. She will travel with you." Elaiya nodded to him solemnly. Her robes were a lighter blue than Priete's, though not by much. Liander returned her nod, hoping she spoke the desert trade tongue. The captain of the ship, a small fierce woman weathered by the sun, with deep brown skin, spoke a smattering. As far as Liander knew, the crew spoke only their own, open-voweled tongue. He and the Ashir would have only themselves to talk with on what promised to be a long voyage.

Liander bid a final farewell to Priete and Dun-Mar, the scope of his task once more pressing in on him as he turned his back on the pleasant white stone of Ileas. Beyond the boundaries of the port, marked by the cradling arms of a rocky bay, the blinding surface of the sea glimmered under the desert sun. As he climbed the ladder to the waiting ship, he felt as if his very soul cried out in protest. There was so long still to go. He had traveled so far, and now not even Liana accompanied him. The vastness of the ocean seemed to mock him with its trackless depths.

"You will do what must be done, Liander," Kabrim said. He once more placed his hand on the prince's shoulder. Liander pulled in a deep breath, feeling the weight slide off of him. One way or another, he would do what must be done.

"My thanks, my friend," Liander said. Behind them, the captain shouted orders. Ropes were cast off, the anchor was drawn. Deep in the hold, chanting began.

"What is that?" Liander asked Kabrim, still at the rail with him.

"They are taking us out to sea," Kabrim said, and Liander felt the ship pull forward, stroke by stroke, heard the long oars splash beneath him, and they were away. There was no longer any turning back.

53 THE PRINCESS

The trade city of Southmark fell quietly.

There was no smoke, no screaming to begin the war that would return the queen to her throne. There was no need for it. One by one, the warriors of the desert tribes took the houses and barracks of the people of Herkunsland. Most simply woke to find their families already corralled in the street. There was shouting, of course. Babies cried. A few of the soldiers rattled their swords, but the nominal but ineffective guard posted here had been shipped off for their loyalty to King Alexander. The desert folk had never threatened them, and they did not so much threaten them now as suggest, strongly, that it was in their best interests to leave their swords and join the crowds gathered in the square that served as the central market. It was at the heart of the city, and was usually filled with colorful stalls, squalling goats, and spry desert horses. Now it was filled with people, young and old, men and women and children. All of the desert tribes had sent their children and elders as well, and the Herkunslanders relaxed some to see it. They were still angry, but they were not afraid.

That had been Sayala's recommendation. Fear would not serve, here. Not yet.

Liana appeared to her people on the balcony of a building abutting the square. It was a tannery, but most of the tannery's activities were halted today, as all nonessential work had halted throughout the city. Still, the smell of the vats was at best bracing. Tanning was a desert trade, not a trade of her people, and she was, regardless, a princess. There were many things that Liana had never experienced firsthand, and the tanning vats were among them. It was a reminder that she had far to go to be fit to be queen.

"People of Southmark," she said, nearly shouting to be heard. There was a trick to this speaking, to giving words weight and volume almost conversationally. Her father had made sure she learned it. Liana knew many in the square would not hear her still. It did not matter. Those who did hear would speak of it, after, and that would be enough. One thing people could be counted on for was storytelling.

The milling crowd had quieted now. Liana spoke again.

"People of Southmark, you have been called here to witness a rebirth. Two years ago, my own uncle Drummond rebelled against Herkun's will. He imprisoned King Alexander and sent assassins after his children.

"Since this treachery, Herkunsland has fallen further and further into ruin. Crops die in the fields, and the very ground shakes in its rage."

The crowd murmured and stirred. The quakes had stretched even here, small tremblings. This was a trading town, though, and they had all heard stories of the damage in Herkun's City - fires and collapsed buildings, tears in the very earth. She had made sure of it.

"This ill use has been for what? To feed the largesse of a power-mad second son? To gild the robes of the fat priests of the temple? Their hearts are as black as the night. They do not hold Herkun's fire."

Anger now, and dismay, rising up from the crowd below her like a perfume. Liana did not smile. Shouts began, curses and bitter agreement. Liana held up her hands, and the shouts died.

"Fear not," she said as the quiet settled again. "Fear not, for Alexander's daughter did not die. What fire could kill Sermund's brood? She stands before you even now, her chosen people.

"I am Liana Auge von Herkun, daughter of Alexander Auge von Herkun, and I pledge to you this - I will take back the throne of my father. I will put this unquiet earth to rest. And I will lead our people into an age of prosperity not seen for a hundred years. I swear these things on the blood that flows in my veins. It is Sermund's blood, the blood of God on earth, and it will not be denied!"

She dropped her hands. Behind her, from the tall spire of the tannery's flagpole, a banner unfurled. It was her banner, not her father's golden sun on white, but that same sun on a background of red, red as blood, red as vengeance. Liana had picked this building for the height that banner would reach. It should be seen. All should see it, and know that her fire was coming.

"For blood," she cried, lifting her fist, "and for justice!"

The tribes let out a loud ululation, clapping and cheering. Most of the Herkunslanders looked shocked, but some clapped and cheered along with their desert neighbors. Others began to join them more slowly.

It would have to be enough. Liana would not turn back. She would have her throne, and her kingdom.

Then, she would find her son.

EPILOGUE

The canal gleamed in the dying light, though it was still early in the spring. Bertrun dipped his head so that his low hat blocked the daggers of sun spearing his eyes. The scarred Shadow had brought him here as Syria had bade him. He held back as Bertrun approached the small canal door to the temple complex. Better to wait, if this were another trap.

There was a man ahead in the brown-red robes of an ascetic, his head clean shaven, pulling water from the canal. This high in the city, the water was still clean enough to pull directly. Below the temple complex, it would not be. Bertrun paused to watch as the man poured water over his head, drenching himself. He had to fight a sympathetic hiss.

When the water had ceased falling, the man did not seem cold. His body steamed in the sunlight, though the morning air was not warm.

Bertrun had heard of men who were so divine. He had never before met one, but his grandmother had told him that in the deserts, there were men called to the water who could heal mortal wounds, and that further south there were women whose visions moved nations. He had heard tales from his soldiers that some of the priests could walk through fire. He had thought it superstition.

Yet when the man turned to him and fixed him with warm brown eyes, Bertrun felt certain that he had been wrong.

The man gestured. His robes were nearly dry now, and Bertrun felt his throat tighten at this display of power. Alexander had never done anything so odd - but then, Alexander had exercised little more than his right to rule, when it came to his heritage. He had estranged himself from the temple. Bertrun had always thought it was the priests' corruption, and maybe that was so. But for all that the gods had put a strong hand on his life, the king had never prayed to them that Bertrun had seen.

"Your sister said you might come to me," the man said, once Bertrun had come closer. His voice was reedy with disuse. Bertrun said nothing, eying the man with an expression he tried to keep calm. The ascetic gazed down at his robes and laughed.

"If I had known you were so skittish, I would have waited to take a bath," he said. He held out his hand. "My name is Fredrick. I know yours."

Bertrun hesitated, then grasped the proffered palm. It was dry and callused, and just slightly too warm, as if Fredrick had a fever. Bertrun released it quickly.

"I don't understand -" he began.

"Have you ever dreamed, captain? You know the kinds of dreams I mean." Fredrick met his eyes, gaze steady.

"I - yes." He had not meant to say yes. But the visions of Jassas had come back to him, the fire and the jackals.

"So have I. Did you mention your dreams to your companion?" He gestured. The Shadow was standing where Bertrun had left him, he noted in surprise. The Shadows were not usually so overt.

"No," Bertrun said slowly, turning back to Fredrick.

The priest shrugged. "You should have."

He picked up his bucket, and headed back towards the small door, gesturing for Bertrun to follow.

"I will keep you here, for a time. Until Herkun's avatar comes to reclaim her city, you will be safe." He opened the door in the white stone wall, pausing in its frame.

"And I will teach you, captain, about your dreams. It will do you good."

Fredrick vanished inside the complex. Bertrun cast one last look back at the Shadow.

He was gone. Bertrun was alone. But he would return.

The Shadows always did.

ABOUT THE AUTHOR

Amanda J. McGee is a writer by night and a mapmaker by day. She lives in southwest Virginia with her two cats and the love of her life. Someday, she'll get around to weeding her garden.

You can find out more at www.amandajmcgee.com.

ACKNOWLEDGEMENTS

It takes a lot of work to write a book, but none of that work is possible without the people who make life worth living.

As I sit and type this, I'm conscious that I have only been fed and functional today thanks to the labor of others. So, though so much of this work has been mine, it has not been possible for me to give this manuscript my focus without other people picking up the slack in the rest of my life, listening to me rant about my characters when they weren't doing what I wanted, helping me come up with sales pitches, and generally being long-suffering about it all.

Thanks are owed to Rose and Kendall, for reading this story and liking it; to Ember, for bothering to listen; to all of those who have provided me critique, including the multiple members of my sadly defunct writing group. We shall rise again, probably. Thanks to Steve and Jerry for being rabidly supportive and to Eric for dragging me to the gym. Special thanks also to my mom, for always believing in my work and being my first and best fan, and to my husband, for feeding me. Seriously, the food is perfect.

Thanks also to my Patreon supporters, and to all of the writers who have shared their knowledge and time with me.

Lastly, to all of the lovely folks who buy my books: you rock.

CPSIA information can be obtained
at www.ICGtesting.com
Printed in the USA
LVHW022050210321
682022LV00007B/1456